EverQuest

Truth and Steel

Other titles in the exciting series

EverQuest: The Rogue's Hour
EverQuest: Ocean of Tears

EverQuest

Truth and Steel

THOMAS M. REID

cds
BOOKS
NEW YORK

Copyright © 2006 by Sony Computer Entertainment America Inc.

EverQuest is a registered trademark of Sony Computer Entertainment America Inc. SOE and the SOE logo are registered trademarks of Sony Online Entertainment Inc.

All rights reserved. No part of this publication may be reproduced, stored in a retrieval system, or transmitted, in any form or by any means, electronic, mechanical, photocopying, recording, or otherwise, without the prior written permission from Sony Computer Entertainment Inc. Printed in the United States of America.

For information and inquiries, please contact:
CDS Books
387 Park Avenue South
12th floor
New York, NY 10016
1-800-343-4499

Library of Congress Cataloging-in-Publication Data

Reid, Thomas M., 1966-
Truth and steel / Thomas M. Reid.
p. cm. — (EverQuest)
"Sony Online Entertainment."
ISBN-13: 978-1-59315-223-9 (pbk. : alk. paper)
ISBN-10: 1-59315-223-X (pbk. : alk. paper)
I. Title. II. Title: Everquest : truth and steel.

PS3618.E548T78 2006
813'.6—dc22
2006018212

Designed by Holly Johnson

CDS books are available at special discounts for bulk purchases in the United States by corporations, institutions, and other organizations. For more information, please contact the Special Markets Department at the Perseus Books Group, 11 Cambridge Center, Cambridge, MA 02142, or call (800) 255-1514 or (617) 252-5298, or email special.markets@perseusbooks.com.

06 07 08 / 10 9 8 7 6 5 4 3 2 1

For Bob, who made it happen, and who reminded me what this art isn't as much as taught me what it is.

And for Veronica, whose patience and encouragement were limitless.

Thanks to both of you for making this a better book.

EverQuest

Truth and Steel

1

"CAREFUL, LAD. IT'S A LONG DROP FROM UP there," Bruigan cautioned from the base of the bluff face, maybe 30 feet below.

Khaniel, his fingers and toes clenching the rock face, glanced down to where the dwarf peered up at him, shielding his eyes from the sun with one gnarled hand. "Would you like to do this yourself?" the mercenary asked. He knew he sounded testy, but he couldn't help it.

"No," Bruigan answered quickly, shaking his head and causing his gray-flecked beard to waggle across his belly. "Have you ever seen a dwarf climb anything?"

Khaniel smirked and replied, "No, I can't say that I have."

"There's a reason for that. Dwarves build things, we don't climb them. We're experts at erecting scaffolding, you know."

Khaniel laughed. "Well, why didn't you say so before? We could construct some right here and you could search for moss to your heart's content."

"Son, the only thing I've climbed in the last thirty years is a staircase, and I usually have to stop halfway up to catch my breath."

Khaniel laughed again, but his chuckle died away as he studied his companion's features. Bruigan's wiry beard, a bit matted and greasy from the morning's breakfast, only partially hid the dwarf's ruddy and lined face. His leather jerkin, worn over a faded and threadbare wool shirt, seemed a size too big for him lately, and Khaniel recalled that he limped as often as not when he walked, especially during the cold mornings. The dwarf indeed showed his age. "You're not *that* old," he lied.

"Well, I'm old enough," Bruigan said, a bit defensively, perhaps sensing Khaniel sizing him up. "And definitely too old to be dragging your corpse back to Freeport. The last thing I need is you cracking your head open out here in the middle of nowhere."

"I'll try to be careful, old-timer." When Bruigan folded his arms and glared, the mercenary laughed. "I'm almost to the top," he said more seriously. "Sit tight."

Khaniel turned and eyed a stunted tree protruding from a crack in the rock next to his head. The mercenary reached out, took hold of the rough trunk, and tugged a couple of times. Though it sagged, the tree felt well anchored, so Khaniel shifted more of his weight upon it. Satisfied that it would support all 225 pounds of him, he began to pull himself up. He swung a leg over the trunk and moved into a sitting position, then rose to his feet. The tree sprang with his weight, making it tricky to keep his balance.

Khaniel spent a moment taking in the view. The Serpentspine Mountains hovered on every side of the long valley he and Bruigan had followed the last few days. The golds, reds, and oranges splashed across the slopes in contrast to the icy blue skies gave testament that autumn was in full swing. Even the air felt crisp, something so rare in the hot plains of the Commonlands to the north. Khaniel breathed it all in as he studied the valley below him.

A glint of light caught the mercenary's attention just as he turned back to the task at hand. The flash had come from an open area, a meadow following a stream through the middle of the valley. At first, Khaniel assumed the water sparkled, but he realized that the morning sun behind him would not cause a reflection in front of him. No, something else glittered, and as Khaniel watched, it moved.

"There's someone in the valley," the mercenary called down. "I can see the glint of armor."

"Are they following us?"

"Maybe," Khaniel replied. "They're coming up the same route we followed at daybreak."

"Well, let's find my moss and worry about them later," the dwarf said.

Khaniel nodded and turned back to his work. Standing upright on the stunted, springy tree, Khaniel could just reach the ledge overhead. He stretched to his full six-foot, three-inch height and grabbed a protrusion of rock with both hands. He then swung one muscular leg up and to the side, hooking his heel on the ledge. He hoisted himself higher, reached out to drag himself the rest of the way up and over—and wound up with a handful of coiling muscle.

A massive, wedge-shaped head snapped up, and a forked tongue darted out toward Khaniel, smelling the air. The mercenary flinched back in shock and jerked his hand away, then froze, staring directly into the flat, black glare of the unmoving reptile. His arms and legs quivered with the strain of holding so perfectly still in such an unnatural pose, but he dared not move suddenly and provoke the thing. His muscles began to ache, and Khaniel feared that he would begin to cramp up.

The cream- and brown-striped reptile, a rock adder as thick as Khaniel's thigh and maybe three times as long as he was tall, slid ever-so-slowly forward, tongue flickering. The mercenary knew it possessed enough venom to kill a giant. He suspected that it had coiled up on the small ledge to sun itself.

"So?" Bruigan called from below, eager. "Do you see any moss? How much is up there?"

Khaniel, his breath coming in nervous gasps, ignored his companion.

The adder paused, motionless.

Heart pounding, Khaniel pulled his hand back, an inch at a time. He readied himself to drop down out of sight, back to the tree.

Not too fast, he silently insisted. *One strike, and it's all over*.

At that moment, the portion of the ledge beneath his foot crumbled away, and he slipped with a yelp halfway off the precipice, scraping his ribs. A cascade of detritus tumbled down.

"Hey!" Bruigan roared from below as soil and pebbles showered upon him. "Watch it!"

With a hiss of fury, the adder lunged.

In a panic, Khaniel released the ledge and seized the snake by its neck with both hands. The reptile's fangs slashed the air scant inches from his nose as he snapped his own head back in desperation. The jolt from the snake's momentum shoved him backward from his perch on the rock. The undersides of his arms scraped against the sharp edges as he slipped down and backward into open space. The mercenary's stomach lurched from the sensation of a terrifying plummet as he clung to the snake, hanging in space.

The rock adder hissed again in rage and thrashed back and forth, trying to dislodge Khaniel. The mercenary clung to it with all his strength, trying to sink his fingers into the scaly flesh, frantic not to lose his grip. At the same time, his legs kicked and flailed uselessly beneath him, unable to find any sort of foothold.

The majority of the snake's weight remained on the ledge, keeping them from plunging to the ground, but the adder's wild efforts pummeled the man against the face of the bluff, bruising him and knocking the wind from his lungs.

"By Brell's beard!" Bruigan shouted. "Let go of it!"

But Khaniel dared not. The snake kept snapping at him, its speed undiminished, and he feared it might manage a lucky strike before he tumbled beyond its reach. The thought of those glistening fangs, each as long as his index finger, piercing his face, made him shudder. Another smack against the rock face of the bluff made his head bounce. He saw spots.

The rock adder tried to pull back, to drag itself and its unwelcome rider back up to the top of the ledge. Its body wasn't made for such a retreat, though, and it couldn't muster the strength. Slowly, with each whipping twitch, the snake slipped a little farther over the side. Without any idea how to extricate himself from the predicament, Khaniel held on, waiting in dread for the inevitable plunge to the hard ground below.

Suddenly, the warrior smacked hard against the stunted tree he had stood upon earlier. Its gnarled trunk cracked the mercenary in the ribs, sending pain through his chest. He grunted in agony and felt his grip begin to slip. Struggling to ignore the injury, the mercenary fought to clamp down harder on the snake. He flung one leg over the springy tree, trying to hook it behind his knee. Using the adder as a makeshift rope, Khaniel strained to hoist himself up, fighting both gravity and the thrashing beast. Finally, he managed to pull himself upright enough that he could sit on the trunk. The tree sagged dangerously low with the combined weight of man and giant snake.

I hope to hell this works, Khaniel thought, eyeing the drop below him.

Gasping for breath and still fighting the furious, twitching snake, he dived off the other side of the tree, praying that it would hold and not rip free of the bluff face. As he fell, dragging the head of the snake with him down one side of the sagging trunk, the rest of the snake's body began slipping over the ledge. The mercenary kicked his feet against the wall, desperate to force himself *down,* hoping to pull enough of the snake's weight to his side of the makeshift pulley so that the two halves would be balanced. The snake snapped at him over and over, jerking its head from side to side, trying to work free of his grip. Khaniel's arms felt like lumps of pudding as he fought to keep out of range of the deadly bite.

He knew he couldn't hold on much longer.

As the last of the snake's torso cascaded off the ledge, Khaniel bounced to a stop, hanging by his aching, trembling hands from the adder's neck. The trick worked. The reptile's tail thrashed next to him, the beast bent double across the trunk of the tree above.

"My axe!" Khaniel called down at Bruigan. "Get ready!"

"I can't swing that oversized cleaver of yours!" Bruigan bellowed.

Khaniel growled in exasperation. "Not you!" he yelled as the snake whipped him about, slamming them both hard against the bluff face. "Just be ready to hand it to me!"

Bruigan answered something Khaniel couldn't make out, but when the dwarf called that he was ready, Khaniel acted.

The mercenary released the snake's neck and jerked his hands away lightning-quick, just fast enough to avoid getting bitten. As gravity pulled him away from the snapping jaws, he grabbed the adder's tail. The shift in weight proved to be enough. Khaniel began to slide downward, toward the ground, accelerating as the snake's head rose upward and more of its body looped over the tree.

When most of the adder's length had slid across the trunk and the thing's head reached near the apex, Khaniel released the snake and dropped the rest of the way to the ground. He landed hard but went into a tumble, springing to his feet, movement made easy by years of training in the practice yard. The rest of the snake followed its torso down, rapidly becoming a writhing coil of reptile flesh near the man. As its head reached the ground, it bounced hard a few feet away, dazed.

"Now!" Khaniel said, and he gestured frantically toward where Bruigan held the head of the massive axe in both hands.

The dwarf stared in awe, but he reacted quickly at the mercenary's demand. With one mighty shove, Bruigan tossed the blade handle-first toward Khaniel.

As the axe arced through the air, the rock adder reared up, turning toward Khaniel. Its eyes glittered with anger as it opened its mouth wide and lunged forward, aiming another strike at the man's face. Fighting off the dire urge to flinch away, Khaniel twisted and grabbed the handle of the huge blade out of midair. Though his arms felt like jiggling jelly, desperation lent the warrior a last bit of power. Continuing the quick, clean motion, he swung. The blade sliced through the snake's neck, separating it from the body, which fell away, jerking in death spasms. The head continued forward in a spurt of blood, right over Khaniel's shoulder. The wide mouth snapped open and shut several times as it sailed past, fangs still gleaming with venom. It tumbled into the tall grasses a few feet away.

Khaniel let the axe head drop at his feet. He sagged to the ground beside it, breathing hard. "Next time," he said between rasping gasps, "get your own damned moss."

Bruigan stood and stared for a moment, his mouth gaping. He nudged the still-twitching torso of the snake with the toe of his boot.

Khaniel couldn't help but smile a tiny bit at his companion's reaction. *That* was *pretty impressive,* he thought.

Finally regaining his wits, the dwarf said, "I think I'll pass, thanks. Besides, that's what I pay *you* for. You're the muscle, I'm the brains. Remember?" He glanced up at the top of the bluff. "So, did you see any bluemoss?"

Khaniel drew in another lungful of air and shook his head. "I don't recall. I was a little distracted." The mercenary felt a little wounded by the dwarf's lack of appreciation at what he had done.

"Well, climb back up there and see!"

Khaniel stared at his companion, wide-eyed in amazement. "Are you serious?" he asked, feeling put out. He looked pointedly at the body lying between them. "Did you not notice the giant snake that tried to *eat* me?"

Bruigan nodded, a faint hint of a smile playing across his crinkled face. "Yes, I noticed. But you dealt with it, and now it's done. I can't brew a keg of Faydwerian Double-Sour Stout without bluemoss, so earn your coin, lad, and find me some."

Khaniel shook his head in consternation, but after a few more moments of catching his breath, he climbed to his feet. "I think you've pickled those brains with that orc-piss you brew," he muttered as he prepared to scale the bluff one more time.

"Hey!" Bruigan blustered, "Keep talking like that, and you won't get any."

Khaniel could hear the amusement in the dwarf's voice. "Promise?" he teased as he began feeling for finger- and toeholds once more.

"I knew it all along," the dwarf muttered. "He's loopier than a sarnak."

The ledge where Khaniel had disturbed the snake proved to be a treasure trove of bluemoss. The plant preferred growing upon certain striations of rock, some of which lay exposed high along the bluff. Khaniel gathered several thick handfuls and tossed them over the side to Bruigan. Before he made his descent once more, he peered back down into the valley again, hoping to catch another glimpse of sun reflecting off armor. He did not see that, but something else did catch his attention, down in the soft soil in the shade of a copse of trees nearby.

Tracks, large and humanoid, indented the earth—made with feet the size of Khaniel's chest.

Trouble, Khaniel thought. He looked wistfully down at his armor and weapons, lying in a heap at the base of the bluff. He always hated removing them, but he could never have climbed in all that gear.

The mercenary took a coil of rope and draped it over the stunted tree, employing it in the same way he had utilized the giant snake to get him down before. Once he descended the bluff face, he released one end of the rope and drew the whole thing down.

Bruigan sat busily dressing the snake, slicing large hunks of the reptile's flesh and cutting it into strips, which he rolled into an oiled cloth. The dwarf shoved the cloth into his pack, which already bulged with numerous things the pair had foraged or scavenged over the last week. The snake meat would supply the pair's next few meals.

"Hurry with that," Khaniel instructed as he began donning his armor. The molded metal plates fit over his body like a second skin. "We may have unwanted company."

Bruigan paused in the middle of his work. "The shine of armor you saw?"

Khaniel shrugged. "I don't know," he admitted. "But there are tracks in the mud over there." He pointed. "They look like cyclops."

"Right," the dwarf said, renewing his efforts. "Almost done."

By the time Khaniel finished adjusting the straps of his armor and replacing his weapons, Bruigan had gathered up all the snake meat and stood expectantly, his pack high between his shoulders. "So, what are we hunting next?" the mercenary asked.

"Nothing. I've made a good haul, and that snake was a nice boon to cap off the trip. I got its fangs, its venom sacs, and more meat than we'll eat in a week. I can sell some of that when we get back to Freeport."

"Then let's get going," Khaniel suggested. The pair turned and set off in the direction they had come, working their way back into the valley.

Khaniel took the lead, stopping briefly to examine the large tracks he had spotted from aloft. The warrior knelt down and ran his finger along the edge of the depression. "I'd say cyclops, or maybe a young giant," he said at last, rising again and dusting his hands off. "Probably came through here yesterday."

"You think it's still around?" Bruigan asked, turning to peer about. Worry deepened the lines on his face.

"I doubt it," Khaniel replied. "They aren't known for patience. No reason they'd be hiding and waiting to jump us. If they lurked nearby, we'd already know it." Bruigan nodded but said nothing else. Khaniel turned, and the two of them resumed their journey.

The sun warmed the day nicely as they hiked through the meadows, passing between copses of trees. Bruigan did his best to keep up with the human's longer strides, but Khaniel still had to slow his pace for the dwarf. It allowed him to keep an eye to the ground, searching for more tracks, but he found nothing.

Eventually, the pair descended to the floor of the valley, where they picked up an animal trail that followed the stream. Khaniel let Bruigan take the lead then, allowing the dwarf to set the pace, while he relaxed his vigil a bit and let the sun warm his face. The mercenary felt happy to be going home.

"It'll be nice to get back to Freeport," Bruigan commented as they walked, echoing the mercenary's thoughts. "I could use a night in a bed instead of on the ground."

Khaniel grunted his agreement. "At the Bunker, you can't tell much difference between the two." His companion laughed at his jest. "Still," he continued, "I suppose it's time I paid the place a visit again."

Bruigan snorted. "What? After all this time we've spent together, you still prefer the company of your thick-necked friends whacking on one another with padded swords to gathering berries and fungus for a drunk old dwarf with aches in his joints? I'll wager none of the Steel Warriors has ever taught you how to brew a fine ale."

"No, they haven't," Khaniel admitted with a chuckle. "Nor do they tell stories quite the way you do." He let his smile fade. "But I'd like to see the new crop of recruits, find out how their training is going."

"You mean, you'd like to see if any of those recruits is impressive enough to unseat you as Cain Darkmoore's favorite son, don't you?"

"What do you mean?" the mercenary asked, though at hearing the dwarf's words, he puffed out his chest and raised his chin.

"Don't pretend you don't love it when Darkmoore dotes on you," Bruigan answered with a hint of rebuke in his voice. "I can see the pride in your eyes whenever the praise starts up."

"I suppose," the warrior admitted with a slight grin. "It is nice to be flattered. But if it's true, then why shouldn't I be proud? Master Darkmoore always said he never trained anyone with more talent."

Bruigan snorted. "That may be, but don't let it go to your head. There is such a thing as being too impressed with yourself. Just when you start to believe it, thinking you're the best in the business, there's something out there that can take you down. That snake almost got you today."

Khaniel shrugged. "A snake is hardly worthy sport," he argued, feeling a bit defensive. "At least, it shouldn't be. I just got complacent. A few hours in the practice yard will solve that problem.

No one fights better than the Steel Warriors," he boasted, "so there's no one better to train against. Besides," he added, "snakes don't buy you a round of drinks and talk about how hard you hit afterward."

Bruigan sighed. "I don't deny that you're a fine piece of work, lad. They trained you well at the Bunker. If any of those recruits turn out even half as good as you, then Darkmoore's got nothing to worry about from Sir Lucan D'Lere. But there is more to life than being the best with an axe."

Khaniel couldn't help but grimace a tiny bit. "So I've heard," he said, refusing to agree with his companion's assessment. "But it's been enough for me so far."

Bruigan didn't reply, so they continued along the trail in silence for a time. Khaniel knew they would be drawing near to where he had seen the telltale glint of the sun, so he began to study their surroundings again, watching for evidence that they were no longer alone. He didn't want to be surprised.

He needn't have worried.

The sound of voices, an argument really, came wafting over a ridge in the path long before the two of them spotted the source. Khaniel laid his hand upon Bruigan's shoulder, a sign for the dwarf to slow up and allow the mercenary to scout ahead.

Bruigan shuffled to the side, and Khaniel skirted past him.

At the top of the ridge, he could see over a second rise to where two dozen or more humans, armed and armored for battle, had gathered in a large meadow. They all had horses, though some had dismounted. They seemed to have halted for a rest. Three of them had come ahead and stood gathered in a hollow at the base of the ridge, arguing.

The first, a young woman, stood facing Khaniel's direction, though she focused her attention on the man opposite herself, who had his back to the mercenary. The third member of the trio sat on a large rock off to one side, contemplating something far away. At another time, the mercenary might have thought the woman striking, with hair the color of summer wheat framing a narrow face with fine, almost elven features. But at the moment, only her eyes held his attention. The color of the sky, they glared at her counterpart with an intensity born of a fervent and absolute conviction. Whatever driving force motivated her, those eyes told the world that nothing would dissuade her from her path.

"We must keep moving," she said, leaning upon the hilt of a sword she held point-down. A two-handed blade of exquisite craftsmanship that came almost to her chin, the sword complemented her armor, a suit of gleaming plate, all silver and white. The emblem etched into the breastplate marked her as a Knight of Truth, a servant of Mithaniel Marr from Freeport. "This is a holy quest, and the Lightbearer will not permit us to fail. There is no need for your paranoid precautions. We are close to the valley now; I can feel it."

The man to whom she spoke threw his hands out, palms up, in a gesture of exasperation. "I understand your eagerness, Zethamy," he said, "but this is foolish! We have no one scouting ahead, no pickets to either side of the column. We're moving blind through these mountains, begging for trouble." A shining suit of plate mail protected him, too, over which he wore a snowy white fur-trimmed cloak that sported the emblem of his holy order.

The woman drew herself up defiantly. "Your fear is faithless and unbecoming, Gerial," she said. "Do you honestly doubt that Mithaniel Marr moves with us, protecting us from any dangers? His blessings and will grant us the power to defeat anything that would stand in our way. How can you doubt such a glorious truth?"

Khaniel rolled his eyes at the woman's words, but he had recognized the knight's name. Hearing it startled him, and when Gerial spun away from the woman and began to pace, the mercenary confirmed that it was the same man. His plain face featured matted brown hair not quite covering ears slightly too large for the rest of his head. He moved like a career soldier, at ease in his armor. He kept a sword at his hip, and Khaniel could see a quiver of arrows protruding from beneath his cloak.

"Maybe *you* can talk some sense into her, Maix," Gerial said to the third member of the group, the man seated upon the rock, who watched them both with a frown. Unlike the first two, he wore no armor, only a light brown tunic of thick wool with similar but darker pants underneath. "Marr knows, she won't listen to *me*," he added. Then he turned to stalk up the trail, right toward Khaniel.

"Trouble making her see reason, Gerial?" Khaniel asked, moving more fully into view.

Gerial jerked to a stop, reaching for his blade. "What the—" he exclaimed. "By the Lightbearer, where did *you* come from?" he demanded, a smile breaking out across his face. At the sound of his voice, the other two turned in the mercenary's direction.

"From Freeport, the same as you," Khaniel answered with a hint of a smirk as Gerial closed the distance to clasp hands with the mercenary. "Though I don't know what business the Knights have out here in the middle of nowhere," he added.

"No less business than one of the Steel Warriors," Zethamy replied in a haughty tone, bringing her blade up and ready. "Who is this man, Gerial?"

Gerial turned back to the woman. "A good friend, Zethamy, and one who knows the truth of what I speak. He's probably the best swordsman to come out of the Bunker in the last twenty years."

Zethamy eyed Khaniel doubtfully, and he simply returned her stare. Those icy blue eyes narrowed in anger or maybe simply dismissal. He already knew he would find it difficult to get along with her. "You were sent to disrupt our quest," she accused him. "It will not work; we have the power of the Lightbearer on our side."

"So I heard," Khaniel said. "But I'm not here to disrupt anything." He turned and called over his shoulder. "Bruigan, it's all right. They're from Freeport." The dwarf appeared from behind a small clump of bushes and climbed the hill to join the rest of them. "This is Bruigan Stormbarrel," Khaniel said, "a master brewer from Freeport. I am working in his service at the moment, and our meeting with you was chance and happenstance, nothing more."

Gerial nodded as he greeted the dwarf. "I'm Gerial Krean. May I present Zethamy Demarro, the leader of our expedition, and Maix Treganan of the Arcane Scientists?"

Bruigan gave a stiff bow. "Milady," he said, "Master Treganan."

Khaniel nodded slightly at Zethamy, who had not yet lowered her guard, but Maix drew his attention away from her. Gerial's revelation identifying Maix as a wizard gave the mercenary pause. "So what's a mage doing out here with all these Knights?" he asked with a frown. He found the use of magic in battle a bit distasteful, even cowardly.

"I am simply an adviser," Maix replied. "Like you, in the service of another," he added, nodding toward Zethamy.

"Zethamy commands our expedition," Gerial continued. "We seek a lost valley, a hidden holy place where a member of our order once dwelt. He was a hermit, a caretaker for—"

"Things that do not concern them, Gerial," the woman cut in coldly. "If you vouch for this soldier, I will accept his story. But we have no time for social visits."

Gerial turned back to face Zethamy. "I thought that Khaniel and his friend here might know more of the valley we seek. Perhaps they have passed through it."

"We have no need of their aid," the woman said firmly. "My visions guide us well enough. Now, let them pass, and we shall be on our way, as well."

"The troops need more time to rest," Gerial said with obvious restraint. "You cannot push them this hard."

"Nonsense," Zethamy replied. "They are fit young men and women, and their faith and trust in the Lightbearer grants them the strength they need to—"

"Why do you bother bringing advisers on your quest if you won't listen to them?" Khaniel interrupted. The holy aura of superiority the Knights of Truth displayed always rubbed him the wrong way. Gerial, at least, served as an exception to that vain mentality. He was a sensible fellow, not one to blindly pass judgment on those outside his order.

"Excuse me?" Zethamy said, her eyes widening in anger. "You would presume to—"

"Yes, I would," Khaniel interrupted again. "I would very much presume to tell you when you're wrong." Beside him, Bruigan made a show of clearing his throat.

Gerial shifted uncomfortably. "Khaniel," he began in a warning yet sympathetic tone. "Perhaps you and your friend should—"

Khaniel found himself too much into the moment to listen, though. The condescension in the woman's voice had rankled him beyond caring if he upset her. He continued. "I've never put much stock into the idea that some god is going to take care of every last detail of my life for me. I have a much stronger faith in my own skills than some fickle, mystical being."

Zethamy's eyes widened in fury, and she opened her mouth to argue, but Khaniel continued on, not letting her interrupt. "If you want to trust in a god rather than yourself, that's your business, but at least open your eyes and consider that maybe Marr's 'blessings' are appearing in the form of good advice. Gerial here is telling you that you're being a fool. Maybe the mage here thinks so, too. I happen to agree. Maybe, if you hear it from all three of us, you'll get over yourself and be sensible."

The mercenary turned and pointed back the way he and the dwarf had come. "Bruigan and I spotted tracks a bit earlier today, and unless I'm very much out of practice, a cyclops made them. With the size of the force you command, you need to be sending outriders ahead and to the sides as pickets. Hell, the two of us," and he motioned to the dwarf beside him, "managed to come right up on you without you noticing. If I were Mithaniel Marr, I'd be making your life miserable just to teach you a lesson, and I'd be laughing at your misfortune."

"Khaniel, that's enough!" Gerial said, his voice much firmer. "I will not allow you to insult—"

Whatever Gerial intended to say, he never finished it. A spear the size of a sapling ran him through, knocking him backward and pinning him against a low slope fully ten paces away.

2

KHANIEL WHIRLED AROUND, HIS AXE READY. A cyclops rose up from behind a tumble of boulders on the side of a low rise a good 40 paces away. It gripped another two spears in its massive, pudgy hands. The cyclops reared back, ready to throw. Instead of flinching, the mercenary strode forward several steps, past where Bruigan stood staring in awe.

"Hide!" Khaniel ordered the dwarf. "Get out of sight, and stay out of my way!" Moving faster than Khaniel had ever seen, Bruigan hit the ground and rolled beneath a fallen log that rested hard up against a large boulder. "Stay there!" Khaniel hissed as the cyclops hurled the spear at him.

"Fools!" Maix shouted from behind Khaniel. "It's too soon!"

Khaniel watched the spear approach and used his axe to swat it away at the last moment. Then he turned toward the wizard, startled at the man's words. Maix ran out of the hollow, up one side of the flanking hills, where three more of the giant humanoids appeared. The wizard waved his hands frantically, and Khaniel thought he intended to conjure some magic to use against the giant creatures. The mercenary started to call out after him, to warn him that he charged to his death, but the trio of cyclopes had pulled up as if actually listening to him.

"You were supposed to wait!" Maix screamed at the nearest one. "We haven't found it yet!"

Traitor, Khaniel realized. He ground his teeth in hatred, but he had no time to do anything about it. *More of Zethamy's folly,* he decided. He risked a quick glance over at her, actually feeling some level of pity. *All the zealousness in the world, and not a lick of sense.*

The woman had not moved since the attack began. She stood rooted to the spot, staring dumfounded at Gerial's body. Khaniel saw that the paladin was dead, his hands wrapped around the shaft of the massive spear protruding from his chest. Blood spilled from the wound in rivulets, pouring over the surface of his armor and pooling around him on the ground.

In the meadow beyond her, where the rest of Zethamy's band of paladins had congregated, more of the cyclopes swarmed in. Many swung massive clubs in both hands, great wooden weapons as large as a man and covered in gnarled knots. Khaniel saw the human troops rising up, reaching for weapons or trying to mount horses in order to meet the attack. It looked to be a furious fight. He counted half a dozen or so of the one-eyed behemoths already in their midst, swatting at armored soldiers as if they were annoying dogs vying for table scraps. Several more appeared on the fringes of the sudden battle.

It's a whole tribe, Khaniel realized in dread wonder.

"Take the woman alive," Maix commanded from the top of the hill, "and kill the rest!"

Khaniel spared the traitorous mage one last, scathing look. Maix pointed toward Zethamy with one hand while he gestured with the other for the three cyclopes nearest him to move out. They began to lumber down the slope toward her. Thankfully, the wizard's orders seemed to snap her out of her horror. She hefted her sword and stared balefully at the three approaching humanoids.

No time to help, Khaniel realized, turning back to the lone cyclops coming toward him. Its long and pointed head—almost deformed in its grotesqueness—sprouted a tuft of black, wiry hair from the very top, like a stem of rotten broccoli protruding from a garden row. The thing's single eye seemed too big for its head, with a red and puffy lid suggesting that the cyclops had not gotten enough sleep. A crude sleeveless leather jerkin, made up of numerous deerskins stitched together in a mishmash pattern, only half covered similar ill-fitting pants. The cyclops had the pants themselves tucked into soft boots laced on with rope, the frayed ends of which dragged on the ground.

The beast still clung to its last spear, apparently preferring to keep it handy for melee combat. It leveled the huge stone tip, lashed to the shaft with sinew, at Khaniel's chest and broke into a trot.

The mercenary moved forward in a wary half-crouch, watching for the giant to commit its thrust before making his own counterattack. When the cyclops slowed ever so slightly and drew back its arms, Khaniel set his feet and twisted. The axe sliced through the air as the spear point jabbed past his shoulder. The blade of the axe cut through the wood cleanly.

"Stupid," Khaniel growled, following through and spinning, yanking the axe toward the cyclops' knee.

The behemoth saw the attack coming and stepped back to avoid it, still clutching its ruined weapon in one hand. As Khaniel pressed forward, his giant foe tried to pummel him with its free hand, balled up into a meaty fist the size of the mercenary's head.

Khaniel made one smooth shift to his weight and ducked beneath the punch. At the same time, he reversed his axe in his hands and yanked the huge blade upward, raking it along the cyclops' exposed forearm. His attack left behind a horrid gash dripping blood, but he did not remain still to watch the beast's reaction. As the cyclops reared up in pain, howling, Khaniel ducked behind it and reversed the axe once more.

The cyclops tried to back away and turn toward its tormentor, but Khaniel moved too fast. With one more vicious swing, he caught the giant humanoid across the back of its knee. The cyclops' scream of pain drowned out the sound of bone crunching and tissue tearing. Even as its leg lost the strength to support it, the one-eyed monster tried to stagger away from Khaniel. Again, though, the mercenary's faster reactions got the better of the cyclops. The human lunged forward and down, grabbing one frayed end of rope trailing the beast's foot; then he dived to the side, pulling the rope with him and wrapping it around his foe's other, wounded leg.

The maneuver worked. The creature tangled itself up as it took another hopping half-step backward. It could not keep its balance and toppled over, away from Khaniel. He ran forward, axe raised high. Planting one boot against the creature's ribcage, he used his momentum to leap across its body toward its head. He landed near the opposite shoulder just as the cyclops began to roll over. The mercenary's axe came down, splitting the misshapen skull with a loud thunk.

The cyclops spasmed once and then lay still, its sole eye staring vacantly toward the sky.

Khaniel stepped away and turned to survey the rest of the battlefield. In the distant meadow, the screams of men, horses, and cyclopes echoed back to him as a whirl of metal and flesh churned the field muddy. The mercenary would have liked to rush into the fray, to share in the thrill of the battle, but Zethamy still stood between him and the rest of her troops, struggling to hold her own against the trio of beasts Maix had sent at her.

Without a second thought, Khaniel sprinted toward her. He considered switching to his smaller sword for the fight, thinking it might serve him better in such cramped quarters, but against a cyclops, it held minimal value; he could put far more force behind the axe and cut much deeper with it. He had no time for whittling the giants down with the smaller blade.

Zethamy took a strike from a club on her shoulder, and the blow sent her reeling sideways.

She staggered and dropped to one knee just as Khaniel reached her.

"Stay down!" he yelled as he yanked his axe up enough to deflect a second blow aimed toward her head. "Keep out of my way!" He stepped into another swing and slammed his axe hard against a second club, then ducked down as the third beast's weapon whistled over his head. "I can fight better without you interfering!" he shouted.

"I'm no coward!" Zethamy replied, and she tried to rise to her feet again. The move nearly cost Khaniel his life as he tried to step through her space to evade another club blow and instead almost collided with her. The club missed his face by inches, but one of the knotty protrusions on it caught the top of his shoulder.

The force of the strike spun the mercenary halfway around, and he nearly lost his grip on his axe from the bruising pain it caused. Growling in anger, he lunged up and swung his weapon with bestial force, cleaving the club in half near the handle. The cyclops, shaking its hands from the sting of the blow, stepped back, blinking in worry.

Khaniel didn't waste time on that creature, though. He repositioned himself with a lunge and a sidestep so that both the remaining giants temporarily flanked him. He waited a heartbeat for them to draw back their weapons, and then, when it seemed he would be pounded, he tucked into a roll and dived out of the way. The resounding crack of hardwood on leg bones satisfied him. Both of the one-eyed horrors shrieked and hopped back, away from the danger. Each one glared at the other, exchanging snarling, guttural words.

Khaniel prepared to take advantage of the distraction to close in for the kill. He flipped his axe around and hefted it high over his shoulder. The closest cyclops' rump made a perfect target, but before he could initiate the attack, Zethamy darted between the two creatures, swinging her greatsword with furious abandon. The cyclops stepped back, right into Khaniel. Its body, positioned too close to the mercenary, ruined his attack. To add to his frustration, the giant beast stepped on his foot in the process, pinning him in place.

It proved to be the worst sort of ill luck, for at that moment, the third cyclops, the one whose weapon Khaniel had previously ruined, hit him from behind with a powerful punch. The blow caught him square in the side, and Khaniel grunted in breathy agony as he felt the air knocked from his lungs. He heard the crack of bone and felt searing pain shoot through his chest.

She's gone and killed me, the stupid wench, he thought as he sagged to the ground, clutching at his side.

The cyclops reared back for another attack as the one standing on his foot pivoted away to avoid the paladin's slashing blade. Khaniel tried to suck in a breath, to regain his air, but the effort made him wince.

The pain made him furious.

Gripping his axe with one hand, Khaniel shoved himself to his feet with the other. Red rage tinged the edges of his vision as he stumbled back, away from a punch aimed at his head. When the giant's follow-through left a deadly opening, Khaniel struck back with all the strength he could muster. The axe bit into his opponent's side, gouging deeply and ripping a huge chunk of flesh away. Blood spurted everywhere, soaking the mercenary. The cyclops teetered, clutching at its midsection. Khaniel did not hesitate. The second axe blow caught the creature in its gut, slicing through the hands it held there defensively.

With a sickening groan, the cyclops sank to its knees, its single eye gazing at the mercenary. With a lone sob, the creature toppled forward, forcing Khaniel to step away. It flopped face down, squirming and whimpering softly in the dirt and leaves.

Khaniel did not stay by its side to watch its death throes.

The two remaining cyclopes had the better of Zethamy. The first had a single huge fist engulfing both of hers, which still clasped the hilt of her sword. The giant used its height to yank the woman up on her toes, stretching her out so that its companion could attempt to reach down and grab her feet. Zethamy squirmed and kicked, trying to evade, which only served to enrage the one holding her. He shook her back and forth, perhaps hoping to daze her enough to slow her down.

Khaniel lunged toward the beast, aiming his axe at the small of its back. The other cyclops saw him coming, though, and bellowed a warning. The one holding the paladin tried to turn defensively to evade the mercenary, hoping to thrust Zethamy into the path of the blade, but the creature was too big and slow; Khaniel's axe grazed the behemoth's elbow.

The blow didn't ruin the joint, but the cyclops jerked its arm away, releasing its captive. Zethamy tumbled to the ground and rolled to one side.

"Now stay down!" Khaniel bellowed, trying not to clutch at his broken ribs as he stepped nearer to her, hoping to protect her. "Let me finish them!"

Zethamy tried to rise again, nearly shoving Khaniel off balance in the process. "Mithaniel Marr protects me!" she screamed, hoisting her sword once more. "I do not need a common sword-for-hire to 'save' me!" She swung her blade at the nearest cyclops, driving it back with several feints.

At least she knows how to use that thing, the mercenary thought as he turned his attention to the final creature.

The cyclops hesitated, crouched and wary, waiting for him to move. When he brandished his axe, it flinched. Khaniel took a step toward it, and it recoiled a bit, as if expecting him to take a full swing.

It fears me, he thought. *Good. I'll make it run. Less pain that way.*

He gave a great shout and stutter-stepped at the cyclops, swinging his axe fully and wildly, hoping the bluff would make it turn tail and flee.

Instead, the giant twisted around and threw a huge fistful of dirt right in the mercenary's face.

Khaniel flung his arm up to ward off the attack, but in his effort to swing so hard, he couldn't release the axe fast enough. Grains of sand spattered his face, stinging his eyes. He jerked his head back, snarling in pain and trying to wipe the soil from his face with his metal-encased forearm. As much as he wanted to keep his sight on the cyclops, the dirt hurt too much. He tried to stumble away, to get clear of the creature and let tears flush his eyes clean.

The impact of the giant's club slammed hard into Khaniel's hip. Only the plates of his armor kept the blow from shattering his bones, but it still struck hard enough to send him tumbling. He rolled on the ground, smacking his head against the bole of a tree. White lightning streaked across the mercenary's vision; a roar filled his ears.

Get up! Khaniel screamed at himself inside his head. *Fight!*

The myriad pains coursing through the warrior's body galvanized into a single ball of fury. Khaniel began to lose his thoughts as that fury enveloped him, spurred him onward. He felt himself sinking from consciousness, not into unconsciousness but into a more primal thing, a thing bent solely on combat.

The mercenary no longer saw his surroundings; he simply existed as a single compunction. He was a killer, a perfect machine, his body trained and honed to lay waste to his enemies. He did not feel himself swinging his axe, though he knew that his arms did so. He did not sense his legs moving, his feet stepping through routines practiced dozens, hundreds, thousands of times, but he understood that the fluid motions happened. His body did not need his conscious mind to help it work; it fought better without rationality.

After a time, perhaps mere seconds or perhaps long minutes, Khaniel's consciousness began to resume control. The berserk rage drained from him, and he found himself aware once more. The mercenary's sight returned to him in mid-swing. He watched as it cut deeply into the thigh of a cyclops, observed almost in complete detachment as the follow-through spun him around.

He saw with abrupt horror the blade bite into the flesh of Zethamy's face.

In other circumstances, given the time to contemplate it, Khaniel would have considered that face beautiful, with its icy blue eyes and delicate, angled features. He would be drawn to her beauty, enchanted by her intensity, were she not so damned arrogant. But instead, as that face, that visage, erupted in blood, the warrior cringed in abject dread.

The blow didn't strike her fully. Facing him, Zethamy saw it coming and tried to react, tried to flinch outside the arc of his swing. But she couldn't quite evade the whistling blade. The axe grazed against her temple, sliced the bridge of her nose, raked across her eyes.

Khaniel thought too late to pull away, to flinch and let the blade recoil from her. In desperation, he jerked back, drew the axe to himself, tightening the circle of its momentum, but the damage was done. He saw no face any longer, only bloody flesh.

Zethamy Demarro made no sound as she pitched forward into the leaves and lay still.

For a long moment, Khaniel could do nothing but stare. No noise from the battle raging around him reached the warrior's ears. No measure of time penetrated his awareness. He simply stood, numb, his mind unwilling to register what his eyes witnessed.

Zethamy Demarro, Knight of Truth, holy warrior serving in the name of Mithaniel Marr, lay dead, slain by Khaniel's hand.

No.

It is not possible, he told himself. *You did not do that. A Steel Warrior, a honed fighting instrument, could not have slain an ally. You're supposed to be perfect.*

Not when you lose your senses and fly into a rage, another little voice, a challenging, accusing voice, responded. *Perfected fighting machines do not let their emotions take over.*

No!

Khaniel looked down at his hands. They trembled as they gripped the axe, white knuckles spattered with gore. The blade itself dripped with it. Zethamy's blood soaked it. Bits of her face.

Suddenly, everything he had believed in, all the skill, all the prowess that lent him pride, crumbled in the warrior's mind. With one sickening strike, Khaniel had laid bare the fundamental flaw within himself, had torn away the feeble trappings of civility and superiority that hid his true essence. His animalistic nature revealed itself at last. His rage had lent him strength, had given him the will and the power to fight with unparalleled savagery, but it had also denied him his means of differentiating friend from foe.

"No!" he screamed, ashamed.

Khaniel wanted to fling the axe away, but he could not. Pain washed through the mercenary as the last vestiges of that savagery faded, replaced by overwhelming, debilitating agony from old wounds and new. With a cough and a grunt, Khaniel sank to one knee, his axe falling to the ground by his side. His arms felt leaden, quivering with the strain he exerted just to keep them from flopping useless at his sides. He could barely draw breath.

At that moment, as the very core of his being seemed to disintegrate within himself, Khaniel broke down. A single, muffled, choking sob escaped his lungs. Self-pity cascaded through him. He had made a mockery of everything he believed in, everything he had trained to become. It was all gone.

"No," he whispered in utter sorrow and despair. *Not this.*

For long moments, the warrior knelt there in the grass and grieved for himself. He gripped the axe handle as he stared at Zethamy's body. Then, a challenging roar snapped Khaniel out of his trance. Four more cyclopes reared up from the far side of a ridge, leering at him. The nearest one slammed its club against the earth and rock, making the ground bounce beneath the mercenary's wobbly legs.

The four one-eyed horrors came at him.

Khaniel knew he couldn't fight them. He had nothing left. He doubted he could even lift his axe, much less swing it. The cyclopes would simply kill him, let him fall beside Zethamy in ignominious defeat. *A fitting death*, he thought, preferable to facing the world as a wretch, a monster. But Khaniel could not find the courage to die so easily. He knew in his heart it was cowardice piled on top of all his other failures, but he masked that further shame behind the thought that, if nothing else, he had to bear witness to the treachery of Maix Treganan.

Somehow, he found the strength to flee.

Tumbling, half crawling, the disgraced warrior scrambled away from the four giants. He struggled toward the others, the cadre of paladins Zethamy had led into the mountains. He hoped they still withstood the onslaught of the attack, still held their own against the horde of cyclopes that had swarmed out of the mountains. At the lip of the hollow, he saw them. A huddled clump of armored men and women and a few horses stood in a muddy, blood-soaked patch of meadow. Bodies lay strewn all about them, both paladins and giants. The cyclopes, it seemed, had retreated, leaving the humans to collapse in their hollow victory.

Behind Khaniel, one of the cyclopes bellowed at him, and he turned back long enough to see it plodding forward, a wicked-looking spiked club clenched in its hands. The one-eyed beast raised the weapon high as its rumbling footsteps brought it closer to the mercenary. Behind the creature, the other three retreated. Already, they had moved beyond the next ridge, only the upper halves of their torsos still visible.

A shout issued from the remaining paladins, and Khaniel turned back to spy one of the soldiers stand, pointing in his direction. He took another exhausted step toward them, too tired to even shout for aid, but it didn't matter. A trio of armor-clad warriors mounted their horses and galloped near.

The cyclops issued another bellow, a sound filled with rage and frustration, but it did not seem eager to accept the challenge of three well-armed opponents on horseback all by itself. Khaniel sagged to his knees and watched the beast give him one last baleful stare with its single eye. It slammed the ground with its club once more, making the earth beneath the mercenary bounce, and then it turned away to join its companions in retreat.

The three paladins thundered past Khaniel toward the giant, but at the sight of three more of them, discretion overcame their valor and they turned back. The mercenary sprawled onto his side, clutching his broken ribs and breathing hard.

The three mounted Knights approached, their weapons still brandished. "Who are you?" one of the three of them demanded, "and where is the Lady Zethamy and Lord Gerial?" Curly red hair framed a face with plenty of freckles and features belonging to one barely more than a boy. His left arm hung limp at his side, and blood trickled from beneath his mail on his right thigh.

Khaniel tried to draw a deep enough breath to answer them, but the effort sent stabbing fire through his chest. He doubled over in agony.

"Answer me!" the young Knight of Truth demanded. "Where are the lord and lady?" A hint of panic filled his voice.

Khaniel shook his head helplessly and tried to speak again, but another's reply interrupted his own.

"Dead." Bruigan's voice. He stood at the top of the ridge, looking down on Khaniel and his three inquisitors. Mud caked the dwarf and leaves clung to his beard, but he appeared unhurt. "They fell in battle. I watched them both," he said wearily. "The cyclopes took their bodies," he added.

"You lie!" a second paladin yelled, whirling her horse around. If anything, she appeared younger than the first Knight, and her long brown hair matted one side of her face, mingled with blood from a gash in her temple.

Children, Khaniel thought in dismay. *She led children up here. Marr help her.*

The girl leveled a lance at Bruigan's chest as she approached him, but the dwarf only hung his head in sorrow.

"I wish that I were lying," he said, his voice scratchy with emotion. "But I do not. Your Lord Gerial was slain with a cyclopean spear, and the lady . . ." he paused, leaving the sentence unfinished, looking straight at Khaniel.

The mercenary stared back at the dwarf, understanding. Bruigan would lie for him, would spare him the dishonor, if he so wished. Maix and his minions had removed the evidence, had taken Zethamy's body. Revealing the wizard as a traitor would mask the mercenary's crime.

"She fell by my hand," Khaniel said quietly. Bruigan flinched and closed his eyes, knowing they could not undo what was to come. "In the fury of battle, I accidentally struck her."

"Murderer!" the girl screamed, taking another step toward Bruigan. "Both of you!"

"Alisse!" the young man shouted. "Hold! Yours is not to judge or pass sentence," he said. Then he looked at Khaniel. "And what of the wizard, Maix? Did he fall, too?"

Khaniel shook his head. "He is your traitor," he muttered. "Maix was in league with the cyclopes."

"Lies, all lies," Alisse growled. "Don't listen to them, Kerard. You think it's coincidence that they happened to appear the same time the ambush occurred? They plot with D'Lere to foil us."

Khaniel wanted to laugh, but he knew it would hurt too much. "Yes," he said, weariness making his voice weak, "you're exactly right. My brewmaster friend and I are allies of the cyclopes. That's why I have half a dozen broken bones and came running toward you to avoid being squashed into the earth."

The girl had no response to the mercenary's comments, but she continued to glower at him.

"You wear the armor of a Steel Warrior," the third Knight of Truth said. He seemed a few years older, with a scruff of beard on his chin and eyes that studied everything with intensity. "Why are you out here?"

Khaniel cringed, as if the words were an accusation. *You have shamed your order,* they seemed to say.

Bruigan answered. "Because I hired him to help me gather ingredients for my recipes." To show the truth of his words, the dwarf slung his pack down to the ground and opened it, dumping the contents out. "See? We've been gathering supplies so I can brew up some fine ales and stouts back in Freeport. I hired him to accompany me. I'm no weaponsmaster."

Alisse barked one quick, sneering laugh. "So this is what a member of the Bunker has been reduced to? Picking berries in the forest? How noble."

"No less noble than following a madwoman into the mountains to your doom," Khaniel snapped back before he could help himself. He immediately regretted it.

Kerard nudged his horse forward and leveled his sword at the mercenary's throat. "Dangerous words from a man who admits to slaying her. The Lady Zethamy was a great woman, blessed with divine sight by Mithaniel Marr himself. Mock her at your peril."

Khaniel raised his arms in supplication. "I'm sorry," he said, his tone wavering. "Would that I could undo it."

"I doubt it," Alisse said haughtily. Then she turned to her companions. "What now? The lady has fallen. We are without guidance. And these two must be punished," she added, jabbing a finger in Khaniel's and Bruigan's directions. "Whether they speak truth or falsehood, at least one has committed crimes against us."

The third paladin, the older one, nodded and sheathed his sword. "Then we have no choice but to return to Freeport and let Lord Dushire and the other masters of the temple sort this out." He looked first at Bruigan and then at Khaniel. "In the name of the Knights of Truth, I place you both under arrest."

Khaniel closed his eyes and swallowed hard before nodding in acceptance. *And so begins the long downfall of a wretched excuse for a man,* he thought in misery.

3

"IT'S TIME," KHANIEL'S GUARD SAID THROUGH the barred window in his cell door. The prisoner sat on his bed, staring at the floor. He looked up as the guard, another Steel Warrior, unbolted the cell door and swung it into the tiny chamber. Laran Kintz appeared, one of the recruits Khaniel had trained a few years back. A good student and eager learner, Laran had proved a fair shot with a bow, but his friendly smile, always wide across his face, was gone. "Are you ready?"

Khaniel took a single deep breath and nodded. He rose to his feet, started toward the exit, and then stopped. "Just a moment," he said as he turned back toward the wash basin. "Could I have some lantern light, please?" he asked.

No windows to the outside illuminated the small cells in the Bunker, and when Laran stepped into Khaniel's chamber holding a small oil lantern in one hand, the prisoner blinked in its harsh glare. He let his eyes adjust to the brightness and then peered down into the water of the washbasin.

The reflection staring back at him hardly seemed his own. Oh, his features shone in the water, all right, from the prominent cheekbones and the cleft in his chin to the close-cropped brown hair that came down to his ears. Several days' worth of beard had sprouted along his jaw line, actually growing in nicely—*or it would,* he thought, *if I remained alive long enough.*

But the eyes belonged to someone else.

Khaniel stared at them, trying to understand why.

Because they are the eyes of a dead man, he realized. *They've known sorrow and felt pain, and they understand that there is no absolution from what you've done.*

Those thoughts probably should have made Khaniel's gut knot up, but no apprehension arose. He had felt numb ever since the day he and Bruigan had surrendered to the remaining Knights of Truth. The finality of Zethamy's death, a tragedy of his own making, seemed too much for his soul to bear. A trained warrior, an expert at arms and tactics, should never jeopardize an ally, much less injure her.

Much less kill her.

"It really is time," Laran urged.

"I know," Khaniel replied, splashing a bit more water onto that face with those stranger's eyes. He dampened his hair and smoothed it back, but he couldn't wash the deadness from the eyes. "I wish I had a razor," he said.

"You know I can't," Laran said, apologizing.

Khaniel waved it away. "It's all right," he said, reassuring his former student. "I don't really need one. The beard will stop growing after today, anyway."

"Khaniel," Laran started, "they won't—" He paused. "Master Darkmoore won't let them—"

Khaniel turned to look at the younger man, a Steel Warrior at the beginning of his career, with so much promise before him. "If he's half the leader I think he is, he will and he should." When the dismay deepened in Laran's face, the prisoner added, "Even if he has to cast the deciding vote himself."

Laran opened his mouth to protest, then snapped it shut again.

"I'm ready," Khaniel said, turning toward the door. "Let's go."

Solid gray stone blocks, lit with lanterns at regular intervals, formed the featureless halls of the lowest levels of the Bunker. Khaniel had never spent much time down there during his early days at the stronghold, for it consisted of nothing more than storage rooms and cells for prisoners. No one lurked about, for which Khaniel was thankful. He wanted a moment to steel his mind against the stares, the accusing gazes.

Laran led him up the first flight of stone steps to another hallway, and then they found themselves approaching the audience chamber. Khaniel could hear the buzz of voices long before they reached the double doors, and the crowd that had gathered spilled out into the corridor. At the sight of him, the buzz rose in intensity. Khaniel stared straight ahead, avoiding eye contact with anyone.

They can condemn me, he thought, *and I can't blame them. But I won't let them witness me suffer for it.*

Inside the audience chamber, the senior leaders had gathered upon the dais at the front of the room. He saw all the usual faces—Valeron Dushire of the Knights of Truth, Tholius Quey representing the clergy of the Temple of Marr, Romiak Justathorn and Sapphire Moonshadow from the Arcane Scientists, and Khaniel's own mentor, Cain Darkmoore, avowed leader of the Steel Warriors. Each one of them represented his or her respective faction within the alliance arrayed against Sir Lucan D'Lere and his Freeport Militia. They all stared at him with blank expressions as he approached the dais. The crowd quieted to a dull murmur as Cain Darkmoore raised his hands for silence.

"I present the prisoner, Khaniel Devlin," Laran began, "for trial and sentencing in the death of one Zethamy Demarro, a Knight of Truth, while on holy and earnest expedition."

"So let all evidence be heard," Cain intoned. "Everyone be seated."

Khaniel took his appointed chair before the council, with Laran behind him. Custom typically demanded a prisoner on trial have two guards, but in Khaniel's case, Laran's presence was mostly formality. Khaniel and Bruigan had never offered any resistance when the young Knights had chosen to take them into custody. In fact, Khaniel had even explained the proper procedures for prisoner transfer to Nailan, the third of the three who had confronted him and who held seniority among the surviving paladins.

Cain stood and looked over the assemblage. In his impeccably polished suit of plate armor, he seemed the very epitome of all a Steel Warrior represented—power and grace, deadly ability, and perfect control in combat.

Khaniel had once aspired to such an image.

"The nature of these proceedings troubles me deeply," Cain began, looking directly at Khaniel as he spoke. "It is not often that one of our own sits before us, accused of acts unbecoming to his stature and station. That said, I wish it to be known that I will only participate in the hearing of the evidence, not in any decision of guilt or innocence. I find that I am too personally involved to trust my own instincts in such matters. I hope the council will see fit to heed my advice on matters of sentencing, should such come to pass." Then Lord Darkmoore returned to his seat.

Khaniel closed his eyes and lowered his head. He could hear his mentor's unspoken message: *I am too deeply ashamed of your acts to judge you fairly.* He had disappointed Cain in a most profound way.

The court conducted the hearing in a simple and straightforward manner. Various witnesses came forth to recount what they knew of the events surrounding the ambush and of Zethamy's and Gerial's deaths. The three Knights of Truth spoke first, followed by Bruigan, who was also being held in the Bunker's prison, pending his own hearing. The witnesses explained everything directly and without embellishment. No one said any more or any less than the truth, though Alisse painted Khaniel in the most negative light as she recounted her dealings with him.

Khaniel found no fault in any of the testimony, though he did learn more of the nature of Zethamy's quest from Nailan's revelations. The hermit Gerial had mentioned, some priest of Marr named Ushiv Beor from many years previous, had carried several powerful artifacts away with him when he had disappeared from society. The Knights sought to recover those artifacts, and Zethamy had believed that Marr was granting her visions of the secret valley where the hermit had lived out his days. The explanation meant little to the mercenary personally, but it did serve to deepen his sense of guilt.

I have affronted the entirety of the Knighthood and the Temple of Marr, he lamented. *If Marr himself ever turned an interested eye toward me before, he certainly holds no warmth in his heart for me now.*

The leaders called on Khaniel last. He stood before the assemblage of council members, knowing there was little else to add to the proceedings. All that was left was to apologize, to restore some sense of honor to his brethren within the Bunker, and to allow them to distance themselves from him and thereby save face. He eyed everyone in the chamber and spoke softly. "I am innocent in spirit, though guilty in action, of the crimes for which I am accused. I have shamed my order with my reckless disregard of the skills it has taught me and the talents it has honed within me. Though I expect no leniency from the council and I willingly accept whatever fate you deem appropriate, I ask that you exonerate Bruigan Stormbarrel, master brewer and citizen of Freeport, for he played no role in any of the events that occurred. I also ask that you name Maix Treganan traitor and seek to bring him before you to determine the extent of his role in the ambush, for just as surely as my blade took Zethamy Demarro's life, his treachery led her into its path."

Murmurs arose from the crowd as Khaniel sat again. For long moments, none of the council members spoke, though they leaned together to confer privately. Finally, Valeron Dushire, the leader of the Knights, nodded toward Cain.

The head of the Steel Warriors called for silence. When the chamber grew still, he turned toward Valeron. "The council has reached a verdict?" he asked. "And you will not require me to break a tie?"

"It is a consensus," Valeron replied. "We find Khaniel Devlin, member of the Steel Warriors, guilty of recklessly endangering his allies on the field of battle. Through his direct carelessness, a noble and respected Knight fell in combat." The room erupted in chaos, and several Knights in attendance cheered for justice. Khaniel accepted the words as nothing more than the truth that already rested in his heavy heart. Cain motioned for silence once more, but it took longer for the room to grow calm again.

"Furthermore," Valeron continued, giving the contingent of Knights a steady look, "we find

Khaniel Devlin innocent of both treason and murder. And, as such, we will not sentence him for any crimes against this alliance. We believe it to be an internal affair for you, Cain." The room began to roar once more, though Khaniel did not hear the commotion. He sat, stunned, unable to comprehend what had happened. The council did not intend to execute him.

But in his heart, he believed he didn't deserve to live.

The chamber slowly emptied, with most of the audience and the other council members filing out while Khaniel remained seated, Laran at his shoulder. Finally, only a contingent of Bunker leaders, headed by Cain, remained.

Khaniel felt more ashamed at that point than he had during the previous proceedings. He faced his own, and they scrutinized him on a different standard—one of perfection in battle. The masters conferred in whispers for a few moments, until finally they seemed to reach a consensus.

Cain Darkmoore cleared his throat. "It seems," he said after a long pause, "that we find ourselves in a place we have not been before. You are guilty of nothing more than losing control of yourself, Khaniel. I have no doubt that Zethamy Demarro would have died if you had *not* been there, for surely those beasts that opposed her would have overwhelmed her." Several of the other old soldiers in the chamber nodded their agreement. "Nonetheless, your actions have sullied the reputation of the Steel Warriors. We are nothing if not impeccable in our service to those who require our aid. Anyone, from the wealthiest noble to the most lowly of street sweepers, expects to be protected in our presence. By your actions, you have caused many to call that expectation into question."

"I understand, Master Darkmoore," Khaniel answered. "I know I am not worthy to represent the order. I am prepared to die by execution to show the world that the Steel Warriors tolerate nothing less than perfection in their skill at arms."

"Such a sacrifice would be both tragic and wasteful, Khaniel," Cain said with gentle reproach. "You're a good soldier, son, and we put much time and effort into teaching you how to be a good soldier."

Khaniel had been staring at the floor, but upon hearing his mentor's words, his gaze snapped up. "What?" he asked, unsure if he understood.

"We're not going to execute you, Khaniel."

Khaniel shook his head. "But I deserve it! I'm a sham! I went into a berserk rage! I lost control, lost my head! I had no idea what I was doing!" He drew a deep breath. "I'm a danger to everyone around me," he continued, surprised at how earnestly he argued for his own death. "Worst of all, I let all of you down," he added quietly. "I am a flawed result of your teachings."

"No, Khaniel," Cain said. "You're just human."

Khaniel flinched. He did not want to hear those words. He did not think he could tolerate forgiveness right then. Master Darkmoore calling him human implied frailty, weakness, imperfection. He had never seen that in himself previously. He would never see himself as anything else from that point on.

The thought made him want to retch.

That's what I'm afraid of, he realized at last. *That I'm no better than anyone else, that I'm as vulnerable to human foibles as the next person.*

"Khaniel," Cain said, drawing the mercenary out of his thoughts. "You were right about most of what you said, though. And you can't stay here."

Khaniel blinked, not understanding. "I can't—"

"You have to go. Away from here. You can't remain a Steel Warrior, son. We have to show the rest of Freeport that we aspire to a higher standard. I don't think you are such a menace as you perceive yourself to be, but we can't allow those who rely on us to doubt, even for a moment, that they can trust us."

"I don't understand," Khaniel said, his mind scrambling to get a grip on the situation. "I'm not welcome here? I'm not a Steel Warrior any longer?"

Cain shook his head. "No. We have to expel you, son. You've got to relinquish your armor."

His armor. The symbol of everything he had worked for, the visible display of his pride. They intended to take it away. In truth, they already had it, for they had stripped it from him when he had arrived as a prisoner, but this decision meant that he would not ever get it back.

"What now?" Khaniel asked, bewildered. "I don't know . . . I have no idea what to do."

Cain nodded and stood. He walked over and took his protégé by the shoulders. "You will find your way," he told Khaniel. "I know this isn't what you expected, certainly not what any of us wanted, but this is how it must be. In time, you will find a new path. You will still put all that talent, all those skills, to good use. But it can't be here; it can't be with us." The next words Cain Darkmoore uttered sent an icy dagger into Khaniel's gut. "Laran, escort him to the front gate. I will inform the rest of the Bunker that Khaniel Devlin is no longer welcome inside its walls."

For the rest of his days, Khaniel could not recall the walk from the audience chamber to the front gate of the Bunker. He only remembered finding himself standing on the avenue afterward, facing the high walls of the city, hearing the roar of the crowd at the arena nearby. Cain Darkmoore's words echoed in his head over and over as he sat down cross-legged against a signpost: *Khaniel Devlin is no longer welcome inside its walls.* He had been banished from the Steel Warriors.

The mercenary had awakened that morning expecting to be put to death for his role in the disaster in the mountains. The Knights of Truth, he was certain, held him personally responsible for Zethamy's demise, a calamity made all the more tragic by the fact that she had been blessed as a seer, chosen by Mithaniel Marr to lead the order to glory.

Khaniel had ruined all that.

The sun sat low in the west when a voice calling his name drew the warrior from his thoughts. "It's me, lad, Bruigan. What's wrong with you?"

Khaniel looked up to see the dwarf standing over him, peering down with an expression of concern on his aging face. Through a numb sort of haze, Khaniel realized that Bruigan had his pack, still stuffed full of the supplies they had gathered in the previous weeks in the mountains, slung on his back. The mercenary dropped his head again to stare at the pebbles in front of where he sat.

"You're free," he said dumbly, his voice sounding strange to his own ears. "They let you go."

"Of course they let me go!" Bruigan snorted. "You don't think they're going to let a poor coward who hides under fallen logs stay there, do you?" Khaniel flinched at the joke, and the dwarf's sudden and sharp intake of breath told the mercenary that Bruigan realized the implication of his words. "Oh, I'm sorry, lad. That was a stupid, stupid thing to say."

Khaniel shrugged. "You didn't kill her," he said quietly.

"Khaniel," Bruigan said, grabbing his counterpart by one shoulder. "I watched you trying to protect her. You have nothing to be ashamed of."

Khaniel stared up at the dwarf again. "I have everything to be ashamed of, and I have to live with it for the rest of my life. They didn't even see fit to take my head for it."

Bruigan sighed and dropped his pack, then sat down beside the larger man. "Lad, I've been wandering the lands for a long, long time, much longer than you've even been alive, and if there's one thing I've learned, it's that few folk are as good as they think they are or as bad as most others see them. Nothing is ever as simple as it appears where people are concerned. So you made a mistake. You live with it, learn from it, and grow. The worst thing you can do now is let it define who you are for the rest of your days."

"But who I am—who I *was*—is gone now; it *is* defining me. From this point forward, I will always be the warrior who killed a seer and got kicked out of the Bunker." Khaniel clenched his hands together to keep from losing himself in his emotions. The tide of sorrow and shame made his chest ache, made the pit of his stomach cold. "It's the only thing I've ever known," he said at last, in a soft voice. "I grew up there, spent my whole life planning to be a Steel Warrior. The *best* Steel Warrior."

"All right," Bruigan said, kindness filling his voice. "I understand. It's a tough medicine to swallow, I'll grant you that. But we don't have to figure it all out right now, right here in the street. We'll save that for tomorrow. Tonight, we're going to go get ourselves good and drunk. What do you say?"

Khaniel nodded lamely. "Sure," he said, thankful for the small kindness of having Bruigan there as his friend. "But I have no coin," he said. "They took my armor," he added. "I don't even have that."

"Nonsense!" Bruigan said jovially as he climbed stiffly to his feet. "I haven't paid you for your services yet!" He grabbed Khaniel by the shoulder and tugged, convincing the man to rise. "Come on. We've got to find a merchant to take all these goodies off our hands, and then we'll hit Hogcaller's and drown our sorrows together for a while."

Khaniel followed the dwarf as Bruigan led them about Freeport. They made a stop at Torlig's Herbs and Medicines, where the dwarf bartered with the herbalist, selling the excess plants and mosses the two of them had gathered, as well as the snake parts Bruigan had salvaged from the rock adder. Once they had completed their business there, they made their way to Hogcaller's Inn and Tavern.

Stout wooden beams and the soft glow of candles and lanterns filled the homey tavern. A handful of locals sat over their drinks and gabbed quietly at wooden tables and chairs scattered about the common room. A woman dressed in a tight-fitting, revealing leather shirt sat on a stool in one corner and strummed a lively tune on a lute, while a younger man accompanied her on a shrill flute. The man tending bar, Swin Blackeye, nodded and smiled at both Bruigan and Khaniel as they entered, then sent a serving girl over to the table where they sat.

Khaniel dropped his elbows on the rough wooden surface of the table and barely acknowledged the girl, so Bruigan ordered two mugs of beer and flipped her a gold coin with instructions to keep them coming. Once the young server had departed, the dwarf began counting out some coins, dividing them into two piles on the table before him.

"This is only part of what I owe you, Khaniel," he said, trying to sound cheerful. Khaniel nodded, but the shine of the coins meant little to him. Bruigan was trying to help, he knew, but right then, his grief overwhelmed any appreciation he felt.

The girl returned with four mugs instead of two, for which Bruigan laughed and tossed her an extra silver. "Just for being spunky," he said.

The rest of the evening seemed a blur to Khaniel. Bruigan did most of the talking, while the mercenary took great gulping swallows of his beer and tried to act as if he was listening. The mugs stacked up on the table before them, and soon Khaniel felt the wobbly buzzing sensation of inebriation. He welcomed it, hoping it would serve as an ample distraction from his woes. But he found himself only sinking more deeply into gloom, and he finally laid his head down on the table, overcome with emotion at the loss of his stature and honor.

"Lad, you're going to feel a pounding in your head tomorrow whether you stop drinking now or not, so you might as well tip a few more back and get lost in it for a while. I've got to take a walk to the outhouse and return some of this swill to where it came from in the first place, so you order another round and don't wait for me." Khaniel nodded as Bruigan got up from the table and headed toward the back door and the alley behind the tavern.

The girl brought another set of mugs, and Khaniel sloshed a bit on himself as he tipped the first one back. His vision bleary, he stared around the room, which had grown more crowded since sundown. The bard strumming her lute had broken into song, and several of the patrons sang right along with her, laughing and cheering at the lewd verses. Seeing so many people so happy intensified Khaniel's depression, and he reached for another full mug before him.

The noise of the inn echoed shrilly in Khaniel's ears. The room spun and tilted around him, and he couldn't understand how everyone could walk sideways like that. *It must be a magic trick,* he decided. Bruigan would think it funny. The thought of the dwarf sent a tingle of something into the warrior's head. *Bruigan? Where is he?*

The mercenary stared at the table before him, covered with empty mugs. Though his vision blurred slightly, it seemed that he had downed the last four beers by himself. Bruigan had been gone a while.

Rubbing his finger under his nose as if to wipe away the drunkenness, Khaniel stood. The chair tipped backward and crashed to the floor, and he raked an elbow against the nearest mug, sending it over the side of the table to crash, too. A few folk paused in their talk or songs to look at him, but his glare made them turn away again just as quickly.

Bruigan had gone somewhere. But Khaniel couldn't remember what the dwarf had said. The urge to relieve himself came suddenly, and it helped him remember his companion's whereabouts.

Staggering toward the rear door, Khaniel nudged a few other patrons out of the way more out of imbalance than rudeness, but he drew more than a few glares as he passed. He made his way across the floor of the tap room and out into the warm, humid evening. Clouds obscured the moon, making the alley dark, but the light spilling from the open doorway helped the mercenary navigate the route to the outhouse.

"Bruigan," he mumbled, stumbling along the narrow route, watching rats scurry about his feet, angry at having him disrupt their scavenging. He rapped his knuckles on one wall of the rickety wooden building leaning against the larger wall of the inn. "Bruigan?" Khaniel shuffled into the hut, disturbing a few more of the rodents, but the dwarf wasn't there. A moment of concern passed through Khaniel, but the urge to do his business immediately washed it away. He leaned his forehead against the wooden wall as he relieved himself. His vision swam, and he closed his eyes to try to keep the shack upright. When he finished, he stepped back out into the alley, thinking maybe his dwarven friend had slipped past him and back inside, to enjoy another round without him.

Khaniel never saw the pair of shadows that separated themselves from the rest of the gloom of night, approaching him from behind. The last thing he considered as a sap knocked him cold was that the rats would be angry when he fell on them.

4

AT FIRST, EVERYTHING WAS DARKNESS AND pain. As Khaniel became aware, his blindness made him fearful, and his heart began to race. The pounding blood made the base of his skull ache. He tried to reach up to feel the spot and discovered that he could not move his arms. A heavy wooden yoke locked around his neck also encircled his wrists, holding his arms immobile in a position of surrender. He sat slumped against a cool stone wall, stripped naked. With a groan, he tried to stand, only to learn that the yoke seemed chained to the wall.

He wasn't going anywhere.

Sitting in the darkness, the mercenary tried to recall how he had come to be there. The memory of being discharged from the Bunker came back to him, put a ball of cold despair in the pit of his stomach. The time after that grew fuzzy, though he remembered Hogcaller's.

And Bruigan.

What happened to him? Khaniel wondered. The trip to the outhouse came back to the mercenary, of checking to see if Bruigan had gone there. *Someone jumped me,* he decided. *In the alley. Who? Why?* He wanted to make sense of it, but the dull thumping at the back of his head made thought difficult.

"Hello?" he called, softly at first, then repeated the word a bit louder. His voice reverberated back at him, telling him that he sat in a small chamber. A cell. "Who's out there?" he shouted, before quickly regretting it for the pain it caused behind his eyes.

No one answered.

Khaniel sat very still and held his breath, listening. He thought once he heard the distant clank of metal on stone, very faint, but it never repeated. If someone could hear him, they weren't answering.

The mercenary began to feel his restraints with his fingers. The wooden yoke, rough and heavy, made the muscles of his shoulders sore. He could move his wrists a bit, enough to pivot them within the confines of the yoke, and he could run the tips of his fingers along the seam, where the two halves of the wood met. But he could find no hasp, no buckle or lock. Not that finding one would do him much good.

Khaniel next tried to find the point where the yoke connected to the wall. He leaned from side to side and arched his back so that he could run his hands along the surface of the stone. He felt around until he located a pair of iron rings attached there. Thick chain that connected to those rings ran down and out to either side, and when he tugged, he could feel that they pulled on the ends of the yoke. The restraint gave him only enough slack to shift from side to side, perhaps to rise to his knees, but that was it. He could not stand or move far from the wall.

Resigned to the impossibility of escape, Khaniel returned to the puzzle of who might have captured him. His first thought focused on members of the Freeport Militia; perhaps they had jumped him. It would make sense, given the animosity between that group and the Steel Warriors, but Khaniel couldn't explain a reason beyond that. The Bunker no longer welcomed him, and he didn't even wear the telltale armor to suggest otherwise. If some of Sir Lucan D'Lere's men had abducted him, they must have recognized him even without the uniform.

They don't know that the Steel Warriors kicked me out, he realized. *They think they can get something useful out of me. Or they don't care one way or another,* he admitted a moment later. *They just want to vent some frustration on me.*

As if waiting for that precise and terrifying thought to occur to their prisoner, someone threw back a bolt on the other side of a door to Khaniel's cell. The sound made him jump. A thin outline of light formed as the door swung open, and then Khaniel had to squint and turn his head away from the blinding brightness of a lantern.

"Well, look who's finally awake," a man's voice said with a chuckle. "Get him," the stranger commanded.

Khaniel couldn't see anything because of the searing glow of the lantern, but he felt two sets of hands grasp his yoke. Fingers unhooked the chains from the wooden restraint and powerful arms lifted the outcast mercenary roughly to his feet. Using the yoke to steer him, the prisoner's escort shoved him forward, toward the door. He had no means of resisting; he could get no leverage to brace against the floor.

Sudden panic made him try anyway.

Khaniel's guards simply lifted the yoke higher, into his chin, forcing their charge up onto his toes. In such a position, he could either choose to walk with them or hang by his neck and wrists and be carried. Either way, his jailors found it an easy matter to march him out of the cell and into a brighter chamber beyond.

The larger chamber glowed orange from the light of several low-burning fires, or perhaps embers. Khaniel found it warm, almost stifling. He still could not make out much for the first few moments. By the time his vision adjusted, his guards had marched him to a point directly between two stout wooden beams running vertically from floor to ceiling. The space between the two beams was slightly wider than the yoke, with short lengths of chain attached to each one at shoulder height. A quick manipulation by the guards locked the chains to the yoke, and Khaniel found himself immobilized in a standing position.

Khaniel got a good look at his guards as they sauntered off to the periphery of the room. Two big brutes, unkempt and sneering, they didn't much look like members of the Freeport Militia. In fact, the chamber didn't look much like the inside of the militia's barracks, the mercenary thought. *Where am I?*

"We only have a few questions," another man's voice said, emanating from behind Khaniel. The warrior could turn his head enough to catch movement out of the corner of his eye, but whoever stood there remained in the shadows for the moment.

"So do I," Khaniel replied, letting a little defiance mask the fear he felt. "Shall we take turns?"

The man chuckled. "Perhaps, after you hear our questions, you won't feel much like asking yours," he said. He began to walk around to one side, and Khaniel tried to get a better look at his face, but the large beam that held him fast also blocked his sight. Then the figure appeared, and Khaniel felt his knees go weak. Though he didn't recognize the face, the man's clothing proclaimed him a member of the priesthood of Innoruuk, the Prince of Hate. He held a steel rod in one hand, the tip of which glowed orange with heat.

The Church of the Dismal Rage, Khaniel realized in sudden despair. *They've taken me below the city.*

Khaniel knew the stories, had heard the rumors of how an organized gathering of Innoruuk's followers lurked in the sewers beneath the streets, well hidden from the good factions of the city. He had never believed the majority of the tales—a foul temple dedicated to pain and suffering right underneath the citizens' noses just seemed too preposterous. He cursed his own skepticism.

The priest moved closer, bringing the heated poker to eye level between them. The warrior jerked at his yoke, desperate to free his hands and fend off the glowing brand that hovered near his face. "You don't need that," he said, the pitch of his voice high with panic. "Ask your questions; I'll answer them all." He knew his bargaining was futile; the priest would mark his skin with the brand simply for the unpleasantness of it. The followers of Innoruuk knew only hatred. *Why do you have to hate me?* Khaniel thought, trying to back away as the priest stepped closer.

"I imagine you will," the priest replied. He smiled, but the grin showed no happiness. His eyes, embedded in damp, pasty flesh, appeared black and dead. They stared right at Khaniel, as if trying to look inside his head to find the truth, whatever truth he wanted. "Let's start, and see what we know, shall we?"

The priest tapped the brand once lightly against Khaniel's chest. The brief touch sent blinding, stinging pain radiating out from the point of contact. The prisoner screamed and bucked, bruising his wrists and neck in his futile efforts to get away from the scorching of his flesh. As the agony subsided, he sagged, sucking in wind. He tried to get his feet fully under himself to take the weight off his chin and hands. "Gods," he growled, his voice hoarse. "Just ask me!" he pleaded.

"Oh, of course," the priest said, feigning surprise. "We quite forgot to do that, didn't we? All right, then, let's see . . . shall I do the honors, or do you wish to?"

Khaniel realized that the priest did not direct that to him, but rather to another in the room, someone lurking outside his range of vision.

"Let me," a voice said, one that sounded familiar. Footsteps tapped on the flagstones of the chamber floor as a new figure moved into view. Khaniel spotted the tan robes and darker pants before he could clearly see the face, and in that instant, he knew.

Maix Treganan.

Khaniel felt his eyes bulge in surprise. "You!" he said. Anger seethed inside him at the sight of the traitor.

"Hello, Khaniel," the wizard said, a hint of a smile showing at the corners of his mouth. "Where is the hermit's final resting place?"

The warrior started, too shocked at the appearance of the wizard to even lie. "I have no idea," he said. His fingers fluttered in agitation. "But if I did, I'd never tell you, you bast—" He cut his words off with another scream, longer and louder than before, as the priest raked his glowing brand across Khaniel's stomach. It felt as if the mercenary had been split open, that his tormentor had exposed and blackened his entire insides. His scream finally trailed off into silence, but it took Khaniel another few seconds to relax his body and draw a ragged breath.

"Mother of—!" he cried, clenching his teeth and sucking huge gulps of air with a rasp into his lungs. "You touch me with that again, and I swear I'll break every—" The brand tapped against his armpit. Khaniel went rigid, the pain making every muscle in his body chord up. The priest popped him two or three more times in rapid succession. The mercenary shook and spasmed, rattling the chains holding his yoke in place. Finally, the torture stopped, and Khaniel hung limp in his bonds, making hoarse cries as his feet scrabbled beneath him to take his weight.

"Anything you might remember now?" the priest asked, keeping the glowing metal near his prisoner's face while Maix paced.

Khaniel couldn't respond. Multiple points of hot pain throbbed all about his chest and stomach, burns that seemed to grow worse by the second. His throat, raw from screaming, felt dry and cottony. He imagined a cool pool of water, of falling into it. He yearned to be drunk again, to pass out from the pain. "Please," he whispered. "I swear I don't know anything about it."

"That's a pity," the priest said at last, turning away. "It makes you fairly useless to us, then."

"Bring the dwarf in," Maix commanded. "Let's see what *he* has to say."

Khaniel closed his eyes in remorse, knowing that Bruigan had fallen prey to the same captors. He heard the sound of a cell door opening, and an all-too-familiar voice began growling in protest.

"Slow down, you motherless dogs! My knees don't move that fast anymore!" Bruigan cried out in pain once, then gasped and muttered, "Wizard! Well, that explains a few things. And Khaniel! I hoped they hadn't gotten you, lad, but I—ow! That's my beard you're pulling, you stupid—ow!"

"Shut your trap," one of the guards commanded as they toted Bruigan into Khaniel's view. They had the dwarf restrained in similar fashion, and the guards actually carried their prisoner, his feet a few inches off the floor. They hauled him over to a second set of wooden pillars similar to Khaniel's, secured Bruigan's yoke between them in the same fashion, and disappeared once more.

The dwarf looked about the chamber, then returned Khaniel's gaze with obvious fear in his eyes. "What does he want?" he muttered. "Where are we?"

Khaniel didn't know whether his companion really wanted an answer or not. He didn't think it would comfort the dwarf much.

"Perhaps you will be more forthcoming than your friend, here," the priest said, appearing once more with his glowing hot poker. He turned his back on Khaniel and planted his feet in front of Bruigan while Maix watched.

"Hey, there," the dwarf said, sounding nervous. "You don't need to go waving that around. I'll tell you—" His words choked off into a cry that made Khaniel flinch.

"Leave him alone," the mercenary snarled, trying to reach out with one foot to kick at the priest. He managed to land a feeble blow against the man's hip, but he only succeeded in knocking the priest forward. Bruigan let out another howl, much longer and more drawn out.

The priest turned back to Khaniel. "Now look what you made me do," he said in a tone that suggested he was scolding a child. "I went and singed his cheek." He stepped to the side to allow Khaniel a clear view. The sight made the mercenary flinch again. A bright red jagged welt ran almost to the dwarf's right eye. Bruigan panted and blinked back tears.

"I'm sorry," Khaniel said, more plea than true apology. He felt so powerless; he just wanted to do something to stop the torture. He clenched his fists, wishing for the chance to pummel the priest.

The priest turned away from Khaniel once more and asked, "Where is the hermit's abode?" Bruigan didn't answer at first, and then he screamed again and Khaniel could hear the dwarf thrashing about in his restraints. "It's not a hard question," the priest said, mocking them both. "Just tell me where it is."

"Blast!" Bruigan shouted as loudly as he could. "I don't know! I didn't even know about him until that day we ran into *you*," and those last words he directed at Maix, who still stood nearby, watching silently.

Khaniel could hear the hurt and anger in the dwarf's voice. He wanted so badly to kick at the priest again, but he knew it would only serve to further injure his friend. In a fury, he tried to jerk the yoke free of its moorings on the twin pillars. "Coward," he growled at Maix, trying to draw his tormentors' attention back upon himself and away from the dwarf. "Springing ambushes, hiding in the sewers. You're pathetic."

Bruigan gasped. "Khaniel," he warned.

Maix glared at the warrior for a long moment, his jaw clenched in obvious anger. "Leave us," he ordered at last, never taking his eyes from the mercenary. "Take the dwarf back to his cell, then all of you, clear out."

The priest bowed and turned away. As the guards complied with the wizard's wishes, Maix and Khaniel stood, eye to eye. The mercenary could hear the creak of hinges as a door opened and then slammed shut again.

When they stood alone, Maix took a long breath. "You killed her, you ass," he said, his eyes narrowing. "The one person who could lead us to the hermit's abode, and you sliced her face in half."

"I wasn't the one that brought a horde of cyclopes down on her entourage," Khaniel replied, returning Maix's stare. "I'm not the traitor."

Maix laughed. "Oh, yes, always with the self-righteous indignation. You sound like Zethamy." Maix turned away and began to pace. "You spent some time in those mountains, the same mountains where you met us that day. This hermit's abode that she saw in her Marr-cursed visions: it was some secret place near a mountain lake. I want to know if you've ever seen it."

"No," Khaniel said. "I don't know those mountains that well."

"You know, it's funny," Maix said, pacing again, "but when those idiot paladins hauled you back to Freeport, I cursed my ill luck. I followed, wondering how I could get to you, find out what you knew. Then they threw you out of the Bunker, dumped you on the street, and it was almost as if they had handed you to me. That's got to sting a little bit, doesn't it?" he asked.

"What's done is done," Khaniel said gruffly. He didn't want to discuss his own laments with the wizard; he didn't like the idea of Maix using it against him.

"Perhaps, perhaps not," Maix countered. He leaned in close. "But aren't you even a little bit angry? Wouldn't you like the opportunity to pay back that self-absorbed prig Darkmoore for humiliating you?"

"He did what he had to do," Khaniel snarled.

"Oh, come on," Maix said, turning to pace once more and throwing his hands in the air in exasperation. "You're not going to tell me you deserved it, are you? I mean, you're in the heat of battle! People get hurt! It's what combat is all about! If Zethamy had only listened to you and stayed out of the way, you never would have hit her! How is that your fault?"

"Why do you care?" Khaniel said, suspicion rising. "What difference does it make to you what I did or didn't do? I don't know where your hermit hut is, nor do I care. Since I can't help you, kill me and be done with it."

Maix stopped pacing and turned back to his prisoner. "Oh, you'd probably prefer that, wouldn't you? I heard how you so graciously acknowledged that they should have taken your head, but please, let the poor, helpless dwarf go, because he didn't have anything to do with it."

Khaniel didn't answer. He glared at the wizard, but he wondered how Maix would have known about the proceedings inside the Bunker. *He has someone on the inside*, the mercenary realized.

"I don't know," Maix continued. "If I were in your shoes, I might want a little payback. I'd be somewhat insulted that they kicked me out. And if you're really as self-deprecating as you pretend to be, then maybe you're insulted that they didn't care enough about your sins to properly punish you for them." He leaned in closer, emphasizing his final words. "It's almost as if they couldn't care less what happens to you."

"I don't believe that for a moment, and you're not going to turn me against them," Khaniel said.

"Right," Maix said. "There's no doubt at all in your mind that you're right where you should be—unworthy even of an execution. That's too bad, because I had an offer for you."

"I'm not interested."

Maix snorted in disgust. "Of course not. You really do want to die."

"It's better than consorting with Innoruuk's haters," Khaniel snapped.

"Don't be so quick to dismiss the Church," Maix warned. "I have pull. I could work it so you have more power, more prestige, than you could have dreamed of possessing through serving that miserable dump on the Hill. The Prince could do much for you."

Suddenly, Khaniel understood. He nearly shuddered in revulsion. "I'm not becoming one of your shadowknight thugs," he said, shaking his head. "You're wasting your time, dangling it in front of me."

Maix stared for a long time into Khaniel's face, searching the mercenary's eyes. Khaniel glared right back. Finally, the wizard sighed. "You're right," he said. "I am wasting my time. Maybe you'll reconsider after I let my priest work the dwarf over some more."

"Don't you do it!" Khaniel yelled, trying to lunge at Maix, to get his fingers around the wizard's throat. He strained with all his might against the yoke, but Maix didn't even take a step back.

"Your reaction proves how easy it's going to be to break you," he said. "I think you've seen that mountain lake, and you're going to tell me where it is."

Khaniel kept struggling to grab at the wizard as Maix walked calmly away.

SWEAT POURED INTO KHANIEL'S EYES, STINGING them. His hair, plastered across his forehead, stank, as did the rest of his body. His wrists and neck had become three huge bruises, the skin rubbed raw where the wood of the yoke held them fast. He found it hard to breathe.

The mercenary's legs and stomach ached, and the corded muscles in his thighs began to cramp, but he dared not sag down, could not let them touch the floor. Burning embers slowly cooked him from below, a neat bed of them stoked right where he longed to rest his weary feet. The yoke, locked in place between the two pillars, was the only thing supporting all his weight.

He grunted in pain and agitation and shifted his feet out again, doing the splits and wedging the soles of his feet against the pillars. Sighing, he took his weight off his neck and wrists. But it would be only a brief respite; already, the muscles in his hips shook, weakened from prolonged stress.

Khaniel had no idea how long he had been there, in that torture chamber. Days, perhaps. A week. He had nothing left to give, nothing to surrender to his tormentors. They had broken him. Maix had departed that first day, but the priest and his two guards remained, asking the same question endlessly. When he managed to drift to unconsciousness, he dreamed of a mountain lake and a hermit's hut on its shore. It was only an image in his mind's eye, though, a conjuration of his imagination. He wished it were real, considered describing it to the priest in the hopes that the torments would end, but in his heart he knew that the followers of Innoruuk didn't really want anything more from him.

Except to suffer.

Groaning, Khaniel shifted his weight back to his neck and hands and let himself hang there, drawing his knees up once more. He could feel the heat of the embers radiating against his feet and buttocks. His body quivered. Soon, he would no longer be able to fight it, and his legs would burn. He wondered absently if Bruigan still lived. He had not seen the dwarf since that first day, either. A pang of regret, the most recent in an endless series of them, flashed through him.

When his guards swept away the hot coals and released Khaniel from the pillars, he sank to the too-hot floor, crying out from the burns. He tried to crawl away from the heat. Blisters formed on his hands and knees. And then he felt blessed relief as a bucketful of cold water splashed across his smelly, grimy body. Khaniel spluttered and choked on the face-full he got, but he didn't care. He closed his eyes and wept.

His guards allowed him only a brief respite. As they grabbed hold of his yoke and bent him up and backward, the priest approached with a copper cup. The man grabbed Khaniel's face and pried his jaw open, then forced a putrid green liquid into the prisoner's mouth. Khaniel coughed and tried to spit out the vile, viscous glop, but the priest clamped his hands over the mercenary's jaw, holding it shut. Khaniel bucked and tried to pull away, but he could not escape.

He drank the stuff.

They left him alone on the floor for a while after that, where he alternated between wallowing in pity for himself and hatred for his jailors. Soon, though, exhaustion overtook him, and he drifted off to sleep.

KHANIEL FIRST NOTICED THE SOUND OF SEAGULLS as he came awake. They were distant, muffled, but they screamed incessantly. He sensed a gentle rocking motion, and when he opened his eyes, he found himself lying on his back in the hold of a ship. To be more precise, he found himself locked in a cage in the hold of a ship. To his dismay, he realized that he still wore the hated wooden yoke.

"Gods," Khaniel groaned, shifting to sit up.

"I don't think they're listening," Bruigan muttered. Khaniel saw the dwarf, also still restrained, sitting up, leaning against the hull of the ship. His body had been transformed into a mass of welts, bruises, and burns. "Welcome back to the land of the living," the dwarf said.

"Where are we going?" Khaniel asked, finally managing to get upright himself.

"Oggok," Bruigan replied, his tone unmistakably fearful. "The city of the ogres."

5

KHANIEL COULD SMELL THE DAMPNESS IN THE air before he felt it. A cool, misting rain fell, chilling his bare skin, as Bulp led him into the arena by the chain attached to his collar. The rough-woven sack the ogre had tied over the mercenary's head blocked out most of the light, but he could tell by the sound of the murmuring crowd that they had filled the arena. Most of Oggok had turned out to see him fight again. The roar of the crowd grew louder as he appeared.

"I hope you die today," Bulp said, his words rough and guttural, his mouth unused to the human tongue. "I win much gold."

Khaniel ignored the ogre and stood still when Bulp stopped tugging. His hands, eager to hold a weapon but bound with rope behind his back, clenched and unclenched. The two of them stood still, waiting.

A booming voice began to address the ogres in the seats. Kizrak delivered it, Kizrak the Tyrant, king of the city. Khaniel could make out most of the words, though he didn't catch everything the ogre said. He heard enough to know that Kizrak spoke of him. At the end of the speech, the crowd erupted again. The ogres were ready for some blood sport, eager for it.

So be it.

Khaniel felt Bulp remove the chain from the front of his collar. Then the ogre guard began to untie the bindings on his wrists. When the rope slipped free, Khaniel reached up and felt for the tie that held the sack closed around his neck, but before he could locate the knot, Bulp grabbed at his right hand and placed the hilt of a weapon there. The crowd screamed its approval, and Khaniel knew that the fight had begun, whether he was ready or not.

Stacking the odds against me, he thought, but he felt no anger or resentment. *It is what it is.* The weight and balance of the weapon in his hand told Khaniel that Bulp had given him a poor excuse for a hand axe. *Not much use in sawing through the knotted cord,* he lamented. *Got to untie it.*

He knelt down in the damp soil and placed the axe at his feet, then reached up once more to find the knot. His fingers felt along the thick braided leather, woven through crude eyelets around the opening of the sack. He finally found the knot and groaned softly at the size of it. Bulp had outdone himself. The ogre guard's words came back to him, reminding him that Bulp had wagered against him.

The sound of running footsteps caught Khaniel's attention. He closed his eyes and focused on them, sensing an opponent charging at him. The steps sounded rapid and light. *Not human or ogre,* he decided. *But definitely on two feet.* He scooped up the axe and tensed, trying to determine his foe's first move. When the steps closed in directly at him, he knew he dealt with something smaller than himself. And it had a small weapon or perhaps claws. Reacting on instinct, he rolled low and to one side, whipping the axe out beside him as he did so.

Khaniel felt the blade of the axe connect and heard a hiss of pain, very long and drawn out. Lizard man. The mercenary rolled away, listening to see if the creature pursued him. It did not, but Khaniel doubted he had mortally wounded it. The strike had not been that solid. He came up on his feet again and held still.

The rain continued to dampen his skin, made his grip in the axe handle suspect, and the roar of the crowd drowned out any obvious footsteps.

Khaniel crouched lower, trying to detect even the smallest of sounds.

The crowd screamed suddenly, a cheer of delight, and Khaniel knew other combatants fought in the arena, a swirling free-for-all again. *Probably means better weapons scattered somewhere, too*, he thought.

There it was. A soft rustle of footpad on soil, to his right.

Khaniel lunged and swung the axe. He felt pain across his shoulder as something sharp grazed him, cutting his flesh, but he ignored it as he felt the axe head crunch against bone. His foe emitted no hiss that time, but the crowd's roar rose higher with excitement. Khaniel felt confident he had delivered a death blow. He dropped close, feeling for the body, and found scaly skin, sticky with something warm and damp. Blood. The leg he held did not move.

Khaniel felt no panic. He moved his hands methodically, feeling all around on the lizard man's body and on the ground next to it. He caught the sounds of something bestial nearby, a harsh roar of anger or maybe pain. It wasn't too close, not coming closer. He ignored it. He knew a blade of some sort lay within reach; he just had to find it.

When his hand closed on a thin dagger, he grinned to himself. He worked with sure fingers, sliding the blade up inside the loop of cord under his chin and slicing it. The sack opening went slack and Khaniel yanked it from his head.

The brightness of daylight, dim and diffused deep in the gloom of the forest city, still dazzled him. He blinked several times, only concerned with imminent danger until his eyes adjusted.

Most of the ogres filling the seats of the arena watched the main fight. On the opposite side from Khaniel, a massive silverback gorilla stood on its hind legs, bellowing a challenge. Khaniel had seen the beast before, had watched it fight numerous times: it was one of Kizrak's pets. He wondered when they would force him to fight it.

Four more lizard men surrounded the gorilla. The bodies of three of their brethren lay crumpled on the earthen floor of the pit, heads twisted at unusual angles. They undoubtedly had been captured in the Feerott, the forested wilds near the ogre city. The gorilla bled freely from multiple wounds, but the lizard creatures held only daggers, similar to the one the mercenary had claimed. The silverback towered easily twice as tall as the diminutive reptilian beasts, and its long arms made it difficult for them to get close enough to wield their blades against it.

One of us dies today, he thought, admiring the gorilla. The idea didn't bother him at all.

Khaniel understood why the lone lizard man had come at him. It had wanted his axe and thought that, with his head encased in a sack, he would be easy pickings. He looked down at it and saw that he had crushed the thing's skull with his killing blow.

Ignoring the dead lizard man, Khaniel tucked the dagger into the sash of his loincloth, scooped up his axe, and sprinted toward the fight, which had rapidly turned the gorilla's way. Two more of the smaller reptile creatures sprawled in the sand, although one writhed in agony, still alive. The other two no longer tried to do the primate in, but rather only seemed interested in keeping clear of its huge, pummeling fists.

As Khaniel approached, the gorilla, furious with pain and in a raging frenzy, tried to club everything within reach. The lizard men still on their feet backed away, while the gorilla grabbed up their wounded companion, held it by its legs, and began slamming it into the ground over and over. The beast only stopped when its makeshift club had been reduced to a ragged, bloody mess.

The gorilla spotted Khaniel and roared at him, rising up to its full height, a head taller than the human. Khaniel slowed long enough to scoop up another dagger from a dead lizard-man body. Keeping that smaller blade in his off hand, he trotted toward the gorilla, then veered away as the beast tried to lunge at him, both hands clamped together in one huge fist, which it tried to bring down on his head.

The mercenary felt the ground thump as the gorilla's blow missed, and a quick flick of his axe put a huge red gouge on the beast's forearm. The gorilla howled in pain and leaped backward to get clear of its tormentor. The mercenary turned and watched, waiting for another opening.

In the back of his mind, Khaniel felt a brief moment of sorrow for the beast. It had not chosen to fight. Indeed, he doubted it was even all that aggressive in the wilds beyond the walls of Oggok. Those feelings of remorse washed away with the misting rain. Khaniel considered himself a beast, too, and his battle rage made him a deadly killer. That rage made him perfect for the arena, where he would kill or be killed. The gorilla was a victim of circumstance, but nature didn't feel sorry for what lived and what died. Neither would Khaniel.

Out of the corner of his eye, the warrior spotted one of the two lizard men trying to come at the gorilla from behind. He smiled slightly, readying his attack. When the reptilian creature leaped and slammed its dagger into the gorilla's back, Khaniel reacted.

The gorilla reared up and whirled on its new attacker. One huge meaty fist smacked the lizard creature fully five paces to one side. Khaniel heard the snap of neck bones from the blow and knew the reptile would not rise again. But he did not see the creature drop limply against the base of the arena wall; he soared through the air, axe high over his head. He yanked the crude weapon down, driving it deep into the gorilla's neck, slicing across the thick muscles there and severing the spinal cord.

Khaniel felt the handle of the axe snap in his hand, and he had the spare dagger out before he landed on his feet. He spun around, one foot ready to kick high at anything coming too close, but the gorilla dropped without a sound and didn't move.

The ogres in the arena screamed, some in anger, others in approval. Khaniel knew Kizrak would not be happy that he had slain the king's pet. Knowing that gave the mercenary a brief feeling of satisfaction. For a moment, the mercenary absorbed the energy of the crowd, thriving on both the adulation and the vituperation. He excelled at what he did, and the ogres knew it. *It's the only thing you're good at,* he reminded himself. *Just an animal, killing to survive.*

Khaniel turned his attention to the only foe left standing, the last lizard man. It studied the warrior from several paces away, obviously unwilling to do battle with a clearly superior enemy. Khaniel smirked, feeling victory already at hand. He knew the ogres in the seats wanted to see him draw the fight out a bit longer, wanted to watch him stalk and corner the lizard creature before dispatching it, but that was not the most efficient means of achieving victory.

Flipping the dagger in his right hand around, he caught it by the blade and, in one rapid motion, flung it at the reptilian thing. Before it even reached its target, Khaniel had thrown the second one. The lizard man, seeing the attack coming, flinched to one side, allowing the first dagger to sail past its head. But the second blade found its mark while the lizard man still watched the initial weapon. The dagger sank into the beast's eye, and as it sagged to the ground, another smattering of boos mixed in with the cheers.

The fight had ended.

Khaniel dropped to one knee and took a moment to examine his wounded shoulder. The gash was not deep, but it still bled. The rain mixed with the runnels of blood, making it all bright red and thin. Khaniel scrubbed at it with his other hand as he sat down the rest of the way, cross-legged, and waited.

The gate in the side of the arena wall, where Bulp had led him out before, opened. His keeper came running out. The ogre carried the thick chain that would soon be attached to the front of the heavy iron collar around Khaniel's neck.

The mercenary waited dispassionately for his escort to arrive, staring at Kizrak. The ogre king frowned but then gave Khaniel a grudging nod. Then Kizrak rose and began to make his way out of the arena, flanked by his retinue of honor guards and servants.

Khaniel, familiar with the routine, never resisted Bulp, yet still the ogre approached cautiously. When Khaniel did not move against his guard, Bulp snapped the chain onto the ring of the collar. He then yanked the mercenary's hands behind him and looped rope around his wrists, binding them together. When the ogre finished, he pulled Khaniel to his feet by the leash, perhaps a bit more harshly than was strictly necessary. "Let's go," the ogre ordered. Khaniel smiled slightly, wondering how much coin Bulp had lost. He strolled out of the arena, following his escort. A few lingering ogres in the stands screamed at him, most of it unkind commentary.

I'm their favorite pet, he thought wryly.

As Khaniel followed Bulp into the torchlit stone tunnel beneath the arena seats, he reflected briefly on his performance. *Never should have let the lizard catch me with that dagger,* he lamented. *I must learn to tune out the crowd noise better.*

They passed out of the tunnel and into the rest of the city. Khaniel considered Oggok more a village than anything remotely approaching a human city. Still, such a gathering of ogres in one place impressed him. He considered it a testament to Kizrak's power and influence that so many of them could exist together at all.

Crude huts in various stages of stability made up most of the dwellings, though a few constructed of slabs of stone stacked together stood out. The streets, nothing more than muddy routes, ran between houses and the roots of trees. A cave complex dug into the side of a bluff served as the king's "palace." That bluff also defended one side of the city. All in all, it was a fitting setting for the brutish ogres.

It seemed to Khaniel that the citizens of Oggok wanted little more in life than to eat, mate, and fight, with an occasional diversion such as the spectacles at the arena or an organized raid into other parts of the Feerott. Often the smelly, half-dressed beasts struck Khaniel as barely smarter than the dogs that ran in packs through their city.

Khaniel felt right at home.

A few of those smelly ogres glanced at the warrior as Bulp hustled him down a muddy street toward his cage: mostly those who exited the arena. But many more hardly paid him any attention at all. They seemed used to having a human in their midst.

Khaniel almost laughed.

Much had changed from when he and Bruigan had first arrived there several weeks before. Several guards, wary and brutal, remained constantly on hand to deal with him, always keeping him heavily bound. After his first battle in the arena, a full dozen ogres had swarmed out to round him up, throwing nets over him and beating him nearly unconscious before dragging him away. Apparently, his reputation as a fierce combatant had preceded him. Khaniel wondered if Maix had sent word that the ogres should be cautious, or if the wizard had simply encouraged them to find reasons to inflict pain whenever they could.

Bruigan had suffered the worst of it. From the moment the deckhands had thrown the dwarf, bound hand and foot, off the ship and onto the docks along the river, the ogres had taken great delight in beating him, mocking him, and belittling him in every way imaginable. The mercenary knew from Bruigan's fearful explanations while imprisoned on the ship that dwarves and ogres did not suffer one another to live. Bruigan himself did not expect to last long in Oggok and flat out told Khaniel as much.

Thus, when Kizrak had approached the trussed-up dwarf with a large knife in his hand, Khaniel had assumed the worst. But the king had only sliced Bruigan's beard from his chin. By Khaniel's way of thinking, his friend had gotten off lucky, but the act had greatly upset the dwarf. He had not seemed the same since.

The ogres initially kept the two prisoners in a muddy pit, covered with a stout screen of wooden poles weighed down with large stones, and left them there to wallow in their own misery. Bruigan was disconsolate; Khaniel struggled to get the dwarf to eat any of the moldering bread and rotting vegetables the ogres tossed down to them.

"They took my beard," Bruigan would mutter from time to time, staring at his own belly. "They took my beard."

On the fourth day, ogres hauled the pair out of the pit, bound them tightly with rope, and took them to the blacksmith. The ogres had made thick iron collars for each of them, cold black bands without any hinges or locks. Khaniel went first. Two of the ugly creatures simply pinned his head against the anvil while the blacksmith hammered the crude collar closed around his neck with several ringing strikes. Then, while they prepared Bruigan for a similar fate, other ogres dragged Khaniel away and, after cutting his bonds, tossed him into the arena.

The ogres wanted to see if he could fight.

The mercenary's first battle surprised everyone. They pitted him against an ogre—a prisoner, Khaniel learned later. His foe seemed more intent on screaming invective at the onlookers in the seats—particularly Kizrak—than on actually facing off with Khaniel. The creature seemed somehow insulted. For his part, the mercenary hesitated to fight, not knowing how the citizens of Oggok would react if he wounded one of their own. After taking his fourth or fifth wound, however, Khaniel didn't much care anymore; the berserk rage overcame him, and he didn't come to his senses again until he had turned his adversary into a bleeding heap in the middle of the arena floor.

The ogres had loved it.

Khaniel blinked, realizing he had gotten lost in his musings during his walk with Bulp. They had already made their way through the streets of Oggok and stood before the cage he and Bruigan shared. A single squat chamber dug into the base of a low stony hillock, it would almost be cozy if not for the fact that the only exit from the place had a stout gate across it that the ogres always kept locked. Bulp untied Khaniel's hands and shoved him inside, and the clang of steel on stone echoed in the mercenary's ears as the ogre guard slammed the gate into place and clicked the locks shut.

Khaniel stood for a few moments, letting his eyes adjust to the dimness. He shared a simple, nearly empty room with his counterpart. The two prisoners slept on pallets made of animal furs, used a wooden bucket for their wastes, and sat at a low block of stone that served as a table. That was it.

"So," Bruigan said from the dimness on the far side of the room. "Are we going to escape today?" The dwarf posed the same question to his companion every day. It had almost become a joke between them. Almost.

"No," Khaniel replied, turning to watch as Bulp strode away. "No place I'd rather be right now." Always the same question, and Khaniel always had a different answer. Most days, the warrior filled his response with grim humor. "We haven't finished decorating in here," he would say, or, "The ogres are making something special for chow tonight." Bruigan would snort and chuckle at the absurdity of their exchange, and no more would be said about it.

They both knew escape would be nearly impossible, and even if they did succeed, they still invited a death sentence. Either the ogres would track them down and slay them, or they would perish in the wilds beyond the city's walls. Without any food or equipment, they remained prisoners in Oggok, even without the cage door over the entrance to the tunnel.

"You really mean that," Bruigan said. His tone carried a mixture of reproach and sorrow. "You really don't want to get away from here."

Khaniel sighed. He had known that his answer that day would shock his companion. It held no humor. It wasn't a lie. "No," he said. "I don't."

Bruigan got up from his pallet and stalked over to the warrior. The dwarf grabbed Khaniel's arm and tried to jerk him around so they could be face to face. He didn't really have the strength to force the human to turn, but Khaniel faced him anyway, despite knowing what was coming. "What in the blazes is the matter with you?" Bruigan demanded. "They took my beard from me, Khaniel, and I'm not just sitting here wishing they'd kill me and be done with it. Why can't you get over this?"

Khaniel stared down at his friend. "I am what I am," he answered. He spread his hands wide and gestured at himself. "We're all animals, killing to survive. Oh, we pretend that we're not. We pull a cloth over our eyes and imagine that somehow, we're civilized, that we have some higher purpose.

Some of us even invent gods and then convince ourselves that those gods think we're special. It's a sham, a farce!"

Bruigan began to shake his head. "No, lad. Animals can't create art. They can't craft a beautiful chalice, or forge a golden scepter. Or brew a malted beverage that tickles your throat as it glides down to your belly. You're more than just a killer. You think and feel and grieve! You can do all those things! You used to do all those things," he said, turning away finally. "Why don't you want to go on doing those things? Why do you want to stay here and rot for their amusement?"

Khaniel shrugged. "Killing is what I do best," he said simply, turning to look out the gate once more. "And I can do it here without pretense. When the blood spills in that arena, I don't have to tell myself that it was for a just cause, that it was an unavoidable result of an unfortunate confrontation. I don't have to pretend to regret it!"

Bruigan made a strangled noise from his pallet. He drew a deep breath and asked, very softly, "Why do you have to pretend?"

Khaniel pursed his lips, trying to come up with the words to make his companion understand. "Because," he finally said, "I would despise myself too much." He turned to look at Bruigan, but the dwarf just shook his head. Khaniel started to plead with his friend, to try to get the dwarf to realize that he needed to embrace his own savage nature to stay sane, but he had trouble finding the right words. A shadow falling across the doorway saved him from the effort.

Bhaobuk stood there, peering in at them both.

"You fought well today," the ogre said, unlocking the cage door. "But I saw you take a hit. How is the wound?"

Bhaobuk appeared scrawny for an ogre, and he enhanced the image in the way he constantly ducked and nodded deferentially to all the other ogres. Khaniel couldn't much blame him for his obeisant ways, though. Bhaobuk was Kizrak's half-brother, and the tyrant king had little patience for a sibling who didn't exhibit the lordly traits expected of a member of the ruling family. Kizrak cast a very imposing shadow, and the warrior understood that Bhaobuk had grown up deep within it.

"It's just a scratch," Khaniel answered, stepping back to allow the visitor to enter.

As diminutive as the ogre was for his species, Bhaobuk still had to stoop to avoid striking his head upon the low ceiling. He entered the chamber and knelt down. "Let me see it," he urged. "I will heal it, keep it from festering."

Khaniel shook his head. "It's fine," he insisted.

"The Feerott is filled with unclean things," Bhaobuk replied patiently. "You don't want to get tainted water in the wound."

Khaniel sighed. He knew the ogre spoke the truth, but he did not like the magic Bhaobuk used to heal him. A sickly coldness always accompanied it. "Fine," he said at last. "Cast your magic so you can go."

"You do not like my magic?" Bhaobuk asked. The ogre closed his eyes and began to mutter strange words under his breath.

"It always leaves me feeling . . . tainted," Khaniel said. "There's something grotesque in your magic."

Bruigan's sharp intake of breath caught Khaniel's attention. The dwarf stared at him with fear in his eyes.

"It's all right," Bhaobuk said, finished with his efforts. "Khaniel speaks plainly, but he speaks the truth. That taint you feel is the touch of Innoruuk. For one such as yourself, who does not worship the Prince of Hate, it must feel unclean. It always passes, though, doesn't it?" Before Khaniel could answer, Bhaobuk continued. "I thought as much. It is that sort of evidence that makes me question my own devotion to him."

6

"THIS LOOKS PROMISING," BRUIGAN ANNOUNCED. He pointed toward a stand of saplings clustered around the base of a parent bloodbark. Though the larger tree lived up to its name, with its deep red fibrous outer surface, the saplings had more of a muddy hue, with their outer layers noticeably smoother. "The grubs like to feed on the roots," the dwarf explained as he knelt down among the saplings. "But the adult trees' roots are too tough for the grubs to penetrate; they like the younger trees."

To Khaniel, the dwarf looked happy gathering his ingredients. Bruigan seemed at home, his thoughts awash in what he would need to do to prepare a batch of some potent brew. The mercenary wondered if his friend even realized that he had forgotten his miseries for the moment. The warrior squatted down and helped dig.

"I will look for another sweetberry bush," Bhaobuk said, ambling away and peering into the undergrowth of the Feerott.

Khaniel saw Bruigan pause, watching the ogre drift out of earshot. When the shaman walked far enough off, Bruigan began to whisper. "He could help us escape," the dwarf said, resuming his digging. "You heard what he said before."

Khaniel grunted softly. "How many grubs do you want?" he asked, avoiding the suggestion.

"We need a lot," Bruigan replied. "The more you boil, the darker and richer the flavor of the lager. Now stop trying to change the subject."

The mercenary chuckled despite himself. "All right," he said. "Yes, I heard what Bhaobuk said. That doesn't mean he could, or even would, help us escape. Just because he has doubts about his faith doesn't mean he's going to turn on his own kind. What happens to him afterward? Do you think he would be safe remaining in Oggok? Being Kizrak's kin wouldn't protect him—it would probably make things worse for him." Bruigan stopped digging and stared at Khaniel. The dwarf's mouth hung agape. "Don't look at me like I have three heads," Khaniel added. "It was one passing comment."

"Gods!" Bruigan growled under his breath in exasperation. "You act like you care more about what happens to him than to me!" Khaniel looked at the dwarf, feeling a bit wounded. "Aye," Bruigan said, "touched a nerve, didn't I? Well, it smacks of a certain truth, lad." The glare left Bruigan's eyes then, and he continued in a gentler tone. "Look, Khaniel, I'm not saying we dash off right now." He looked wryly at the chain that held them both fast. The length of it ran between their collars, encircling the tree in the process. "I'm not even suggesting we ask him to free us today," the dwarf continued. "But I *am* asking you to think about it, to listen to him, and maybe win him over. First, we have to earn his trust, see if he would consider helping us. He might even want to go with us!"

Khaniel shook his head. "That's too much to ask of him."

"But it's not too much to ask me to stay here and rot as an ogre's slave?" Bruigan said, his voice rising dangerously. "You might be perfectly content to stay here the rest of your days, but I'm not, and if you won't help me, then you're as good as chaining me up yourse—" Bhaobuk stepped back into view, and Bruigan swallowed whatever else he intended to say.

"I found a whole big clump of sweetberries," the ogre announced, dropping an armload to the ground next to the two prisoners. "Do you think that's enough?" Khaniel wondered if the creature had heard the dwarf and was just feigning ignorance.

Bruigan stammered and choked, then nodded. "Yes, that should be plenty." He gave Khaniel one more sideways glance, a telling glare, and went back to digging for grubs.

The mercenary assisted the other two for a while, but he had no interest in their conversation, falling into his own private thoughts. Bruigan's last words had stung.

Is that true? he thought. *Am I guilty by inaction of letting him suffer?* The thought made him uncomfortable, but Khaniel decided it wasn't as clear-cut as the dwarf claimed. True, Bruigan had been a victim of circumstance, caught up in the whirlwind of events that had led to Khaniel's dismissal from the Bunker, but the warrior saw that as a truth for anyone. Nature did not discriminate or play favorites, he insisted to himself. The strong adapted, overcame, survived; and the weak perished. No higher purpose existed, no greater plan for any of it.

If Bruigan is capable of escaping his current circumstances and making a different life for himself, then that's what will happen, the mercenary decided. *I am no more responsible for his plight than I am for that gorilla becoming my opponent today.* Somehow, the conclusion did little to assuage Khaniel's sense of guilt.

Nonetheless, he shrugged it off. *We are who we are,* he told himself. *You are not his keeper.*

"I think we have enough," Bruigan announced, rising from the ground. Khaniel heard the dwarf's knees pop and watched as his friend grimaced and straightened them gingerly. "I only hope that these sweetberries will work as well as kingberries for this recipe. I've never been able to find those anywhere in this part of the world. Always meant to see if I could get some kingberry seeds from back home in Faydwer and try growing them over here, but I never did."

Khaniel sighed softly. *When Bruigan lets himself just be,* the mercenary realized, *he's happy. He brews. That's his calling. He's doing it here, in Oggok, the same as he did in Freeport. Why should the location change anything?*

Bhaobuk took a large iron key from a pouch at his belt and removed the lock that held the chain wrapped around the tree. Thus freed, Khaniel and Bruigan could walk with the ogre, though they remained connected by the links, which gave them some ten feet of play between them.

For a moment, Khaniel considered the dwarf's urgings. With a little bit of luck, the two of them could probably overwhelm the shaman right then and there. The chain held enough slack that the mercenary felt confident he could get it around Bhaobuk's neck and strangle him, and they could run.

But where? he thought helplessly, frustrated at mentally battling himself over the issue again. *No weapons, no food. And with this stupid chain locking us together, we'd never outrun anything. The Feerott is no place to be wandering like this.* He peered into the gloom of the forest. The thick canopy overhead made the days little brighter than the nights. *It would be nearly impossible to keep track of our direction,* he thought, adding to his list of reasons for labeling it a foolish idea. *We'd die in a matter of hours,* he concluded for the hundredth time. No, he would not be facilitating an escape for the two of them. He turned his attention back to his companions.

"You call these 'sweetberries,'" Bhaobuk said as they followed the path back to the entrance to the city. "We call them 'kurdrah.' And what you refer to as bloodbark, we call 'gromj-kak,' which basically means the same thing: 'bark of blood.' That itself is interesting, because 'kak' is only one of several words we have for 'blood.'"

Khaniel listened to the ogre's language lesson intently. Bhaobuk had been teaching him the ogre tongue almost since the beginning of his time in Oggok. They made it a mutual gift, for the mercenary—and later, when Kizrak allowed Bruigan to join them, the dwarf, too—taught the shaman more of the human tongue.

Khaniel had met Bhaobuk in the first few days of his captivity, after that first arena fight. The shaman had come to heal the mercenary's wounds with his magic. The ogre lingered with him afterward, seemingly keen on talking. Khaniel did not understand why at first. He even grew suspicious that perhaps the ogres intended to learn something incriminating from him. It eventually became clear that the shaman only wanted to glean more about Khaniel and his ways. And to avoid his half-brother, the king, the mercenary realized.

Bhaobuk had proven helpful in other ways, as well. He got Bruigan out of the pit and into better accommodations. After that first fight in the arena, the ogre guards had locked Khaniel in the cave rather than returning him to the pit, but they had seemed content to leave their dwarven captive there to rot. Exposed to the elements like that, Bruigan's health began to deteriorate quickly. In desperation, Khaniel searched for a way to convince the ogres to relent, despite their hatred for the dwarf.

Khaniel eventually convinced Bhaobuk that the dwarf could brew a fine tun of beer as a means of getting Bruigan free of the pit. "Doesn't Kizrak enjoy his ale?" the mercenary had asked. "Bruigan can concoct beverages like nothing the king has ever tasted. And you can tell him it was your idea," Khaniel had added. Finally, Bhaobuk agreed to intercede.

Kizrak grew furious at first and berated Bhaobuk—accompanied by a few cuffs to the head—for bringing him such nonsense. But when the shaman suggested that the dwarf might have a useful talent, the king relented. At first, Bruigan remained confined to the cave, while Khaniel and the shaman procured the supplies. Bruigan ranted and raved about the crudeness of the tools the ogres provided him, but somehow he made do. He declared his first batch of beer a miserable failure and wanted to dump it immediately, but Khaniel convinced him to let Bhaobuk sample it. The shaman turned his nose up, but—once convinced that the dwarf had not poisoned the batch—he took some to the king.

Kizrak drank five mugs on the spot and demanded more.

"It simply proves that there's no accounting for an ogre's tastes," Bruigan had grumbled, but Khaniel could tell the dwarf secretly felt pleased. Thus began an odd friendship between the warrior, the shaman, and the brewmaster, one that grew as the ogres afforded Bruigan more freedom to gather his own ingredients and take more time in the brewing process.

Khaniel's thoughts returned to the moment. He had lost track of the things Bhaobuk and Bruigan discussed, but they seemed deep into a conversation about the finer points of fermenting. He let them be.

See? he told himself. *When he's not thinking about how miserable he's supposed to be, Bruigan's actually happy here. Maybe he'll grow to accept it.*

The trio had reached the city gates by that point, and Bhaobuk led them inside. The two guards posted on either side of the large stone entrance eyed them all with a mixture of disdain and concern. "Why do you not keep them bound?" one of the two demanded of Bhaobuk. "They might escape!"

The shaman shrugged, and Khaniel noticed he avoided making eye contact with the burly sentinel. "They have not tried to run," he said. "They have no place to run to."

The guard harrumphed in disgust, but he said nothing further.

Once past the opening in the high earthen wall, Bhaobuk turned to lead his two charges back to their cave. Before they had taken ten steps, however, a group of ogres, seemingly out for a stroll, stepped in front of them. Half a dozen of the hulking, crude humanoids congregated around the trio, and judging by their dress, they were more than mere citizens. Several of them actually wore boiled hide armor and carried thick clubs. Khaniel recognized them as some of Kizrak's soldiers, his personal favorites. They often sat with the king in the arena during the matches. They clustered about another, a smirking ogre dressed in an animal-skin robe, the accoutrements of Kizrak's personal retinue of shamans.

"Hello, Bhaobuk," the other shaman said in the harsh, clipped ogre tongue. "I see you play with your friends again."

Bhaobuk tried to stand a little taller, but his counterpart still towered over him by nearly a full head. "We were gathering ingredients to make Kizrak's beer, Kohd," he explained.

Kohd chuckled, and several of the others joined in. "How nice," he said. "Little Bhaobuk not a good shaman, so he tries to make king happy with beer. Kizrak is proud."

Khaniel could see Bhaobuk's shoulders stiffen, but he knew the shaman would not dare challenge his counterpart. Beyond the fact that Kohd and the other ogres outnumbered him, his own life could become very miserable after arguing with a more powerful shaman.

"You want to talk back, Bhaobuk?" Kohd asked.

Bhaobuk seemed about to retort, but then he let his shoulders sag and replied, "No."

"Good. Innoruuk might grow angry from your words. Go and see Master Zulort. He has training chores for you."

"But I must help—" Bhaobuk began, gesturing toward where Khaniel and Bruigan stood behind him.

"Go now, or Jurn and the others here beat you!" the shaman screamed.

"Yes, Kohd," Bhaobuk, said, ducking his head and hurrying away without another look at his two companions.

"Hey, where's he going?" Bruigan asked. Khaniel remembered that the dwarf did not understand nearly as much ogre as he did. "They're sending him to study for a while," he said, eyeing Kohd warily. The shaman glared at him.

"Talk ogre, slave!" one of the others roared at Bruigan. The towering thug took a step forward and backhanded the dwarf, who grunted in pain and toppled to the side. The action caused the chain stretched between their collars to yank taut, pulling Khaniel off balance, too. He nearly choked as he leaned awkwardly to one side to avoid having to drop to his knees.

After he closed the distance between himself and Bruigan to ease the tension on the chain, Khaniel stood upright again and glared at Kohd. "Stop hitting him," he said quietly in ogre. "You like the taste of his beer as much as the king does." Bruigan stayed down on the ground, watching. Khaniel saw him place one hand against his cheek. His palm came away bloody. The blow had split the skin.

"A slave tells me what to do?" Kohd asked, turning to look over his shoulder at his companions. The question elicited more chuckles from the gathering. "Don't do that," the shaman ordered, staring at the mercenary once more. "Jurn can beat you, too."

Khaniel felt his own rage rising. It would be an ugly fight, one that he almost certainly would lose while chained to Bruigan. They might even kill the two of them out of hand. He clenched his fists, trying to calm himself. "I am sorry," he said at last, making his tone deferential. "I am still learning ogre. I was only asking."

Kohd smirked. "Liar," he said. "What do we do with lying slaves who tell us orders, Jurn?"

The ogres laughed again. Then the one that had struck Bruigan said, "Beat the want out of him."

"Yes," Kohd said, his smirk gone. "A good idea. Beat him," he commanded. "Beat them both."

Khaniel moved to stand directly over Bruigan as Jurn and the others surrounded them.

"Khaniel," Bruigan said, nervous as he eyed the ogres closing in.

"Stay down," the warrior instructed. "Make yourself as small as possible."

"Right," the dwarf replied. He curled into a ball as Khaniel crouched into a defensive stance.

The first of the ogres stepped close and swatted at Khaniel with his club. The mercenary brought both hands up and absorbed the hit with them, catching the head of the weapon. The blow made the bones in his arms ache, but he ignored the pain as he grasped the club and yanked it free of its surprised owner. Khaniel didn't waste time watching the brute's expression. He spun the club behind himself and knocked away two more blows aimed for the backs of his knees and the back of his head.

As the mercenary pivoted in place, warding off blows from his adversaries, Kohd seethed. "Fools!" he yelled. "Hit him together!"

Khaniel saw purplish energy crackle in the shaman's hands as Kohd aimed both sets of fingers directly at him. *So much for a fighting chance,* the warrior thought. Then the arcane blast struck him. He staggered from the tingling pain and nearly went down to one knee.

The ogres saw their chance and came at him in unison. Khaniel managed to deflect the first couple of shots, but with his muscles cramping and his vision blurring from the shaman's attack, he could not hold them all off. He took a glancing blow on one shoulder, very near the wound he had received in the arena. Though the cut had healed, it still felt raw and sore. Khaniel grunted and lurched to the side as a second strike caught him on the hip. The fiery pain shot through his leg. He twisted and fell.

"Khaniel, look out!" Bruigan hollered as the ogres all swarmed in, ready to beat him senseless. Or to death.

One more bruising strike slammed into the mercenary's neck, and spots swam in his vision for a heartbeat or two. And then all the world went black.

KHANIEL OPENED HIS EYES INTO COMPLETE darkness. For a moment, he just blinked, wondering where he was. The smell of sour sweat reeked all around him, not all of it his own. Then the memory of the fight—well, the beating, he admitted to himself—came flooding back into his mind.

I should be dead, he thought. *Or aching in every bone.*

Instead, he realized he didn't feel any pain at all. He lay on a soft pallet made of animal furs, and most of the stench radiated from that. Ogre stench.

This isn't my cave, the warrior realized. *Where am I?*

He rolled over to sit up, and the animal skin that someone had draped across his body fell away from his face. Dim light, most likely the orange glow from a torch, streamed through an opening near his feet. A hanging cloth, like a curtain, covered it so that the light only seeped through around the edges. It looked like a stone doorway.

The king's palace.

Khaniel wondered why he had been brought there instead of to his own locked cave. *Or to the pit,* he silently added. Then he thought of Bruigan and wondered if the dwarf rested in Kizrak's home also. He found the image of his friend's face, terrified as the bullying ogres began to close in around the two of them, gut-wrenching.

I'm a fool, Khaniel thought, rubbing his face in regret. *Why did I think he could learn to like this place? How can I be content here?*

The part of his mind that wanted to accept that, the shamed part of him that tried to hide behind the notion that he was nothing more than an animal acting on instinct, didn't seem so eager to rationalize any longer. He could not explain away their beating as just nature taking its course. Bruigan deserved better than that, no matter how much Khaniel loathed himself.

If he's still alive, the warrior thought, his heart heavy with guilt, *I will find a way to get him free.* The mercenary took a deep breath, washing away his remorse and focusing on his immediate situation. *It's a fine promise to make,* he thought, *but first things first. Why am I in Kizrak's palace?*

He sat very still and listened. The sound of several voices, low and unintelligible, drifted into the room from beyond the curtain. Ogres conversed.

Khaniel rose from the bedding and began to move toward the opening, but the chain still attached to his collar stopped him short. Someone had anchored the other end to a point on the wall opposite the doorway. Khaniel couldn't quite get to the curtain to move it aside.

Sighing, the warrior moved back to the pallet and sat down again. *This is getting old,* he decided in disgust. He wondered whether to bide his time until someone came for him, or if he should call out, let them know he had awakened. Impatience got the best of him.

"Hello?" he called in ogre.

The conversation stopped outside, then Khaniel heard the sound of heavy, plodding footsteps approaching. A hand thrust the curtain aside, temporarily blinding him, before the silhouette of an ogre stood in the doorway, peering at him. "You awake," Bulp said. "Good. Get up."

Khaniel stood as Bulp took a key from his belt. He approached the wall and released the prisoner with a click. Khaniel had once thought to ask Bhaobuk how the ogres had learned the art of forging locks, given the fact that everything else they made was so crude. The shaman had explained that they didn't make them, they stole them from other species. At the time, it had seemed funny to the warrior, locking up their valuables with other people's locks. But being considered a valuable had taken a lot of the humor out of it.

"Come," Bulp said, tugging on the chain. "We go now."

"Where are we going?"

"You will see," the ogre growled, tugging again on the chain. "Come!"

Khaniel followed his jailor willingly, wondering again why he didn't show any effects from the beating he had taken at the hands of Kohd and the others.

"Where's Bruigan?" he asked as they followed a stone hallway lined sporadically with torches. "The dwarf," he added. "What happened to him?"

"Already with king," Bulp replied.

"The king?" Khaniel said, surprised. "We're going to see Kizrak?"

"Yes," Bulp replied. "You his new battle champion."

7

BULP'S WORDS STUNNED KHANIEL SO COMpletely, he nearly stopped walking. "Champion?" he said. "Me?"

"What?" Bulp asked, looking back over his shoulder with a quizzical expression.

Khaniel blinked and realized that, in his surprise, he had used his own tongue. "The king wants me as his champion?" he repeated in ogre.

"Yes," Bulp said. "No more talking!" he growled as he turned back. "Walk faster!"

Khaniel shook his head, trying to get over the shock of that news. *Gods,* he thought. *What happened today?* Then he sighed with a great deal of relief as he remembered Bulp's comment concerning Bruigan's fate. The dwarf was with the king. "Good," he muttered softly. "Then he's still alive."

They passed through a large chamber with multiple exits. A pair of ogre women sat there, one weaving cloth and the other stitching pieces of completed cloth together. Bulp selected one of the other tunnels and continued, while Khaniel tried to ignore the stares of the two women as he followed the ogre up a sloped passage that curved around as it rose, doubling back on itself. Kizrak's palace seemed a maze to the warrior, who wondered how big it was. Dug into the side of a mountain, the series of tunnels and chambers might be expansive, but the mercenary had found it impossible to judge from out in the city.

At one point they emerged from the tunnels onto an earthen ledge cut into the side of the mountain. The ledge sat high above the city and overlooked it. Several other tunnels also emerged there, and two ogre guards sauntered lazily back and forth along the ledge's length, keeping watch. Over what, Khaniel had no idea. Bulp entered a second tunnel, and they continued.

At last, the pair passed into a large, well-lit chamber, obviously Kizrak's throne room. The ceiling there rose higher than in most of the other areas of the palace, and the number of torches gave the entire place a warm glow. Several animal-skin rugs lay scattered haphazardly about the floor before a great stone throne, which sat high on a slab of stone serving as a dais. Kizrak himself sat upon the throne, garbed in his telltale tiger-skin stole. Numerous other figures had gathered about the dais, including Bruigan, who looked positively sullen. Khaniel noted that the chain from the dwarf's collar connected to a large iron ring set into the stone dais.

Bulp led Khaniel over to stand before the throne. Kizrak looked down at the warrior expectantly as the crowd of ogres, engaged in several conversations, grew quiet. The king said nothing for a few moments, and Khaniel wondered if Kizrak actually expected to see him after all. Finally, the ogre king spoke.

"Kohd!" he roared, looking around the chamber.

Khaniel caught movement from one side, and everyone turned to watch as the shaman who had led the assault on the human and the dwarf moved before the throne. He seemed shrunken, craven, and he darted furtive glances full of hatred at Khaniel as he presented himself.

"You and your friends attacked him?" Kizrak asked. To Khaniel's ears, the king demanded more than questioned.

The shaman nodded. "Yes, Lord Kizrak." He seemed to shrink even more at the admission.

Kizrak grunted. "What happened?" he demanded. "Tell all!" he added fiercely.

Kohd looked almost as miserable as Bruigan as he began. "Jurn and others and me found Bhaobuk and sent him away to his lessons. This *slave*"—the shaman uttered that word with complete contempt—"attacked us, so we fought back."

Kizrak snorted, and Kohd flinched at the sound. "You not tell it right," the king growled. "Tell it right!"

Kohd rolled his eyes in dismay and shrugged. Pointing at Khaniel, he began again. "He talked back! He tried to tell us what to do. He is a slave, he should obey! Kohd and Jurn tried to make him obey. He fought back. He killed Jurn, Hurgol, and Drak," the ogre finished lamely.

Khaniel felt his eyes grow large at that revelation. *I did what?* he thought. He looked down at Bruigan, who watched him. "I killed three?" he mouthed, holding up three fingers to clarify. His friend nodded. The look on the dwarf's face seemed very sorrowful. *Oh, no,* Khaniel thought. *My rage . . . I've doomed us both.*

"Is this true?" Kizrak demanded, and Khaniel realized the king stared at him.

He shrugged. "I do not remember it," he admitted. "I blacked out."

"You what?" Kizrak asked, looking confused. "What is 'black out?'"

Khaniel took a deep breath. "I went into a rage," he explained. "It is like sleeping, but my body still acts, still fights."

"Ah," Kizrak said, nodding. "You were taken by battle lust. Innoruuk entered and fought from within your body. You are blessed by his touch."

Khaniel began to shake his head. "I don't think that it's—"

But Kizrak interrupted him, addressing the entire chamber. "Innoruuk touches this slave!" he declared, looking at every face in the room. "The Prince of Hate makes him strong, makes him fight well! He will fight for me, as my champion, when Ghoarg comes to visit!"

Khaniel listened to the words of the king with a mixture of disbelief and dismay. He wasn't sure if he welcomed such attention from the ogre. If Kizrak considered him a champion of the brutal god the ogres followed, how many enemies among the king's other warriors had he just made?

"You," Kizrak continued, looking at Kohd, "are a blight in His sight! You would dare to attack the favored of Innoruuk? Your punishment will be guard duty during the feasting! You will get no roasted meats, no beer, while Ghoarg is here! Now go!" and he pointed vehemently toward the exit.

With one last scathing glance toward Khaniel, the shaman slunk away from the proceedings, disappearing down the tunnel. Everyone watched the wretch vanish, then turned back to their king.

"Return him to his chamber and keep him well fed," Kizrak instructed Bulp. "I do not wish any suffering upon him until the feast occurs!"

Bulp nodded and turned to lead Khaniel away. The mercenary hesitated, pulling against the chain. "Please, King Kizrak," he began. "I would prefer to remain in my cave in the city. I am happy there."

Kizrak stared at the warrior as if Khaniel had declared that he had two heads. "No," he said simply. "You will live in the palace now."

"But what about Bruigan?" Khaniel insisted, still fighting Bulp's pull on the leash. "He needs help with his brewing."

Kizrak's eyes bulged wide, obviously not happy. "The dwarf will live in the cave!" he roared. Then, after taking a deep breath, he continued. "Bhaobuk will assist in the brewing. You are a warrior; warriors do not make beer. That is almost women's work! Now go!"

The mercenary realized the tyrant king would brook no further argument, so he reluctantly turned to follow his jailor back to the chamber where he would be spending his time. He did give

Bruigan one last glance before he left, though, cringing at the dwarf's sad face.

THE ENSUING COUPLE OF WEEKS WENT BY VERY quickly. Though the ogres kept Khaniel confined to the room Kizrak had designated for him, they did allow him out to exercise and hone his fighting skills. The king ordered his guards to permit the new champion access to the best weapons in Oggok, though he also increased Khaniel's guard detail to three ogres at all times. His captors fed him the choicest foods from their larders, with plenty of meat, breads, and hard cheeses. Though hardly exquisite fare, it certainly tasted better than the foul things he and Bruigan had been forced to eat in their first days there, sequestered in the pit.

Shortly after Bulp had confined Khaniel to his chambers, Bhaobuk visited him.

"Who is Ghoarg, and what's going on with Bruigan?" Khaniel asked immediately.

The shaman sat down and faced the warrior. "Ghoarg is the chieftain of a rival tribe of ogres who dwell in the mountains to the north of here. He is particularly bloodthirsty and brutal, and takes great delight in bringing the most savage and fearsome warriors to fight in the games. The last few times that Kizrak has hosted Ghoarg's tribe,

Ghoarg's warriors have not only won the contests, they have butchered the king's own champions."

Khaniel looked at the shaman askance. "So I'm the lucky sacrifice this year, huh?" he said, realizing Kizrak's ploy at last. Bhaobuk tipped his head to one side, as if not understanding. "Your brother has chosen me as his champion because he doesn't want to lose any more of his own warriors," Khaniel explained. "If I win, then he triumphs over his rival, but if I lose, all he's lost is a slave who amuses him from time to time in the arena. Either way, he comes out unscathed."

Bhaobuk nodded. "Yes. It has grown difficult to convince members of his own honor guard to train for the games. They all know what happens to the loser in these fights."

Khaniel had to chuckle. "Very clever," he muttered. "And that explains why no one protested his decision to name me champion. None of your brethren want anything to do with the title. They're happy to see me die. Especially Kohd. I half feared for a while that he would come after me when Kizrak wasn't looking."

"Kohd hates you, but he will not confront you again," Bhaobuk said. "He is not a fool, though he acts like it sometimes. He knows that, should you die at his hands, my brother will force him to replace you in the games. Kohd wants no part of that."

"What of Bruigan?" Khaniel asked, changing the subject. "I haven't spoken with him since Kohd and his muscleheads jumped us."

Bhaobuk's face grew solemn. "Your friend is in a sour mood. I do not know why, but something troubles him. He barely works on his beer at all. If he does not increase his production, Kizrak will become very angry and may punish him. I don't know what to say to make him see this."

Khaniel nodded. "I need to talk to him, Bhaobuk. Can you arrange it?"

The shaman thought for a moment. "I can arrange it so that you two meet during one of your exercise periods. We will come by, pretending to have your guards taste the ales he is making to see what they think of them. They will not turn down such an offer. While they sample his brews, you can speak with him for a few moments. But you may not be alone."

"That doesn't matter," Khaniel said with a grin. "You're about the only ogre in this place who can speak the human tongue; Bulp and his pals won't understand anything we're talking about."

"Very good. Bruigan and I will see you tomorrow, then."

"Bhaobuk," Khaniel said as the shaman rose to leave.

"Yes?"

"Why are you helping us?"

The ogre shrugged. "I don't know," he said with a wistful smile. "I find you . . . interesting. And you do not treat me like my brother and all the others do."

Khaniel just nodded, and the shaman left. Afterward, the warrior sat there thinking for a long time.

THE NEXT DAY IN THE PRACTICE YARD, BHAOBUK brought the dwarf around, as he'd promised. The guards watching Khaniel grew wary at first, but when the shaman explained to them that the dwarf wanted their opinions on the beer he was preparing for the feast, they eagerly agreed to sample it. While they gulped down mugs of the frothy ale, Bruigan sidled over to where Khaniel rested nearby.

"Hello, Bruigan," the warrior said, sitting against a wall, sweating profusely. "How are you holding up?"

"What do you care?" the dwarf snapped. "You've got everything you want. Now that you're Kizrak's dancing pet, you haven't got a care in the world. And so you sleep in the king's palace while I stay locked away in a cave, spending my last tired days brewing orc-piss for ogres who would as soon kill me as look at me."

Khaniel bowed his head at his friend's stinging words. "I made a mistake," he admitted quietly. "I should have listened to you before."

"Well, it's too late for that, now. If we were still together, we might be able to make an escape. But with them keeping us apart, there's little chance of it."

"I'll figure out a way to get you out of here," Khaniel promised. "I owe you that."

The dwarf looked at him for a long moment, as if considering. "You sure that's what you want?" he asked.

Khaniel drew his head back in surprise. "You really have to ask me that?" he said. "I may be nothing more than an animal, living among a tribe of animals, but my failings should not be your punishment. I won't go with you, but I will figure out a way to get you free."

Bruigan snorted. "Don't bother," he said, turning away. "You already know what my chances are of surviving beyond those walls by myself. You might as well kill me right now."

Khaniel watched the dwarf walk away, his heart heavy. He did not know what to do. *How can I save him without condemning myself?* he wondered. *I cannot return to the lands of men. I am too dangerous, too feral. This is where I belong now. It's where I've always belonged; the Bunker was merely an illusion of civility. But he shouldn't have to pay for my shortcomings.* He had no answer for Bruigan. And in the middle of it all, Khaniel actually wondered how much he was trying to convince himself.

AS THE DAY OF GHOARG'S ARRIVAL DREW NEAR, preparations went into full swing. The hunters went out into the Feerott and returned laden with fresh meat, which ogre women promptly began roasting on spits over fires that burned day and night. Guards actually spent time cleaning armor and polishing their few steel weapons. Some even took the time to craft fresh pieces, greaves and breastplates and shields of wood and hide, brightly painted with the symbols of the clans of Oggok. They cleared the commons of sticks, stones, and grazing animals so that Ghoarg's followers would be able to erect their tents for the duration of their stay.

Khaniel saw it all as he worked with Kizrak's best warriors. The ogres allowed him little free time, but he could sneak a peek every once in a while, during a break or while being escorted by Bulp to or from the practice yard. Kizrak even appeared on a few occasions to supervise his champion's training, explaining to the man some of the common dirty tricks Ghoarg's warriors liked to employ or techniques to combat the more unusual ogre weapons that his foes would certainly bring.

Each night, he went to bed exhausted, only to be kicked awake the next morning to do it all again. Bhaobuk came to him more than once, at Kizrak's orders, to cast healing spells upon the mercenary's cuts and bruises or even to soothe his aching muscles so he could sleep better.

Through it all, the mercenary missed Bruigan. He spotted the dwarf once, when Bruigan and Bhaobuk returned from the gates, apparently out on another ingredient run. The dwarf either didn't see him or refused to look at him. Khaniel considered calling out, forcing his friend to acknowledge him, but his heart wasn't in it. Bruigan had made up his mind that Khaniel's path was anathema to the dwarf. Khaniel couldn't change that unless and until he freed his friend.

The day before the impending arrival of his guests, Kizrak took Khaniel to the arena. The warrior had not been there since the day he had battled the lizard men and the gorilla, and he hardly recognized the place. The ogres had added a wide variety of obstacles and dangers to challenge the combatants.

The battlefield consisted of a series of seven platforms formed of rough logs set high above the floor of the pit, with narrow spans connecting them in such a way that the whole resembled a great wagon wheel with six spokes. Platforms stood at the north and south points of the compass, as well as at the northeast, southeast, northwest, and southwest. Pathways connected the outer ring of platforms to form a great six-sided circle, and additional routes led from the perimeter to the central platform. Each pathway connecting platforms featured unique obstacles. Along one route, Khaniel saw low walls to climb over and others to duck under. On another, the path actually consisted of a series of knotted rope swings. Sharpened wooden stakes lined most of the open ground beneath the upper areas, a deadly fall for anyone unlucky enough to slip or be pushed.

"Learn it," Kizrak ordered. "Know it well. It will help you during the fight." Then the king led Khaniel to a spot beneath one low bridge, to the left of the southernmost platform, in a place with stakes spaced farther apart. "A secret for you," the tyrant said, picking his way carefully through the dangerous spikes. The more slender Khaniel could move through them with greater ease. When Kizrak reached the underside of the bridge, he pointed. "For you," he said, "if you lose your other weapons."

Khaniel saw the handle first, and then, leaning farther underneath, he discovered a huge and wicked-looking axe. He reached up to take hold of it, and immediately, Kizrak went on guard. Khaniel froze and turned to look at the king. "I need to feel the balance," he said, backing away from the weapon. "That's all."

Kizrak regarded the warrior critically for a moment, then he stepped back and nodded. "Only for a moment," he warned.

Khaniel nodded back and reached in, pulling the axe free of its hiding place.

He held a magnificent weapon. The craftsman had forged the polished steel blades, two wicked half-moons, with a hint of blue pigment to give them an eerie glow. Intricately carved scrollwork adorned them, detail so fine that Khaniel had to squint to see the individual lines. The wrought blackwood handle felt stout and hard as a rock. The leather grip slipped into his hand perfectly.

For a moment, Khaniel closed his eyes and let the axe be a part of him. He hadn't felt so perfect a weapon since his time in the Bunker, and maybe not even then. He took one experimental swing with the axe and hardly had to shift his weight. It flowed like water through the air, never pulling him even a fraction of an inch from his intended motion. He went through a couple of simple paces, nothing elaborate, but enough to know in his heart that the craftsman had forged the axe just for him.

"Put it back," Kizrak commanded.

Khaniel opened his eyes and looked at the king, who stared at him sternly. "It's perfect," he said. "I could win any battle with this weapon, defeat any champion Ghoarg brings—"

"Put it back!" Kizrak demanded, his voice growing sharper. Around him, the guards who had accompanied the two of them to the arena became more alert, more attentive. They could hear the concern in their king's tone.

Khaniel reached under the bridge and replaced the axe in its hidey-hole. "Why can't I fight with it from the start?" he asked as Kizrak gestured for him to step away and follow.

"You would look too powerful," the king answered as they left the arena. "Ghoarg's champion will be wary if you are armed with it. But if you appear in the battle with only your puny sword, then his champion will take you lightly, and you will surprise him with your prowess. You may go for the axe after the battle begins."

Khaniel considered the ogre's words and decided that the king had devised an interesting plan.

He wasn't sure how much he liked being the pawn in Kizrak's game, but he had to admire the ogre's clever thinking.

At last the day of the festivities dawned, and Oggok buzzed with excitement. Ogres hustled everywhere in the city, dealing with numerous last-minute preparations. They set up a great feast area outside, in an open space along one side of the common, with row after row of long wooden trestle tables flanked by benches. Already, platters of smoked meats, wheels of cheese, and kegs of Bruigan's beer covered the tables.

When Ghoarg's entourage finally arrived, dusk had nearly settled. Kizrak waited upon a raised platform built at one end of the common. His various confidants and trusted warriors clustered around him in a show of force. Khaniel watched from off to one side, on the grass, with Bulp serving as his keeper, chain-leash in hand. Ghoarg marched in to much fanfare, with his own honor guard of ogres surrounding him to the cacophony of strange horns sounding a battle call. Kizrak waited expectantly for his counterpart to approach. As Ghoarg climbed the steps to the top of the platform, Kizrak met him with two mugs. The two leaders each took a long draught from their respective mug, downing the entire contents. When they both finished, they rammed the two mugs together, shattering them. A cheer arose from both groups of ogres, and the feast was on.

It took some time for the rest of Ghoarg's tribe to arrive. Even as more and more of the visiting ogres streamed into the city and servants began to set up tents on the common, Kizrak and his guest took their places at the main table. The king and the chieftain dug into the heaps of food with gusto, and as soon as they began to eat, the other ogres, from both Oggok and the neighboring tribe, started to fill the benches at the surrounding tables.

Khaniel sat near one end of the head table, a fact that seemed to displease a few of the ogres in attendance. Most of those scowling at him were visitors. At one point, the warrior overheard a rough-looking guest with one ear missing and very few teeth make a rude comment about having to eat with the chained animals. Khaniel started to retort, but he snapped his mouth shut again when it occurred to him that the ogre merely described precisely what the mercenary had said about himself since arriving in Oggok.

As the meal continued into the evening and the ogres appeased their ravenous appetites, conversations began in earnest and grew louder. Eventually, Kizrak and Ghoarg got into a lively debate on the relative value of owning slaves and their merits. Khaniel could see the twinkle in the king's eye as he spoke of a surprise for Ghoarg, and when the visiting chieftain could stand it no longer, Kizrak finally revealed what he had been holding back.

"There," he said, pointing to Khaniel. "My champion. You will not win our bet this time, Ghoarg."

The chieftain took one look at Khaniel and nearly choked. "That puny human? Ha!" A smile played across his lips. Then he burst into full laughter.

Kizrak bristled at the rudeness of his guest. "Wait and see," he growled.

Many of the other ogres also stared at Khaniel, chortling. The warrior said nothing and concentrated on his food, avoiding the stares. He suddenly felt very much like a prized bull being inspected at market and found wanting.

"Well, if you have pets at the feast table, then me, too," Ghoarg announced. He turned to one of his attendants. "Fetch me Dakkas," he ordered. The attendant ran off toward the burgeoning tent city.

The comment puzzled Khaniel. The name the chieftain had used meant "dog" in ogre. He wondered for a moment if Ghoarg had given an unoriginal name to a true pet, some sort of hound, or if he had simply misunderstood the reference as a proper name. He watched for the attendant's return, eager to see what sort of beast might emerge from the shadows of the tents.

When the ogre came hustling back, Khaniel felt dismay surge through him. The attendant held a leash, but instead of leading some sort of actual dog, the ogre kicked a humanoid, driving it toward the head table.

Khaniel seethed at the sight of it. *That's barbaric,* he thought before he realized how utterly foolish such outrage sounded. *Of course it's barbaric; they're ogres!*

The scrawny wretch crawled on hands and knees, and for a moment, the mercenary wondered if it might be a halfling, thin from hunger. But as the so-called pet grew closer, he recognized it as human, though filthy and dressed in torn rags. Ghoarg's attendant gave it one final kick to the ribs, and a high-pitched whimper issued from the slave. At the same time, Khaniel noted distinctly feminine curves showing through the tattered rags the slave wore.

Not a man, he realized. A woman.

"See? This is Dakkas," Ghoarg announced proudly. The poor woman crawled the rest of the way to the chieftain's feet and huddled there miserably.

Kizrak sniffed. "A good name," he said, feigning contempt. "She looks useless," he said, though the gleam in his eyes told Khaniel that the king thought anything but that.

"Ha!" Ghoarg said, laughing at the insult. "She's good at fetching, Kizrak. And look," he said, reaching down and grabbing the slave by a handful of hair. "She cannot see!" He hoisted the woman up to her feet hard enough to make her gasp, giving everyone a good look at her face and scar-clouded eyes.

It was Zethamy Demarro.

8

KHANIEL ROSE FROM THE BENCH, STUNNED TO be seeing the face before him. His chest tightened from the shock; he could barely breathe. Bulp yanked on the chain leading to the warrior's collar, forcing him to sit down again. When Khaniel glanced at his guard, the ogre glared at him, and the mercenary could see that he had knocked over a platter of gnawed rib bones in his shock.

The rest of the table paid no attention to him, though. They all either talked and laughed among themselves or watched with bemused grins as Ghoarg paraded his pet in front of Kizrak. The chieftain turned her back and forth by his grip on her hair, letting his host see her from all angles.

Khaniel stared at the paladin's face, unsure he could trust his own sight. But he had not mistaken the identity of the slave. An ugly scar ran straight across the bridge of her nose, a perfect line connecting her eyes. The orbs, once such an intense blue, had become cloudy white, sightless. She stumbled about helplessly as the ogre twisted her head back and forth, letting his counterpart get a good look at her countenance.

Khaniel shook his head, unable to turn away, trying to understand how she could have survived. He had watched the blade of his axe rake across her face. He had seen her fall, the blood everywhere. He had been certain she was dead. He had been wrong.

The mercenary finally tore his gaze from her unseeing one and stared at his lap. "The cyclopes," he muttered, low enough that no one around him could hear. *They dragged her away,* he thought. *And healed her? How is that possible? And how did she end up in Ghoarg's possession?* Khaniel couldn't think clearly. Nothing made sense.

"She cannot run away, but I like to keep her on her leash, anyway," Ghoarg said. "My little Dakkas." He reached out with one huge, callused hand and lewdly caressed the inside of her leg.

Zethamy jumped at his touch, spinning away to evade his groping fingers. She struck a mug of beer with one flailing hand. It tipped over, right into Kizrak's lap. Beer soaked the king's trousers, and he leaped up from his seat in a roaring rage. Ghoarg jerked Zethamy away, as if to prevent her reckless act, but the damage had already been done.

The festivities came to a sudden, silent halt as everyone turned toward Kizrak. The ogre king stood fuming, looking at the beer dripping from himself. Then he gave a hateful stare at Zethamy, whose sightless eyes stared at nothing, while her hands clenched and unclenched at her sides. With one sudden and ferocious motion, Kizrak slapped her, a powerful smack that twisted her face around, despite Ghoarg's hold on her hair.

The paladin grunted in pain and brought her hands to her stung cheek. Her knees grew wobbly, but she braced herself and would have stayed on her feet, if Ghoarg had permitted it. Instead, he shoved her down to her hands and knees and thrust the end of her chain to the attendant.

"Take her to my tent," he commanded. "I will punish her later." The attendant turned to leave.

"No!" Kizrak snarled. "Your Dakkas has insulted me! I want her head!"

Upon hearing Kizrak's demand, the crowd began to murmur. No one spoke about the fate of the slave, though. Everyone wanted to see the two tribal leaders square off.

"She's mine," Ghoarg said, challenging Kizrak. "You have no right."

"I will take her," the king warned. "You cannot stop me."

Ghoarg reached for the hilt of his weapon, a wicked iron mace with sharpened flanges all about the head. Kizrak growled and stepped back, overturning his chair, and grabbed at his own weapon, a curved sword with a barbed tip. The two leaders dropped into defensive crouches as the other ogres cleared out of the way of the impending fight.

Khaniel felt sick to his stomach. Zethamy was alive. He had not slain her in the mountains so many weeks ago. Elation surged through him with that knowledge, a glimmer of hope that he was not forsaken after all. But in one fateful moment, right in front of him, that hope threatened to slip away again. Ghoarg's attendant departed, towing her along on her hands and knees once more. The sight of the once-proud paladin, reduced to feeling her way along the ground while the ogre kicked at her, sickened the mercenary. Even as Bulp drew sharply on the chain connected to his collar to move him out of the way of the coming scuffle, Khaniel made up his mind.

"Wait!" he shouted, moving to step between the two angry ogres. He nearly had his head taken off, but he only flinched slightly as Ghoarg pulled his strike, barely missing the mercenary's skull. "Foolish slave!" the chieftain yelled. "Move, or I will cut you down to get to your gutless king."

"Gutless?" Kizrak said, his eyes wide with insult. "When I cut you open, *you'll* be gutless, you dog!"

Khaniel shook his head, resisting Bulp's efforts to drag him out of the way. "Stop fighting!" he shouted.

Kizrak swore and grabbed at the warrior's leash, jerking it from Bulp's hands. He tugged Khaniel toward him, fury in his eyes. "You are making me angry," he said through clenched teeth. "You are not a good slave. Sit down!"

"I won't let you kill her," Khaniel said, not budging. Inside, his own audacity stunned him. *Fool!* he chided himself. *You will get her* and *yourself killed!* He didn't care.

For a moment, Kizrak's rage seemed limitless. With a tremendous growl of fury, he drew his arm back. Khaniel stood still, not backing down. He braced himself for the coming death blow.

Suddenly, Bhaobuk stood at the king's side. He whispered something to Kizrak. Whatever words the shaman spoke, they did not seem to have much of an effect at first, for the tyrant shook his head and tensed, ready to slay his unruly slave. But Bhaobuk persisted, and finally, Kizrak drew a deep, calming breath and lowered his arm.

Ghoarg barked a derisive laugh. "You cannot even hit your slave," he said. "You are a weak king."

Kizrak pointed his blade over Khaniel's shoulder, right at Ghoarg. "Be silent!" he commanded. "I will listen to my adviser's words, *then* kill my slave! I am a smart king." He turned back to his half-brother and placed the blade in his hand against the shaman's throat. "Say your idea, and be prepared to die with him if I do not like it."

Bhaobuk nodded, his eyes betraying his worry. "Buy her," he said simply.

Khaniel's gut churned, hope springing anew. *Would Kizrak consider such a course?*

"Buy?" Kizrak asked, looking unconvinced.

"With coin," the shaman said. "Give him gold."

Kizrak considered Bhaobuk's proposal. Then he looked at Ghoarg. "Will you sell her?"

Ghoarg smirked. "You have nothing I want, except your throne."

The king shook his head. "You cannot have my kingdom," he said, his tone determined. "But I will give you gold and gems."

Ghoarg considered for a moment, then shook his head. "No. I have enough gold. I like my Dakkas. You must kill me to take her from me." He seemed almost eager.

Khaniel's heart fell. He had thought that letting Kizrak purchase Zethamy might defuse the situation, let the two leaders settle their argument without bloodshed, while still saving face. There would be time to convince the king not to harm Zethamy later.

Then Khaniel had an idea. "I will buy her," he offered. Everyone looked at him.

Ghoarg seemed amused. "You? You have nothing. You are a slave."

Khaniel held up his hands. "I can fight," he said simply. "I will entertain you."

Ghoarg laughed. "I will get to see that tomorrow anyway. No."

"Then make it a wager," Khaniel said, not giving up. "Bet her as stakes for the battle tomorrow."

Ghoarg looked intrigued. "A bet?" he asked, looking at Kizrak. "I like that," he said, smiling.

Kizrak nodded. "But not with him," he said, jerking his head in Khaniel's direction. "He is *my* champion. Bet with me." Khaniel grimaced at being undercut, but he dismissed the frustration again just as quickly. If he had the two leaders talking rather than fighting, that was worth something. Anything to buy Zethamy time.

Ghoarg shrugged. "But you still do not have anything I want," he said. "It's not better than buying."

Kizrak snarled and threw his hands up in disgust. "Then we fight," he announced.

"Wait," Bhaobuk said, stepping between the two as Khaniel had done before. "Change the fight."

Both Kizrak and Ghoarg stared at the shaman as if he were mad. Khaniel could see that they grew tired of the interruptions to their impending battle. "How does that help?" the chieftain asked.

"Yes, how?" Kizrak added.

"Let him fight two champions," Bhaobuk suggested, pointing to Khaniel. "Give better odds," he added.

Ghoarg tilted his head to one side, considering. "Your one champion against my two?" he asked.

Kizrak looked at his half-brother. "Is that what you mean?"

Bhaobuk nodded. "It is a harder fight, so if Khaniel wins, it is worth more."

Kizrak smiled. "A good idea, little brother." He turned to Ghoarg. "Will you do that? My champion against two of yours? If mine wins, I get the slave."

Ghoarg frowned. "Your puny human slave against my two best warriors? Why do you think you could win? My champion has beaten yours many times now."

Kizrak shrugged. "He is a strong warrior," he said. "Are you afraid?"

Ghoarg glared. "I am never afraid! But I still do not think the odds are good. I like my Dakkas. Let him fight three of my champions," he suggested smugly. "I will be the third," he announced with pride. "I want to take the head off this foolish slave that forgets who is the master."

Khaniel's stomach did a flip-flop. *All three?* He felt a cold chill settle over him as he remembered what Kizrak had told him before. Ghoarg's warriors were brutal and savage. It would not be an easy fight.

"Done," Kizrak said, agreeing. "Tomorrow, my champion against you and your two champions. If mine wins, I get your slave, and her head will roll."

"He will not win," Ghoarg said, smiling. "He is nothing but a puny human slave."

"Maybe," Kizrak admitted, "but you have not seen him fight yet." Then he turned toward Bulp. "Take him back to his room," the king commanded. "He must rest. He has to be ready for tomorrow."

Khaniel allowed himself to be led away from the feast, lost in a swirl of thoughts. He had to fight three ogres. Not the best of prospects, he concluded. He stole one last look back toward the tent city, hoping to catch a glimpse of Zethamy, but she and her attendant had already disappeared.

Night had drifted well into the small hours of the morning when Khaniel awoke to the realization that someone had entered his chamber. He sat up, instinctively reaching for a weapon that he did not have.

"I am sorry to wake you," Bhaobuk said. Khaniel relaxed with a sigh. "I came to say I'm sorry."

"For what?" the mercenary asked. "You helped me. I know that girl. I can't let her die."

Bhaobuk seemed taken aback. "You know Dakkas?"

"Yes. I met her once, not so long ago." He pursed his lips in remorse. "I was the one who blinded her," he added quietly. "My axe made that scar and took her sight."

"That is why you risked your life tonight on her behalf," Bhaobuk said, sounding surprised. "I did not know."

Khaniel shrugged in the dim light. "I am responsible for her predicament. I have to find a way to save her."

"But you did nothing but condemn her, or yourself," the shaman said. "If you win, my brother will take her head."

"That's why I need your help again," Khaniel said earnestly. "Help me figure out a way to convince Kizrak not to kill her. There's got to be some reason he would want to keep her alive, and you've got to make him think about it."

"You have to win tomorrow, first," Bhaobuk said. "That will not be easy."

"You let me worry about that," Khaniel replied. "I can win that fight, if I can get to that axe."

"I can help you win," Bhaobuk said hesitantly. "With my magic."

Khaniel considered the suggestion. "Won't you be seen? If Ghoarg sees us cheating, won't that ruin the bet?"

"He will not see me," the shaman responded firmly. "I will be subtle."

Khaniel shrugged. "All right," he said at last. "What will you do?"

"I will give you great strength and uncanny speed," Bhaobuk answered. "And I will draw your injuries from you if you are struck."

Khaniel nodded. "That would be good," he said. "It might tip the balance." When the shaman didn't say anything further, Khaniel changed the subject. "How's Bruigan? I haven't seen him since Ghoarg and his group arrived."

"He is very tired," Bhaobuk said. He sounded worried. "I think he is sick. He has worked very hard, making the beer for the feast. But he does not talk much anymore."

Khaniel felt pangs of guilt blossom in his gut, but he had no time for the dwarf's laments right then. Khaniel had to help Zethamy first. He'd figure out a way to deal with the rest of it later, even if it meant that all three of them would escape Oggok. Bruigan had to know that Khaniel was planning something.

"I need to talk to him," the mercenary said. "Can you arrange it?"

"I don't think so," Bhaobuk answered. "You have too many guards around your chamber. Kizrak is fearful that Ghoarg will try something before the fight. He doesn't want you sabotaged beforehand."

Damn. There had to be a way to get a message to Bruigan, something that only the dwarf would understand. Then he had it. "I need you to tell him something for me," Khaniel said. "I need you to let him know that Zethamy was right: his beer needs more bluemoss, and I know where to get some. Tell him I said we'll go there tomorrow."

Bhaobuk cocked his head to one side in confusion. "Bluemoss? Tomorrow? I don't understand. You can't gather ingredients tomorrow; you must fight."

"Just tell him for me, Bhaobuk," Khaniel begged. "He'll know what it means."

"All right," the shaman answered, though he sounded doubtful. "I will go see him tonight. Now, you must rest."

WHEN KHANIEL AWOKE THE NEXT MORNING, the palace bustled with activity. The warrior stretched on his pallet and lay there for several minutes, thinking about what he faced. The battle would demand everything he knew, every combat trick he could muster. And victory would still require him to be a little bit lucky.

Kizrak had seemed so eager to agree to Ghoarg's final terms. As a warrior himself, the king must have known the odds weren't in Khaniel's favor. *He has a lot of confidence in me,* the mercenary thought. *Can I live up to it? Can I survive at all?*

Bulp came for Khaniel not long afterward. The ogre guard led his charge through the halls of the palace and into Kizrak's throne room, where the king and many of his retinue waited expectantly. A long table sat to one side of the throne, and on it, Khaniel saw a wide assortment of weapons. He also spotted several suits of armor, from individual and mismatched padded cloth pieces to an entire suit of chain mail.

"You may pick from any of them," Kizrak said. "They are the best in Oggok," he added proudly.

Bulp released the chain from Khaniel's collar and the mercenary walked over to stare at the collection of armaments. Kizrak's standards were laughable. Most of the weapons had been poorly forged or showed signs of many years of use and lackadaisical care. Rust pitted the blades, and cracks ran along many of the handles. Grips looked old and worn or did not exist at all. The armor appeared no better.

Khaniel eyed it all critically, but he did his best to hide his dismay. *How can you have such a wonderful axe and then hide it away?* He thought dismally. *It's by far the best piece in the lot, and it's not even here.* Finally, he settled on a small, one-handed sword that appeared to be in decent shape. He hefted it, feeling the balance, and examined the edges. Khaniel instantly recognized the quality of the weapon, but it suffered from a lack of care. It needed a new grip and a good sharpening, but otherwise, it suited him well.

"This one," he said, drawing a frown from the ogre king.

"It is so puny," Kizrak said, shaking his head. "You need a bigger weapon to win today."

"Speed will be my ally," Khaniel explained. "The obstacle course will hamper a large weapon. It's going to make fighting more difficult for

Ghoarg and his champions. But I will be quick and deft, and they will not be able to keep up with me. Long after they are tired of chasing me, I will still be nimble and deadly. This is the weapon I need. But I need to work on it. It needs regripping."

Kizrak stared at Khaniel for a long moment, as if considering. Finally, he nodded. "Get him everything he needs," he told Bulp. "What about your armor?" the king asked.

Khaniel pursed his lips and examined a collection of mismatched leather pieces. Some of it would never fit him. He wondered how the ogres had come to possess such a motley assortment, but decided soon after that he'd rather not know. He rummaged through the pieces, settling on a boiled breastplate, a pair of vambraces, a scabbard he could wear on his back, and greaves. Finally, he took a buckler from a selection of shields and added it to the pile. "This," he said, gathering the pieces he had chosen. When Kizrak frowned again, Khaniel added, "As with the weapon, I'd rather be fast than loaded down. These will work fine."

Kizrak nodded again, content with his champion's decisions.

Back in his room, Khaniel began unwrapping the grip on the sword and cleaning it. When Bulp arrived a bit later with fresh leather and wire, Khaniel had already begun working on adjusting the breastplate to fit him. The ogre stood and watched as the mercenary began to cut a new grip for the sword. Eventually, though, the guard grew bored and left. Khaniel spent most of the rest of the day repairing the sword and adjusting the fit of his armor.

When at last he felt satisfied with everything, it was nearly time to venture forth to the arena. The mercenary slipped the armor on, testing the fit. He stepped through a few routines, practicing footwork, getting a feel for how the armor constricted his movement and how the sword felt. He had done a decent, if not spectacular job on the grip, given the time and materials he had available. It would have to do. He hoped he could get to the axe, but if not, he trusted the sword well enough.

The day had passed into late afternoon before Kizrak's champion entered the arena. Bulp led Khaniel from the gated tunnel out into the open. Ogres, cheering and chanting, packed the seats surrounding the open pit. The warrior followed Bulp over to the edge of the new construction. The ogres had dug a trench around the perimeter of the obstacles, like a dry moat a good ten feet below ground level. Outside that, they had erected a palisade, all thick tree trunks topped with sharpened points. The workers had designed the whole thing to keep the contestants inside the battle area.

Khaniel considered it to be an effective enclosure; a plank laid across the stakes at the southernmost point offered the only means of getting into or out of the pit.

Khaniel could see that his adversaries had arrived before him, waiting upon the high platform in the middle of the wheel-shaped obstacle course. Ghoarg and his two warriors had outfitted themselves in heavy plate mail, and each of them carried a different weapon. The chieftain held a long hooked pole with a spike at the end, good for tripping and stabbing. One of his companions hefted a weighted net, while the other lazily swung a large spiked club back and forth. Each opponent also wore a sword sheathed on his back. They intended to work in concert, hoping to trip or trap Khaniel before closing in for the kill.

Khaniel waited while Bulp unhooked the chain from his collar. Then he walked across the plank to the opposite side. The ogre pulled the plank away, effectively trapping him within the enclosure. He moved to a ladder and hurried up it to the southernmost platform as Kizrak began to speak. One of his shamans must have somehow magically augmented the king's voice, for it boomed loudly over the din of the crowd.

"Today, champions fight for honor!" he shouted, making the crowd roar. "If mine wins, I claim the slave Dakkas for myself." He pointed to a spot on the opposite side of the arena, and for the first time, Khaniel saw that a cage sat there, raised high on a scaffold for the entire assembly to see. A lone figure huddled inside. "If Ghoarg somehow cheats well enough to win"—a cacophony of boos rippled through the crowd—"then he may keep the wretched creature. Afterward, we will drink and eat!" The crowd screamed its approval.

Kizrak turned to face the arena, a red flag in his hand. He raised it high and held it there. When he lowered it, the battle would begin. Khaniel scanned the crowd near the king, looking for Bhaobuk. He couldn't see the shaman. He wondered where the ogre might be, or if he would keep his promise of magical aid.

Better not count on it, Khaniel thought grimly. *Do it yourself.*

Taking a deep, calming breath, the warrior looked at his three foes, who watched Kizrak, eagerly awaiting the signal to start. A narrow bridge between their central platform and his perimeter platform served as the most direct route between them. Khaniel wondered if they would try to come at him together, or if they would split up and attempt to surround him.

Better for me if they divide up, he decided. *I can outrun them and pick them off one at a time.*

Khaniel surreptitiously eyed the location of the hidden axe, beneath the bridge immediately beyond the southwestern platform to Khaniel's left. To reach it, he would have to swing across the series of knotted ropes he had spotted the previous day. The ropes hung over a field of sharpened stakes. If one of the ogres followed the path to the southwestern platform, Khaniel would either have to rush across the ropes before he got cut off or delay reaching the axe until later in the fight.

Kizrak jerked his arm down.

The crowd went mad, shouting encouragement to one side or the other. Ghoarg and his two minions fanned out to come at Khaniel from three different directions. The one with the net headed straight toward him, while the other two took the paths immediately on either side. The warrior could see the chieftain grinning, but no mirth showed in that smile. The ogre was eager for the kill.

The ogre with the club went to Khaniel's left, crossing a rickety bridge toward the platform on the far side of the rope swings, just as he had feared. However, he didn't seem to be moving all that fast. The warrior suspected the ogre would wait until the other two closed in on him, possibly even contained him, before he tried to cross the rope swings. No one would want to be caught hanging there with a foe waiting on the opposite side.

Khaniel needed to take out that enemy first. He couldn't allow the one with the net to reach him, and he didn't like his chances against Ghoarg, with his weapon's extended reach, while the other two roamed free. He needed to eliminate the club-wielder.

Making a snap decision, the warrior ran to his left, toward the ropes. He launched himself out from the platform, bypassing the first couple of ropes as he sailed through the air. The crowd's roar rose in pitch and volume as the onlookers watched him execute his daring maneuver. He kept his eyes locked on the rope itself, refusing to look down. He grabbed it and let his momentum carry him to the next rope. Swinging like a monkey in a tree, Khaniel raced across the series of swings. He saw the club-wielder speed up, trying to cross the rickety bridge to intercept Khaniel before he crossed the ropes. The bridge shifted and rocked beneath the foe, nearly causing him to lose his balance; the ogre had to pause and stabilize himself before continuing.

If he makes it in time, I'm in trouble.

Ignoring that thought, the warrior focused all his concentration on swinging from rope to rope. It was going to be close, but Khaniel leaped from the last rope and rushed across the platform to the path on the far side—the one leading toward the northwest platform—just as the club-wielder also arrived. The ogre lunged at Khaniel, but the mercenary dodged to the side and kept running. He reached the bridge where Kizrak had hidden the axe and dropped down into the field of sharpened stakes. Picking his way quickly but carefully, Khaniel reached up under the bridge.

The axe was not there.

9

"**D**AMNATION!" KHANIEL SHOUTED. KIZRAK had betrayed him, had set him up. The axe, the absurd wager, even Bhaobuk's promise of covert magical aid, all trickery from the start, he thought.

He was going to die.

No. You are a fighter, the best Cain Darkmoore ever trained. You can still win. Become the beast.

Whirling about, he saw that the ogre pursuing him had reached the point where Khaniel had jumped down from the platform into the stakes. The club-wielder eyed the gap in the spikes uncertainly.

He couldn't go back up that way; the ogre would pulverize him from the high ground. He had to find another route. Turning, he ran north along the length of the bridge, directly underneath it where no one had bothered to erect stakes. He reached the base of the northwestern platform at the far end and stopped to listen. Even over the roar of the crowd, he heard the heavy footsteps of the plate-armored ogre running that way. Khaniel snatched up one of the sharpened stakes, yanking it out of the ground, and positioned himself under a particularly wide crack between planks. When the ogre drew near, Khaniel thrust his makeshift weapon up. The sharpened end slid easily between the planks and right into the soft sole of the ogre's boot. Khaniel lunged upward with all his might, shoving on that spike, driving it into the creature's flesh.

The ogre let out a howl of pain and, in the next instant, toppled to the bridge with a resounding thud. Khaniel jerked the spike free and saw that the tip had broken off. He hoped he had wedged it deep in the fool's foot. The warrior sprinted back the other way, picking his path through the spikes, and then clambered back to the bridge. A quick look over the battlefield told him that neither of the other two ogres had gotten anywhere close; they had decided against trying to cross the ropes and had instead rushed back to the central platform to reach their target.

Khaniel turned back to the club-wielder. The ogre sat up and struggled to bend forward far enough to reach the broken end of the spike and remove it. His heavy and inflexible armor made the effort futile. Realizing his predicament, the ogre began trying desperately to unbuckle the straps holding his mail on.

Khaniel pulled his short sword out and charged across the bridge toward the downed foe. The ogre frantically redoubled his efforts but, when he realized he would never finish, grabbed his club, which lay beside him on the bridge. As Khaniel approached, the ogre began swinging the weapon back and forth. The warrior understood the tactic clearly; the ogre simply wanted to hold Khaniel at bay long enough for his allies to reach him.

Instead of trying to get inside the powerful club swings, Khaniel timed his approach and leaped directly over the ogre, kicking at the club as his opponent tried to strike him in midair. The mercenary came down easily on the far side of the bridge and spun back around. With his back to Khaniel, the ogre found himself in an even more awkward position, unable to turn and face the warrior. He tried to spin around on the bridge, but Khaniel darted in and slashed hard with his sword, catching his opponent on one elbow. He felt the blade slip between folds of armor and strike flesh, and the ogre grunted in pain. He nearly dropped his club but retained a grip on it with his good hand. His wounded arm hung limp at his side as he managed to turn so that he faced Khaniel once more.

The mercenary feinted another attack, and the ogre tried to counter it. With only one good arm, though, he swung awkwardly, and he allowed the weight of the weapon to carry too far. Khaniel struck again, ramming his sword up into a soft point in the creature's armor at the armpit. The blade sank deep.

The ogre whimpered in pain and stared fearfully at Khaniel, but the mercenary had finished with him. Knowing that he had already effectively eliminated his first foe from the combat, Khaniel turned his attention to the other two, slipping his sword into its sheath on his back. He saw immediately that they were trying to flank him, come at him from opposite sides.

Ghoarg turned down the same rickety bridge the club-wielder had followed to reach the southwestern platform, immediately to Khaniel's right, while the foe with the net headed directly north, to a platform two spots to the left of the mercenary's position. At first Khaniel wondered why the ogre had skipped the more immediate northwestern platform, since it left the warrior with a way to cut between the two ogres and head toward the center platform, evading their flanking maneuver. But then he took a closer look at the route between the northwestern platform and the central hub and understood his foe's reluctance.

The ogres had made that route one of the most difficult to cross. It consisted of a series of log pillars set vertically into the ground and spaced apart like elevated stepping stones. The gaps between the logs would force anyone attempting to navigate them to jump from pillar to pillar, and of course the builders had lined the ground beneath with a multitude of sharpened stakes. An ogre in heavy plate armor would be loath to attempt such a difficult balancing act.

But Khaniel realized the ogres hadn't accounted for a more nimble human when they had constructed the battlefield. They'd been watching contests between big, armor-encumbered ogres for years; it had limited their mindset. The warrior felt confident he could cross the obstacle with little difficulty.

Quickly, before the ogres could make up any more ground on him, Khaniel raced the rest of the way to the northwestern platform and right to the edge where the log pillars began. He appraised the distance to the first pillar, retreated a step or two, and leaped. He landed gently atop the log on one foot, planning to use his momentum to keep going.

The log lurched beneath the warrior's weight, nearly tossing him over the side.

The crowd roared with delight as Khaniel realized to his dismay that the logs weren't anchored into the ground. He staggered and swayed, flailing his arms about to maintain his balance. The pillar teetered beneath him, rocking back and forth as he tried to compensate. He could not stay upright, though, and as the log began to tumble to one side, Khaniel desperately leaped off it and back toward the platform.

He managed to grab hold of the very edge as the log fell away with a thundering crash to the ground below.

Idiot! he fumed as he hung there, trying to catch his breath. The near-catastrophe only served to remind Khaniel that Ghoarg and his minions knew the battlefield better than he. They could use it as an advantage against him. *Never assume!*

Knowing that the two ogres had indeed trapped him between them, Khaniel scrambled back to the platform and stood up. He could still choose the place to make his stand, and he wanted it to be where he could take best advantage of his quicker reactions, and where the ogres would have the most difficulty employing their larger, more cumbersome weapons and armor. He surveyed the pair's progress and determined that Ghoarg would reach him first, if he chose to stand and fight there on the platform. That didn't seem too promising, with the visiting chieftain's longer hooked weapon.

Khaniel turned back the other way. Along that route, between the northwestern and northern platforms, Kizrak's builders had constructed a very narrow bridge with a series of bisecting half-walls. Anyone crossing would have to duck beneath and climb over them in an alternating sequence. Because of the way the workers had laid them out, opponents on opposite sides of the bridge could not see one another. Khaniel wondered if the netthrower had realized that when he had chosen his route.

Khaniel considered the obstacles both a hindrance and a boon to him. They would make it difficult for his foe to employ the net, but it would also mean that Khaniel would not be able to dodge other attacks if his enemy decided to use his sword. And if Ghoarg managed to close the gap between them and come at Khaniel from the back side, he was dead.

The mercenary settled on a tactic and began to navigate the walkway, really little more than a beam. Khaniel focused on placing one foot directly in front of the other, ignoring everything else around him. He reached the first of the obstacles, a waist-high wall. He jumped onto it rather than trying to climb over. While he balanced there, he turned back to judge Ghoarg's progress. The ogre chieftain had reached his ally, who lay writhing in an expanding pool of blood. He did not stop to check on his companion but kept coming, reaching the edge of the narrow bridge. Ghoarg gave Khaniel a glaring smile.

"Come here and let me bleed you a little," the ogre taunted.

In response, Khaniel dropped down on the other side and darted forward, ducking under the next obstacle. That second wall rose well above Khaniel's head but left a gap not quite waist high at the bottom. Beyond it, another waist-high wall stretched across the beam. Khaniel stood again, unable to see beyond the immediate set of obstacles on either side of him. He couldn't see the other ogre's progress, but he knew Ghoarg would not be far behind.

With only a heartbeat's hesitation, Khaniel hopped atop the second low wall and then used the additional height to leap toward the next high wall. Stretching his hands out, he caught hold of the top of that taller wall. Swinging from side to side, he managed to kick one leg up to the top of the wall, in the same way he had scrambled to the top of the bluff face a lifetime ago, and drew himself up and into a sitting position. From that vantage point, Khaniel could see the entire arena, as well as the tops of the most immediate series of high walls still along his path. He counted five more of them.

The crowd screamed its delight when Khaniel appeared, and he took a moment to look over toward Kizrak. The king of Oggok stood, waving his arms along with everyone else, genuinely into the fight. Khaniel had half-expected the tyrant to be frowning.

Maybe he didn't double-cross me after all, the mercenary thought. *But then where in the hell's the axe? And what about Bhaobuk?*

As if the shaman had read Khaniel's mind, a sudden and almost sickening wave of miasma cascaded over the warrior. Through the taint of what he knew to be Innoruuk's touch, he could sense his agility heightening, his strength increasing. He felt more completely alive, more deadly, than he had ever imagined possible.

Khaniel grinned. *That's more like it,* he thought.

He turned and leaped easily from the top of the wall upon which he stood to the top of the next high wall. He crossed a span of at least eight feet, with a low wall in between, but the jump gave Khaniel no difficulties, requiring little effort at all. He continued the motion, launching himself toward the next wall and then the next.

Below the warrior, he could see the ogre with the net struggling to climb over the low wall directly in front of him. As Khaniel jumped again, he passed over the ogre and settled on his feet atop the next-to-last wall. He noted that his foe did not see him. Taking a chance, Khaniel dropped down on the far side of the wall, catching the top of it with his hands, and hung there. Then he released his grip and settled lightly to the beam, going instantly into a low squat and pulling his blade free at the same time. He could see his opponent's feet, up on tiptoes, still working to clamber over the low wall. The ogre had his back to Khaniel.

The mercenary darted under the low wall and came up to the deafening screams of the cheering crowd. The sound must have tipped his enemy off to his presence, for just as Khaniel drew his blade back for a killing blow, the ogre kicked out at him. The blow did not connect fully with the mercenary, but it struck well enough that Khaniel stumbled back, nearly losing his balance in the process. His blade swished through the air and left the warrior teetering with his arms wide to regain his balance.

The ogre, meanwhile, turned around and pulled his sword free from his belt. Khaniel took a swipe at his foe, but his smaller blade struck metal plating and bounced harmlessly off. The ogre counterattacked, and Khaniel had to duck low to avoid having his head taken from his shoulders.

"Quit wiggling and let me spit you!" the ogre yelled, swinging again. Khaniel ducked once more and then hit the ogre's blade as hard as he could with his own sword. He hoped to knock it from the beast's hand, but it didn't dislodge. The blow did, however, shift the ogre's weight enough that he swayed a bit on the beam.

Khaniel needed only that small opening.

Spinning, the mercenary snapped his foot up, ramming it hard into the ogre's hip. The blow sent his foe, arms flailing like twin windmills, tumbling over the side of the narrow walkway. With a yell of frustration coupled with sudden fright, the ogre plunged to the ground below, collapsing on top of several rows of sharpened stakes. The stout wooden spikes impaled the ogre, punching all the way through both armor and body to protrude from the opposite side.

The crowd's fever pitch rose higher. Khaniel stared down at the ogre, feeling a sense of satisfaction. He had reduced the fight to one-on-one. He could defeat Ghoarg alone in a face-to-face fight in an open space. He turned to move on, away from Ghoarg and to the next platform beyond, when the chieftain lunged up suddenly from behind the low wall to the warrior's rear.

With a savage cry, Ghoarg jammed the pikelike weapon at Khaniel.

The mercenary managed to evade the stab, but Ghoarg seemed to expect the maneuver, for he immediately reversed course, catching Khaniel's shoulder with the hook. The chieftain yanked hard, pulling the mercenary to one side and off his feet. Khaniel flipped forward, landing awkwardly atop the narrow walkway. In his desperate effort to avoid slipping over the side, he lost his grip on his sword and watched it fall to the ground far below, helpless to stop it.

"Now I'm gonna gut you!" Ghoarg screamed in triumph. He drew the weapon back once more, lining up for a deadly strike right at Khaniel's torso.

Rather than trying to scramble back to his feet, Khaniel slipped over the edge of the walkway and hung there by his hands. The pike slammed into the wood right where he had lain a moment before. The mercenary could feel the bridge vibrate with the force of the blow. With a hand-over-hand sideways motion, he pulled himself along the causeway, putting distance between himself and his foe.

He passed beneath the next low wall just as Ghoarg reached down with his hooked pike and tried to stab at him again. Khaniel shifted his weight so that the weapon slithered past his hip, and rolled that hip to the side to evade the hook on the return. Then he rotated his body and moved one hand under and around to the other side of the walkway so that he hung straight down beneath it, one arm on either side, making himself a more difficult target. When Ghoarg's pike darted into view again, Khaniel kicked at it, trying to dislodge it from his enemy's grip. But again, Ghoarg expected such a tactic and jerked the weapon out of reach.

Not waiting to see if Ghoarg would attack again, Khaniel began to move backward, brachiating his way along the walkway. He knew he could move faster that way than Ghoarg could navigate the obstacles topside, especially with Bhaobuk's magical enhancements making him so strong and agile. He passed beneath the final low wall and then the last of the high walls. Turning once more to cling to one side of the bridge, Khaniel executed a reverse somersault, kicking his legs forward, up and over himself so that his belly rested on the walkway.

The warrior felt Ghoarg's weight as the ogre landed hard on the bridge. *Probably just got over that wall,* he surmised.

Without waiting to see, Khaniel shifted around, got to his feet, and ran along the last few feet of the beam and onto the northern platform. He peered around, feeling helpless without some sort of weapon. He briefly considered hopping down to ground level and retrieving either the net-thrower's blade or his own, but he felt uncertain he could navigate those stakes as easily as the ones near where Kizrak had hidden the axe. Besides, he reasoned, Ghoarg could get to him from above with his longer weapon if he did that.

No, he would have to find another weapon. The other club-wielder.

Khaniel turned, prepared to sprint south along the connecting bridge to the central platform, intent on circling around to reach his first opponent. Before he took a step, though, agonizing pain gripped him. A fiery ache made every muscle lock up, and the warrior tumbled to the boards, paralyzed with torment. He could feel the taint of Innoruuk's magic coursing through his body along with the agonizing spasms. He first thought of Bhaobuk, but that made no sense. Someone else had cast against him.

One of Ghoarg's own shamans.

As with Bhaobuk, the offender could go unnoticed within the crazed, screaming crowd; even if Khaniel could sit up and peer about, he would never find the culprit, much less do anything about it. Through the pounding in his ears, Khaniel could hear the intense boos of the crowd, protesting the obvious cheating. When the magical affliction finally faded, the warrior could only lie there for a moment afterward, panting.

The platform beneath the mercenary bounced with vibrations. He rolled to one side and scrambled to his feet as Ghoarg charged toward him, his pike angled at Khaniel's chest. The hidden spellcaster's assault had accomplished more than just injury. The attack had also allowed the chieftain to overtake his quarry.

Khaniel crouched, wary of the approaching ogre. Ghoarg slowed a bit, clearly understanding that he held the advantage because his adversary had no weapon. As he drew nearer, he tried a couple of experimental thrusts, watching to see what Khaniel would do. The mercenary dodged to the side, slapping the end of the hooked pike away. Ghoarg tried a different tactic, sidestepping in a wide circle as if trying to come at Khaniel from the side. The warrior could easily keep his foe in front of him, but the chieftain's intentions became clear.

Ghoarg intended to herd the human toward the edge of the platform, trying to pin him into a corner.

Ghoarg made a more vicious lunge, and Khaniel almost didn't evade it. When he did step to the side, the ogre swatted him in the side of the head. The strike stung, and Khaniel grunted and grabbed at his ear. Ghoarg used the brief distraction to his advantage, dropping the head of the pike low and hooking Khaniel's ankle. The mercenary managed to shift his weight enough to prevent his foe from tripping him, but the effort spun him part of the way around. Khaniel teetered off balance and turned away.

Ghoarg dropped his pike and charged forward.

Khaniel, balanced on one foot, couldn't react to evade. If the chieftain struck him squarely, he would go over the side. Deadly spikes awaited him below if he fell, so the warrior did the only thing he could. He dropped to the deck.

Ghoarg adjusted his charge and aimed a vicious kick at Khaniel. Around them, the crowd roared in excitement as the chieftain slammed his metal-shod foot into the mercenary's ribs. Khaniel rolled away from the blow and tried to rise to his hands and knees, but Ghoarg pounded him again. The mercenary felt his ribs crack as the blow drove the wind from his lungs. He dropped completely prone, unable to overcome the injuries.

Ghoarg sneered, "Puny human. You cannot defeat me!" As the ogre shouted those words, he let his voice rise in volume and began to strut around the platform, his arms aloft in a gesture of victory. The crowd of ogres roared a mixture of praise and dismay at the sight. Ghoarg soaked it in as Khaniel tried to catch his breath. He struggled up again, breathing hard, thankful for the chieftain's vanity.

Khaniel welcomed every second he could gain for recovering his wits.

When the ogre chieftain saw his opponent on the verge of standing, he stomped across the platform toward Khaniel again. The crowd inundated them both with encouragement and catcalls. Khaniel's tender ribs protested as he drew in a deep breath.

Bhaobuk, this would be a fine time for some of that healing magic, he thought.

Ghoarg closed with Khaniel and drew his foot back for another strike. Desperate to avoid any more punishment on his ribs, Khaniel went into a roll. He shoved with all of his strength toward his foe's feet. The maneuver disrupted the timing of the kick and shoved the ogre backward in the process. Ghoarg stumbled a few steps in an attempt to keep his balance, and Khaniel took advantage. Lurching up off the rough wooden decking, the warrior gathered himself and charged toward Ghoarg, lowering his shoulder. The ogre saw him coming and tried to ram his mailed elbow down on the mercenary's back, but Khaniel bowled him over. They both went tumbling to the deck.

The crowd screamed once more, thrilled at the prospect of the fight continuing. Khaniel's tumble jarred his ribs again, and he almost blacked out from the pain. But instead, he felt himself becoming enraged, and for once, he didn't try to fight it. The warrior knew it was time to let the fury take over, time for him to succumb to it, become a savage, blind killing thing.

Rising to his feet, Khaniel fed the fury, imagining the injustices inflicted upon Zethamy during her captivity. He directed that hatred and rage, focused it at the ogre before him, who struggled to roll over in his cumbersome suit of mail. The anger surged, and the mercenary began to lose himself in the tempest.

Another spasm of fiery pain shot throughout his body.

Ghoarg's hidden accomplice had done it again. Khaniel dropped to the platform in agony once more, fighting the effects of the debilitating magic that coursed through him. The attack further infuriated him, but his anger grew chaotic, unfocused, and he knew the moment of attaining that berserk nature had passed.

As the magic's effects slowly faded and Khaniel lay panting on the platform, he could hear the crowd, lustily bellowing its disapproval once more. The warrior managed to open his eyes and gaze over at his foe, who rested on one knee.

If he gets to me while I'm down again, I'm done for.

Summoning some hidden will, Khaniel managed to get to his feet about the same time Ghoarg did. They looked at one another. The ogre chieftain seemed wary, showing an expression that seemed to Khaniel to be grudging respect.

"I'm tired of this fight, pesky slave," Ghoarg growled. "It's time for you to die." He reached back and slid his fat-bladed sword from its sheath on his back. "No more playing." He took a step forward, then another, coming right at Khaniel. The warrior still had nothing to use to defend himself. He eyed the wicked blade in dismay, then did the only thing he could to survive.

Khaniel turned and ran.

The warrior sprinted as fast as his wounded body would let him toward the causeway leading to the center platform. His lungs burned for air, and sharp, stabbing pains from his ribs jolted him with each step, but he dared not falter. He could feel Ghoarg storm after him, heard the ogre shout a curse at having to chase the smaller, more nimble combatant.

The ogre builders had constructed a rope bridge for the middle third of the causeway between the northern platform and the central one. Khaniel knew it would either be his salvation or his undoing. If he sprinted across it quickly enough, he would easily outrun the larger and slower Ghoarg and might even manage to circle around and retrieve the club-wielding ogre's sword. If he stumbled or missed a step, he would undoubtedly become entangled in the ropes, and Ghoarg would cut him down then and there.

He could not miss a step.

Blocking out the protesting pain in his body, Khaniel focused every part of his attention on the rope bridge and his feet. He sprinted across the short bit of solid walkway and then began to navigate the expanse of knots and lines, placing each foot directly on a support strand. It resembled running in sand, the warrior supposed.

Almost at the far end, Khaniel felt the rope vibrate sharply beneath him. The sudden bounce ruined his timing and placement, and his foot missed the next step. He went plunging down, one leg pinned under his body while the other hung beneath him in open space. Below, the ground brimmed with sharpened stakes.

Kizrak must really like to witness impalings, the mercenary thought in a moment of desperate humor. He turned back to see what had caused his slipup, and spotted Ghoarg standing at the far end, jumping up and down on the rope. *Very clever,* Khaniel reluctantly admitted.

Seeing his quarry upended, Ghoarg stopped his bouncing and started crossing the rope bridge.

Khaniel began to extract himself, flailing about as he tried to climb back up onto the rope bridge. With the ogre chieftain bearing down on him, the mercenary had to fight the urge to rush the process. It didn't help matters that he still felt considerable pain and found it difficult to breathe. At last, he managed to draw himself to a standing position.

Immediately, Ghoarg began bouncing again, but Khaniel braced himself for it that time, and he didn't fight the rhythmic vibrations. Timing it perfectly, Khaniel leaped from the rope bridge and landed on the solid footing of the far side. Breathing a sigh of relief, he took off, racing up the path toward the central platform as fast as his cracked ribs would permit. From there, he knew he could circle around and reach the extra sword. Ghoarg could not move fast enough.

When Khaniel reached the central platform, he drew up short, filled with dismay. The club-wielding ogre stepped into view, a wicked smile playing across his face. He appeared healthy and hale, and he blocked the path. Behind the mercenary, Ghoarg approached, and Khaniel could hear him laughing.

He had nowhere to run.

10

KHANIEL EDGED AWAY FROM THE MOUTH OF the bridge behind him, where Ghoarg approached. The other ogre shifted with him, keeping the warrior at bay with his club. The mercenary feinted to one side or the other a couple of times, but the ogre, suspiciously spry, always managed to take the proper angle. Some of the crowd hissed in disapproval, but for most of the ogres watching, bloodlust prevailed, and they screamed for Ghoarg and his minion. They wanted to see carnage, to see a winner emerge triumphant.

It looked to Khaniel as if they would get their wish.

How can he be standing there after the wounds he took? the warrior wondered. *Of course,* he realized. *Ghoarg's accomplice must have healed him from afar.* The thought infuriated Khaniel. *No wonder Ghoarg's champion wins the contest every year.*

At that moment, Khaniel noticed a pile of weapons stashed near the center post of the platform. He saw an odd assortment, including everything from greatswords to spiked clubs to bolas. Then he remembered that the three ogres had begun the contest at that spot. Suddenly, it made sense. Ghoarg and his minions had brought a wide variety of armaments with them, in order to choose appropriate weapons after they had surveyed the battlefield.

Very smart, he thought grimly. *Plan for all contingencies.* Then the handle of a very familiar axe peeking out from the collection attracted the mercenary's attention. *They grabbed it before the battle,* he realized. *Someone tipped them off to its whereabouts. Or else Kizrak's tricks are old hat by now.*

By that point, Ghoarg had reached the platform, too, and both ogres maneuvered around their foe, maintaining flanking positions while preventing him from darting away. "Your time is short, puny slave," Ghoarg gloated. "You've given quite a show, but you are no match for me."

"What a shame you have to cheat to win," Khaniel replied, desperate to buy himself even a little more time. If he could slip past them and reach the pile, he had a chance. But then, he realized they knew that too. "I wonder how great a warrior you really are. You let magic do your work for you."

"Shut up!" the ogre chieftain ordered. "I could kill you with my bare hands!"

Khaniel laughed, though the effort hurt his ribs. "I doubt it," he said, still grinning. "From what I've seen, you couldn't kill a gnome by yourself."

Ghoarg let out a roar of fury and took two menacing steps toward his adversary. He drew his sword back wildly, intent on slamming it into Khaniel as hard as he could. The mercenary started to dart to one side, away from the second ogre. Ghoarg's minion, upon seeing Khaniel beginning to flee from him, took a step closer in pursuit, just as Khaniel had anticipated. When that happened, the warrior whipped back the other way, cutting between the two of them. In Ghoarg's furious desire to cleave his foe in two, he overswung and discovered too late that his companion had moved within reach of his blade. Ghoarg tried to pull back, and armor absorbed some of the impact, but the blade still dug deep into his minion's flesh. The other ogre let out a groan and sank back as blood flowed from the new wound.

Khaniel, meanwhile, had launched himself across the open decking of the platform, coming to land near the pile of weapons. Without hesitation, he grabbed up the axe. It felt so good in his hands, like an extension of himself. He turned, rising to his feet in a fluid motion, ignoring the aches in his battered body, and faced his opponents. The crowd chanted and cheered as loudly as ever.

Ghoarg spat. "What did you say about cheating?" he snarled. "Hiding axes is the same."

Khaniel shrugged. "Whatever it takes," he said. "One of us dies; the other lives to cheat another day."

The other ogre struggled to rise to his feet again, but Khaniel decided he'd had enough of dancing with his foes. He feinted at Ghoarg, driving the suddenly cautious ogre back a few steps, then turned and swung his axe at his wounded opponent. The blade whistled smoothly through the air and separated the ogre's head from his shoulders. Khaniel hardly had to recover from the strike due to the superb balance of the axe. Even as he followed through, he locked eyes on Ghoarg again.

The crowd went mad.

The ogre's body toppled back to the decking, seeping blood. The head tumbled over the side, out of sight. It was down to one-on-one.

For a while, the two combatants simply circled one another. Khaniel made an effort to hide how much he hurt, but he found it difficult. Ghoarg, on the other hand, didn't need to pretend. He had not taken a scratch to that point. Khaniel darted forward once, slicing at the chieftain, but the ogre skipped out of the way and took a counterswing at the warrior. Khaniel lunged a bit awkwardly to evade the great blade, twisting around and aggravating his ribs. With a gasp of pain, he set his feet and readied for another attack.

Back and forth the pair went, driving each other one way, then retreating another. The sounds of their weapons clanging together rang through the arena, even over the sound of the madly screaming onlookers. Ghoarg proved the stronger of the two, and each time he hammered a blow down on Khaniel, the mercenary had to muster all his strength simply to deflect it. Even with the perfectly balanced axe in his hands, the exertions took their toll.

Khaniel knew he could not stand toe-to-toe with his foe much longer.

When a particularly vicious hit caught Khaniel directly on his buckler, the warrior went down to one knee. His forearm felt fractured; he could hardly hold it up. Ghoarg stepped in and tried to finish the fight by slicing Khaniel's head off, but the mercenary ducked low and rolled to the side. Ghoarg followed, swinging for all he was worth. Each time, Khaniel barely evaded the strike, and each strike slammed against the planks of the platform, splintering wood. On the fifth such attack, the ogre chieftain actually got his blade lodged in the wood, caught in a crack between two boards.

Khaniel used the reprieve to struggle away and clamber to his feet. He stood there, panting, while Ghoarg furiously worked his blade free. The warrior had nothing left. He could barely hold his axe aloft, especially with his other arm next to useless. His ribs burned. Ghoarg seemed destined to win by sheer attrition. Khaniel needed something, a trick, to catch the more powerful ogre off guard. Suddenly, he had it.

Ghoarg finally wrenched his sword from the wood and spun, expecting an attack. When he saw Khaniel standing only a few feet back, trying to catch his breath, the ogre chuckled. "It won't be much longer," he said. "You cannot keep fighting; you are not as strong."

"I'm strong en—"

Then it happened. The crowd watched in awe and wonder as Khaniel went rigid, his muscles clenched. He staggered and fell, crying out as if in intolerable pain. Ghoarg's hidden minion had struck again, it seemed, had felled the human warrior with cunning magic.

Ghoarg crowed in delight and raised his arms in triumph. He gave the crowd one quick salute, spinning in place, and came full circle to stare down at Khaniel once more. Then, with a hateful grin on his face, the ogre chieftain raised his sword high, blade tip pointing down, ready to drive it into his foe's chest.

He never struck.

Right when the ogre had his weapon at the apex of his strike, Khaniel dropped the feint and whipped his body around, swinging his axe with all the remaining force he could muster. Ghoarg, caught by surprise, tried to block the blow, but his effort came too late. The mercenary's cut struck sure and went deep. The armor divided in half, hardly even crimping.

Ghoarg, the ogre chieftain, stood still for a moment, blinking. He seemed unable to comprehend the image before him, the evidence of his own demise, as his entrails slid from his belly onto the wooden planking. For that instant, as Khaniel sat upon his knees, totally spent, and watched, the crowd went silent. It lasted only a heartbeat, only long enough for the trickery to register with them.

Then, as Ghoarg toppled forward, falling into the mess that his own insides had become, the onlookers roared one final, deafening time. Khaniel sagged, clutching at his side. The axe lay on the platform next to him, forgotten.

His whole world had become pain.

NIGHTFALL SETTLED OVER THE CELEBRATION. AS before, Khaniel received a seat at Kizrak's head table, but he drew much more attention than he had the previous evening. The mercenary had expected many of the visiting ogres, those who had come to Oggok with Ghoarg, to be sullen and angry with him. In fact, he had almost expected a riot in the arena after he managed to defeat the chieftain. But the ogres seemed to shrug the whole incident off.

After he had sliced Ghoarg open and won the day, ogres came to cart the three dead combatants away, and Bulp appeared with Bhaobuk in tow to retrieve the victor. The shaman healed most of Khaniel's wounds, granting him relief and renewed strength at the same time. Khaniel gave the shaman a meaningful stare as Bhaobuk worked his magic, but the ogre did not respond to the mercenary's unspoken question. Khaniel would have to find out some other time why Bhaobuk had been unable to assist him more effectively.

Some among the guests began vying for the position as leader of the visiting tribe. A few issued formal challenges to combat, intending to fight after the feasting and drinking. Others began to barter for support with one another, looking to become kingmakers if they could not be king themselves. Khaniel didn't completely understand the process, but however it would be decided, choosing a successor did not interfere with the celebration. Both hosts and guests appeared more interested in toasting him for his battle prowess than in worrying about the death and replacement of a chieftain.

Kizrak acted a bit odd during the course of the evening. On the one hand, he clearly relished finally defeating his rival in the martial contests. But though he praised Khaniel repeatedly for his show of battle savvy, he also remained subdued while at the table. Khaniel accepted the accolades graciously, though he couldn't have cared less at the time. He worried about Zethamy.

Kizrak had ordered the paladin's cage taken to his palace, and a handful of his attendants had seen to that, hauling it away with the woman still inside, looking as miserable as ever. Khaniel desperately wanted a chance to speak with her, to tell her he would try to free her, but winning the contest had not allotted him any more freedom. If anything, it seemed that he had come under more severe scrutiny, albeit supportive rather than suspicious.

As the feasting proceeded, some of the attention paid Khaniel finally subsided. The ogres turned their attention away from him and toward the savory meats and brewed delights before them.

Khaniel tried to enjoy some of the food placed in front of him, but his concern over Zethamy's well-being interfered with his hunger. He feared that Kizrak would make good on his promise to put her to death that very night—or that he had ordered underlings to deal with it for him. The king's odd mood did nothing to assuage Khaniel's fears.

Bruigan appeared suddenly at the main table, toting a tun of something dark and foamy, which he used to fill each mug. As he proceeded around the table, the dwarf laughed and smiled and patted the keg enthusiastically, as if to say, "Drink up! It's good stuff!" When Bruigan reached Khaniel's side, he began filling the mercenary's mug.

"I need to speak with you," the dwarf said softly, under his breath. "Get away from here; tell them you're tired or something. But whatever you do, don't drink this."

Khaniel gave his friend a startled stare, but Bruigan never made eye contact. Instead, he proceeded to another table and continued filling everyone's mugs.

Khaniel waited a few moments longer so that his departure would not seem to coincide with the appearance of the dwarf and thus draw suspicions. But none of the ogres gave Bruigan even a glance, completely caught up in laughing and consuming everything in site.

A fortuitous night for espionage, Khaniel decided.

The mercenary feigned exhaustion from the day's events and requested permission to return to his own quarters. Kizrak gladly allowed it, and Bulp escorted the warrior back to the palace. The guard seemed to weave ever so slightly as they walked, and Khaniel briefly considered getting the jump on the ogre at some out-of-the-way place. He decided it wasn't worth the risk. Whatever Bruigan had planned, Khaniel didn't want to ruin it by getting into trouble.

Bulp locked the warrior's leash to the wall in his room and departed hastily and without comment. Khaniel could see that the ogre wanted to get back to the party. When Khaniel finally found himself alone, he set about trying to yank the chain from the wall. When the lock proved too durable, he turned his attention to the connection on his collar. That, too, remained stoutly secured, beyond his means to detach. He grew frustrated as he began trying to pry the collar itself apart. Finally, with his hands raw from grasping the rough metal, Khaniel gave up. He had hoped to meet Bruigan somewhere outside the palace, but the dwarf had to come to him, if he could. Khaniel could do nothing more.

Bruigan took a long time to appear. Khaniel nearly fell asleep waiting, truly tired despite Bhaobuk's ministrations. The dwarf slipped inside the curtain and knelt down next to the warrior, about to shake his shoulder softly.

"I'm awake," the mercenary whispered. "What's going on?"

"You're in trouble," Bruigan said. "Kizrak intends to kill you tomorrow."

Khaniel sat up. "What?" he asked, stunned at the dwarf's revelation. "Why?"

"You actually won today," Bruigan replied. "He sees you as a threat. He worries that the rest of Oggok will come to view him as soft and weak compared to you. You're quite the hero after today. Even for a slave." Khaniel could hear the sarcasm clearly laced in those final words.

"How do you know this?"

"I overheard Kizrak talking to a couple of his honor guard earlier, before you came out to the feast."

"How could you understand what they were talking about?" Khaniel asked, a little surprised.

"What?" Bruigan snorted. "You think you're the only one here who can learn a new language?" When Khaniel only grinned, the dwarf added, "Bhaobuk has been teaching me every day. I got tired of not knowing what in the five kingdoms everyone was talking about."

Khaniel grinned a bit more, but then he shook his head. "All the more reason to get out of here," he said. Then he remembered that he had not seen the dwarf in several days. "Hey! Did you get my message? Zethamy's here! She's alive!"

"Yes, I figured it out," Bruigan replied. "You had Bhaobuk pretty confused, but I got the message. Can't say I understand how it happened, but I guess she—and you—are lucky."

"Not so lucky," Khaniel said, brooding. "She's blind. I took her sight from her, Bruigan. And Kizrak intends to kill her. I've got to save her, get all three of us out of here."

"Oh, so *now* you want to rescue someone and escape. What if *I* don't want to leave? What if *I* like it here now?"

Khaniel could hear the jest in his friend's tone, but the words stabbed him with guilt all the same. "I'm sorry, Bruigan," he said in earnest, feeling genuine remorse. "I did you a bad turn."

"Yes, you did, Khaniel," the dwarf replied, not pulling any punches. "I'm not saying your life here has been a sweetcake, but to even *think* that I could bear living among ogres, my hated enemies, for the rest of my days and somehow find a way to like it—well, it doesn't say much about your consideration for our friendship. I could never like this. Never."

Khaniel let the words wash over him. He had to accept the dwarf's anger; he deserved it. "I know I lost my head for a while, thinking I belonged here: it was a lie. I should never have convinced myself that I—or you, for that matter—could be happy living this way. You have every right to be angry, and I won't blame you if you won't help me now, but I hope you will." He drew a deep breath before continuing. "I still loathe myself every day for what happened in those mountains, and I don't yet know what I can do about it, but if I can save her, along with us, maybe I can redeem myself a little bit. Will you help me?"

Bruigan sat there beside Khaniel for a long time in the darkness, as if thinking. The warrior began to worry that his friend actually needed to consider whether or not to help him save the paladin. Finally, the dwarf spoke. "I've been waiting for you to admit that for such a long time. It was so nice to hear it finally, I had to soak it in." Then he rose to his feet with a soft groan of age. "As for the escape part, I've already started working on that."

"The beer?" Khaniel asked, feeling a growing sense of elation come over him.

"The beer," Bruigan confirmed. "Remember those grubs we gathered? Well, they weren't for flavor, my friend. Tonight, I served up my special batch of stout—the one with the powerful sleeping nectar in it. In the last hour or so, everyone who's had even a sip started sawing logs. They'll stay down until well past sunup."

"You're brilliant," Khaniel said, beaming with genuine admiration. "You've been planning to escape even without my cooperation."

"I told you there was no way I would stay here for the rest of my life," the dwarf said with a chuckle. His next words sounded far more serious. "I would rather die out there in the stinking Feerott than rot here as an ogre's slave."

Khaniel nodded. "You may yet get your chance," he said solemnly. "But before that can happen, we've got to get me free of this damned chain."

"Again, I'm already ahead of you, my friend," Bruigan said, producing a set of keys. "Bulp was my first stop."

The dwarf manipulated the lock, and the chain dropped away from Khaniel's collar. With a sigh of relief, the warrior stood up. He hadn't realized how good it would feel to be free of that restrictive iron leash.

"Let's go," Bruigan urged, turning toward the doorway.

"First the throne room," Khaniel said. He turned and led the dwarf through the tunnels, remembering the route from before. Along the ledge that opened to the outside, he listened for a moment, wondering if anyone remained awake. The only noise he detected came from tree frogs and insects; the city seemed unnaturally quiet otherwise.

In the throne room, Khaniel and Bruigan found the cage used to house Zethamy. The paladin slept inside, and for a moment Khaniel stared at her, still trying to wrap his mind around the fact that she lived. She looked thinner than he remembered, and her hair, so long and lustrous before, had become a bedraggled mess. The ogres had stripped her to her smallclothes, tattered garments that barely covered her. Bruigan began working through Bulp's keys, looking for one that would fit the lock of the cage.

"Zethamy," Khaniel called softly. "Zethamy, wake up."

The woman stirred, then sat upright with a strangled whisper. "Who's there?" she called out, her tone uncertain. Her sightless eyes peered around, her expression filled with apprehension.

Khaniel realized she was listening, not looking. "Zethamy, it's—" He hesitated, uncertain how she would react when she learned his identity. "—a friend," he finished. "We're getting you out of here. We're escaping."

"You aren't an ogre," Zethamy said, still sounding hesitant. "Who are you? How do you know me?"

"Later," Bruigan said gruffly as he twisted a key. The lock sprang open, and they wasted no time drawing the woman out of the cage. "Right now, we've got to go."

"Wait," Khaniel said, turning toward the long table. All of the weapons still lay there, including the ones he had taken for himself before the contest. The leather armor, the buckler, and most importantly, the axe all rested right where Bulp had placed them after the fight. Khaniel grabbed them up, donning the armor. "Find something for yourself," he said to the dwarf. "Hurry."

"I know your voices," Zethamy said, standing where Bruigan had let go of her hand to sort through the weapons. "I've met you before. But where?" she finished, trailing off.

"Yes," Khaniel said, grabbing up a padded jacket. He turned toward Zethamy and held the quilted armor up, judging its size. "Put this on," he said, holding it out and guiding it around her shoulders. Absently, the woman slipped her arms through the sleeve holes. The garment sat a little loose on her, but it would do. As Zethamy laced it shut, Khaniel grabbed a pair of leggings and some soft boots. He handed them to the paladin, who slipped them on.

Finally, Khaniel grabbed up the short sword he had regripped and slipped it into Zethamy's palm. When she felt it, she jerked her hand back as if the weapon had burned her. The sword dropped to the floor with a ringing clatter.

"Shhhh!" Bruigan admonished. "They won't sleep through much more of that!" he said in hushed tones.

"Take it," Khaniel said, picking up the sword and placing it in the paladin's hands again. "You might need it."

"No," the woman replied, trying to hand it back. "I can't see. I can't fight." Her words sounded thick, as if she fought back tears.

"I know," Khaniel said softly. He gave her hand a gentle squeeze as he closed her fingers around the hilt. "But just in case," he added.

Zethamy gave a reluctant nod.

Khaniel turned toward Bruigan. "What did you pick?" he asked, peering over at the dwarf.

"I'm not worth much with a blade," Bruigan said, "but I can maybe cut some damned ogre down to size with this," and he held up a hand axe. The weapon appeared sturdy, if not much to look at. "And if nothing else, I can chop wood for our cozy little fireside chats," he added. In the dwarf's other hand, he held a large round shield covered in boiled leather. "And this is what I will cower behind the rest of the time."

Khaniel nodded. "Excellent choices," he said. "Now, let's get out of here." He turned toward the exit of the throne room, ready to depart.

Bhaobuk stood there, watching them.

11

"I FEARED THIS FROM YOU," THE SHAMAN SAID, frowning. "Your cryptic message made me wonder, and then when everyone at the feast began to fall asleep, my suspicions proved right."

"Who is that?" Zethamy asked softly from beside Khaniel. "What's happening?"

"Our escape plan has hit a snag," the warrior explained under his breath. "Bhaobuk, please," he pleaded, louder, so the ogre could hear him. "We can't stay here. You more than anyone in Oggok should understand that. And no one among your kin is dying. The sleeping effects will wear off by tomorrow."

"You betrayed my trust," the shaman said. "You used me, convinced me to help you, and made me the fool. My brother will not look kindly on it or on me for letting it happen."

"The same brother that beats you and ridicules you," Bruigan countered. "And for every demeaning thing he does to you, multiply it tenfold and think of me."

"Yes, Bruigan, I sympathize. But the dwarves and the ogres have been mortal enemies for many years. It is more than one shaman can undo in a single lifetime."

"Bruigan," Zethamy said, tilting her head to one side in puzzlement. "A dwarf..." And then it hit her. She stiffened, horror playing across her face. "You!" she cried. "It's you! Get away from me!" she yelled, backing away, swinging the sword in her hand wildly about. "You bastard!"

Bruigan hissed a warning for quiet.

Khaniel flinched at Zethamy's sudden outburst, and then he tried to go to her, to calm her down. "Stop," he said, wanting to reach out, to take her by the arms. But she kept flailing about in panic. The mercenary knocked aside one aimless swing of her sword with his buckler and grabbed at Zethamy's wrist, restraining her to prevent her from hurting either of them. She jerked and screamed again.

"Stop it!" he insisted. Then he began twisting her arm down and away, keeping the sword low. "I know," he said, using a soothing voice as he grasped her other arm. "I know. You have every right to hate me. But I'm trying to help you now. Please, calm down."

"Let me go, you unholy bastard! I hate you! I hate you!" and her defiant invective broke down into a whimpering moan as she collapsed, still in Khaniel's grip. The sword fell from her grasp. "You took everything from me," she sobbed. "My eyes, my life, all of it. Why? Why are you tormenting me?" she howled.

Khaniel opened his mouth to speak before he realized that Zethamy was crying out not at him, but at the ceiling. *No, to her god. She speaks to Mithaniel Marr.* "Not tormenting," he said at last, dropping down beside her, wrapping his arms around her to offer comfort. "Salvation, perhaps. A second chance at redemption. An opportunity for me to make amends. Come with us, and maybe I can restore what you've lost."

"No!" Zethamy shouted, her anger renewed, her voice hoarse. "Don't touch me!" she yelled, flailing at Khaniel, pounding at his head with her fists. Khaniel fended them off as best as he could, finally trapping her arms by her sides with his own again. "There is no redemption!" she cried, sagging down once more. "He betrayed me, torments me."

Khaniel looked at Bruigan and Bhaobuk helplessly. *Has she really lost so much faith that she would blaspheme her own god?*

The dwarf shook his head, dancing from one foot to the other. "If she doesn't stop that shrieking, the whole city is going to wake up and come find us," he warned. "We have to go."

Khaniel nodded and turned back to Zethamy. "Shhh," he said. "Bhaobuk, can you heal her?" the mercenary asked. "Restore her sight with your magic?"

The shaman shook his head. "My magic is not that powerful. I can mend the bones and flesh, take away the scar, but I do not think it will help her," he said sadly. "And even if I could, why would I do this? You cannot really think to ask me to aid you further! What right do you have to ask anything of me right now?"

"Because you're a good person, Bhaobuk, and you know what we do is right," Khaniel responded, still holding Zethamy. She had given up trying to drive the warrior away from her and simply sat there, crying. "I know it's a lot to ask. I know if you are discovered, it could mean your death. But without your cooperation, we won't get out of here. And I think I speak for all three of us when I say we'd rather die than stay here."

"You can count my vote twice on that," Bruigan said. "You're a decent fellow, ogre, but if you stand there tonight and try to keep me from walking out of this city, then you're no better than the rest of your kin. And if that's true, then I have no compunction against striking you down where you stand, right here, right now."

Bhaobuk drew himself up, insulted. "And what makes you think you can do that, dwarf?" he asked.

"Because I would be right beside him," Khaniel answered. "I owe him that, and a whole lot more."

Bruigan turned to look back at Khaniel and nodded his appreciation. Then he focused his gaze on the shaman once more. "So. What's it going to be? Are you going to step aside and let us run, or are you going to see if your magic will drop us before both Khaniel and I can get to you? After witnessing the battle today, I know on whom I'd wager *my* coin."

Bhaobuk looked from one to the other of them. He frowned, shaking his head.

"Please, Bhaobuk," Khaniel said, rising. "Don't make it come to this."

"I will not try to stop you," the shaman said at last. "But you must do something for me in return." He paused, drew a deep breath, and said, "I would go with you."

Khaniel did a double take in surprise. "What?"

At the same time, Bruigan snorted. "You're loopy."

"I want to accompany you. Out of the city. Forever. I'm ready to leave Oggok behind, and this may be my best opportunity. Take me with you."

Khaniel looked helplessly at Bruigan, who looked back at the warrior and shrugged. "What choice do we have?" the dwarf asked. "If he lets us escape, it could be his death sentence when the rest of them wake up."

"Can you keep up?" Khaniel asked.

Bhaobuk spread his hands apart in a gesture of supplication. "As well as she can," he said, nodding in Zethamy's direction.

After a moment's hesitation, Khaniel nodded. "All right," he said. "Let's get out of here, then." He started to rise, pulling at Zethamy's arms. "Come on," he said. "We're leaving."

"No," she said, sullen. "I don't want anything to do with you."

"You'd rather stay here and be treated like a dog than escape with us?"

"Yes." She folded her arms across her stomach and hunched down, looking very much like a spoiled child.

Khaniel sighed and looked over at his two companions, feeling helpless.

Bruigan stalked over to stand in front of the woman. "They will kill you, lass," he said.

"I don't care," Zethamy replied, her voice quavering and tears running down her cheeks. "Leave me alone."

The dwarf's sudden slap surprised Khaniel as much as it did Zethamy. The paladin gasped and grabbed at her cheek. "Stop feeling sorry for yourself!" Bruigan nearly shouted. "Martyrdom doesn't suit you! Now get up and walk, or Khaniel will hoist you over his shoulder like a sack of beans and carry you. Do you understand me?"

Zethamy's face grew red with indignation, but she did not retort. Instead, she climbed to her feet and glared at nothing. Khaniel was glad to see some of her old fire come back, the part of her personality that he remembered from before.

"That's better," Bruigan said, turning back. "It's good to see the damned ogres didn't beat *all* the sense out of you." He stomped toward the exit from the throne room without looking back.

Khaniel had to smile. He'd never seen his friend so gruff before. *But,* he had to admit, *he is a dwarf.* He reached out and tentatively took Zethamy's hand. She stiffened momentarily, but she didn't jerk away, so he led her from the room.

The four of them made their way through the halls of the palace. Along the way, they gathered up a pair of satchels that Bruigan had loaded with supplies—meat and cheese and skins filled with water. Bhaobuk went to his own quarters and pulled together a few more things. Then they made their way out into the night.

With Bhaobuk in the lead, they moved through the city like four cats hunting mice, sliding from shadow to shadow. Though the vast majority of the citizens had feasted and were undoubtedly under the influence of Bruigan's special brew, there might still be a few ogres who had avoided the drink or had simply missed out altogether.

As they crept along, Zethamy continually slowed, tugging against Khaniel's grasp. He turned a glance back her way more than once and saw her with her free hand outstretched, feeling the air before her, and she took small, shuffling steps, her face a mask of uncertainty.

"I won't let you run into anything," he promised quietly. "Trust me."

"Never," she sneered, shaking her head. He could see her hatred for him.

The group neared the gates out of the city, and Bhaobuk motioned for them to wait a few moments in the shadows of a building. He slipped ahead to scout out the route.

As they waited, Khaniel studied Zethamy's face. A haunted visage, like something surreal from beyond the grave, gazed without sight back at him. Somehow, despite the scar and the ruined eyes, he found her beautiful to look at. He still could not understand how his stroke had not dealt a killing blow. He caught himself reaching up to run his finger across the bridge of her nose, along the scar. He jerked his hand back down. Such a touch would only infuriate her.

"Stop staring at me," she said, her voice quiet.

"How can you tell?" he asked, startled.

"I just can," she answered, sounding tired. "I can feel your eyes."

Khaniel hesitated. "I'm sorry," he said.

"For what? Staring, or for slicing me open?"

Khaniel shuddered. She wasn't going to let it go. He couldn't really blame her. "What happened that day?" he asked at last.

Zethamy frowned. Perhaps she hadn't expected him to be so blunt in return. "You hit me with your axe," she said. "Dropped me like I was one of the cyclopes. What do you think happened?"

"I mean afterward," he said.

"What do you care?"

"Please," he said. "Just tell me."

"I don't remember much," she answered, getting a distant look on her face. "There was so much pain, I'm sure I blacked out for several minutes.

When I awoke, I couldn't see, and I thought at first that I had passed on, that . . . he had brought me to be with him in the Halls of Honor."

She stopped then, swallowing hard, and Khaniel felt sympathy for her. *To believe that your god had been watching over you,* he thought, *only to have those beliefs dashed.* He shook his head. *No wonder she's so bitter.*

"I realized when I could still feel all the pain that I was not dead. And I could tell that I was moving. Being carried, over a giant shoulder, like a . . . a sack of beans," she said, adding emphasis to those last words. "It was terrifying."

"What of your own curing touch? Couldn't you heal the damage? Restore your sight?"

Zethamy winced upon hearing the warrior's words. She drew one shuddering breath. "No," she said.

"I don't understand," Khaniel replied. "A servant of Mithaniel Marr as dedicated as you, one of such favor in his eyes, surely you had the power to—"

"No, I didn't!" Zethamy blurted, louder than she should have. Bruigan gave them a warning shush. In a quieter voice, she added, "Not by then."

Khaniel cocked his head to one side, puzzling over that statement. Then he understood, and the realization felt like a cold knife rammed into his gut. She had turned from Mithaniel. She had forsaken him, because she had felt betrayed. "You lost faith," he said, not knowing why he would put words to her pain.

The sob came out soft, almost muffled, and anguish shone in her milky eyes. "He didn't protect me," she whispered. "He turned away from me, first. I was supposed to lead everyone to greatness. I was his spiritual beacon, his avatar." Then she grimaced. "It was all a bunch of lies. He didn't care about me at all." She reached out and grabbed Khaniel's arm. "Leave me here," she pleaded. "There's nothing left for me out there."

The mercenary opened his mouth, then snapped it shut again. Her torment tore him apart. He wanted to heal her, body and mind. But he didn't know how. "I can't," he said, feeling helpless.

She let out a short, mirthless laugh. "Why not?" she asked. "Don't tell me the arrogant mercenary suddenly feels guilty for destroying someone's life."

Khaniel didn't answer. He had to turn away from the accusing stare she gave him, even though he knew she couldn't see the pain on his face. *Yes,* he thought. *And this is my penance: saving someone who doesn't want to be saved.*

Bhaobuk returned then, stealing into the shadows and crouching down. "There are only two guards at the gates," he said. "You both know where they are. There's no way to get past them without them seeing us."

"Can you lure them away?" Bruigan asked.

Bhaobuk shook his head. "I don't think so. They don't think too highly of me as it is, but they know Kizrak would have their hides if they leave their posts."

"Is there another way to get out of the city?" Khaniel asked.

"I'm afraid not."

"What are our chances of outrunning them?" Khaniel asked. For answer, Bhaobuk grimaced and pointed at Zethamy. "Right," he said, giving up on that idea. "I guess we don't have a choice," he said, raising his axe and adjusting his grip.

"No," Bhaobuk said, reaching a hand out and taking hold of Khaniel's arm. "I can't be a part of that."

Bruigan snorted. "How are we going to get out of here, then?"

"You're not," a sneering voice said from behind them.

Khaniel whirled around to see Kohd and three other ogres standing there. They had fanned out across the path leading to the gates. The shaman had an unpleasant smile on his face.

"Kizrak cannot be angry with me if I kill you while you're trying to escape," Kohd said, laughing. "Thank you," he added.

Khaniel silently cursed, remembering the punishment the ogre king had handed down to Kohd after their confrontation. No feasting for him. The mercenary rose to his feet. "Watch her," he whispered to Bruigan, then he stepped out into the street. "You think you can do better than Ghoarg did?" he asked the gloating shaman.

In answer, the ogre began mumbling nonsensical phrases as he gestured at the warrior. A flicker of purple energy cascaded up and down his arms, and then he flung it at Khaniel. The glowing force arced between them, slamming the mercenary backward. Cold gripped him, turning his blood to ice. He recoiled from the excruciating pain and fell to his knees, moaning in agony.

Not again. Fight fair, damn it!

Then, as quickly as the attack had started, it stopped. Khaniel unclenched his eyes to see Bhaobuk gesturing at Kohd, who was engulfed in a swirl of orange flame. The other shaman jerked and twisted around, trying to escape the conflagration. Two of the ogres with Kohd stood mesmerized by the sight of their leader burning alive, but the third recognized Bhaobuk's hand in the matter.

That one strode forward, raising a thick club to bash in his skull.

Khaniel shook off the lingering effects of the magic and leaped to his feet. He intercepted the guard and knocked the club away with a flick of his axe. The ogre growled and dropped back a step, wary. The other two, seeing the battle joined, began to rush forward as well, ready to pounce on the rest of the group. Khaniel stepped to the side and spun, sweeping the broad head of his weapon around, driving them back again.

He became furious. Freedom so close, and he could see it all slipping away. "Come on!" he screamed at the three ogres, challenging them. "Who's first?" He spun his axe through the air once for emphasis.

The closest of the three, startled by the mercenary's vehement outburst, blinked in surprise, and that was enough. Khaniel leaped forward, a whirling force of destruction. He cut down hard, letting the blade bite into the ogre's shoulder. Before the creature even had a chance to scream, Khaniel kicked out, knocking the ogre back with a foot planted against his chest and freeing his own weapon. Then he moved on, sliding past that fallen foe and toward another. He brought the axe back around again, aiming low, intending to cut his next opponent's legs out from under him. The ogre saw the strike coming, though, and jumped backward. Khaniel advanced again, stepping precisely through martial forms as he twirled the axe around and around. The blade whistled through the air as he spun it over his head and out to either side. The ogre grimaced, shrinking back from the whirlwind of death coming at him.

A shout from behind him drew Khaniel's attention away for a moment. He stole a glance back and saw the third ogre and Kohd working against Bhaobuk and Bruigan. The dwarf desperately defended himself with his shield, working hard to block each of the ogre's club strikes. But the ogre stood much taller, and each blow drove the dwarf back a step. Bruigan staggered against the onslaught.

Behind Bruigan, Zethamy cringed with every crash of weapon on weapon, every grunt of pain. She had dropped down on her hands and knees, and she cowered against the wall of the closest building, trying to make herself small. The dwarf defended her, but the two of them would soon run out of room.

In the meantime, Bhaobuk and Kohd circled one another. Bhaobuk held his staff in both hands, jabbing and poking at the other shaman with lightning-quick flicks of his wrists and elbows. Kohd countered with a black mace, keeping the smaller ogre at bay; Bhaobuk couldn't aid Bruigan and Zethamy any time soon.

Cursing, Khaniel turned back to his own opponent. The ogre's club came at his head, and the mercenary had to duck to avoid having his skull smashed. The brief distraction had almost undone him. With a primal snarl, Khaniel launched himself at the ogre guard, bringing every last bit of his fury to bear. The axe sang as he swung it in great arcs, slicing through the air relentlessly. The ogre parried the first couple of attacks, but he could not withstand Khaniel's prowess and rage.

The third great clash of weapons sent the ogre's club tumbling off into the darkness. The guard blanched and backed away, but Khaniel would not be denied. He charged closer, his footwork precise, his balance pure as he prepared to make the killing strike. The ogre, seeing annihilation blazing in Khaniel's eyes, turned to flee. The warrior never relented, and his foe's death wail echoed off the walls of the buildings as Khaniel cut him down.

Spinning back toward his companions, Khaniel charged at the ogre who beat on Bruigan. The dwarf had dropped to his knees and simply cowered behind the shield, which disintegrated under the assault. The next blow shattered the shield, and Bruigan sagged down in a limp heap. Behind him,

Zethamy held her sword in both trembling hands, jabbing blindly into the air before her.

"Enough!" Khaniel shouted, rushing toward the third guard. "Try me, you dog," he challenged. The ogre, club already raised to strike at the woman, turned to the new threat. Seeing the enraged warrior charging him, he abruptly shifted around to receive the attack. The ogre swept his club at Khaniel, who altered his axe swing to deflect it away. The powerful maneuver knocked the ogre's arm out to the side, and he spun half around from the momentum. Khaniel stepped into the opening in his foe's defenses and sliced the guard from collarbone to groin. The ogre died before he hit the ground.

A shadow fell across the periphery of Khaniel's vision. Turning, he saw two more ogres coming at him. One of them swung a club right at the mercenary's head. Khaniel twisted around to evade the blow, but it caught his shoulder. With a grunt, Khaniel tumbled to the side, and the ogres, seeing their chance, leaped at him.

The guards, he realized as he rolled away. A club head pounded the earth right next to his arm as he scrambled to put space between himself and their onslaught. *They must have heard the fighting*.

When the next ogre smacked the ground beside him, Khaniel grabbed at the weapon and used it to brace himself as he kicked at the guard. He caught the ogre squarely in the stomach, and the stricken creature doubled over with a sudden gasp.

Khaniel reversed direction and used his axe to block the other ogre's next strike. He kicked again, sweeping his foot around and behind that ogre's legs. The blow landed against the back of the guard's knees, buckling them. The ogre dropped into a kneeling position as Khaniel flipped himself upright and stepped back a pace. The glare he gave his two opponents felt bestial.

"Let's end this," he said as the second ogre climbed upright once more. The first one remained hunched over, trying to regain his breath, but Khaniel didn't have the angle to get at him.

An opportunity lost, he lamented. *But not for long.*

The second ogre came at the mercenary, swinging his club for all he was worth, back and forth, perhaps trying to drive Khaniel into retreat. With a laugh, the warrior parried the strikes, jerking his axe into the path of the club each time. On the fourth swing, he shifted the blade around and cut cleanly, splintering the weapon in two. The ogre stared dumbly at his ruined club, and Khaniel finished him with a cross stroke that opened his chest.

By the time Khaniel returned his attention to the first ogre guard, that foe stood upright again.

With an animalistic snarl, the ogre rushed at him. Khaniel set himself to receive the charge. As the ogre closed within striking distance, he swung his club at the warrior's head. But Khaniel no longer stood there. With a sudden sidestep, the mercenary ducked in under the swing of the club and raked his axe through the ogre's gut. The strike, driven deep by the ogre's own momentum, cut clean through the guard. The body tumbled to the ground in a sickening, twisted heap as blood spilled everywhere.

Khaniel spun away, looking for another foe to take down. Only Kohd remained. He loomed over Bhaobuk, who at some point had moved to defend the fallen Bruigan. But the king's brother, overmatched by the large Kohd, lay crumpled on the ground, feebly trying to keep the other shaman at bay with his staff.

"Kohd!" Khaniel snarled, approaching. "I'm the one you want to kill. Come try," he taunted.

Kohd turned toward Khaniel, smiling. "Yes," he said, stepping away from Bhaobuk. "I will kill you," he said, twirling his mace, which had begun to glow with a sickly green light. "It will feel good to watch you die."

Khaniel easily deflected the ogre's first swing, but the jarring impact caused the mace to flash with green energy. The burst sent bolts of pain shooting up the warrior's arms. He grunted and faltered a step, his arms half numb.

"See?" Kohd gloated, coming at Khaniel again. "Innoruuk no longer protects you, slave."

Khaniel gritted his teeth and braced himself for the pain as he parried the mace again. The blow sent needles all along his arms, and he felt his grip on the axe weakening. He couldn't fight the shaman that way.

In inspiration, he let the axe fall and spread his arms wide. "Hit me," he dared Kohd. "Try it."

The shaman frowned for a heartbeat, hesitant. Then the ogre gave a shrug and licked his lips in anticipation. He swatted at the weaponless warrior, expecting Khaniel to leap back, out of harm's way. Instead, the mercenary stepped into and under the swing. Kohd's mace shot through the air over Khaniel's head, and the warrior came up again on the back side. With blurring speed, Khaniel rammed the palms of his hands into the ogre's elbow. The jab sent Kohd's arm too far around, wrapping across the shaman's neck. The momentum of the mace caused it to smack against the ogre's back. Kohd grimaced in pain as he suffered the debilitating energy from the magic of his own weapon. Khaniel threw a pair of quick jabs into the ogre's nose, followed by a right hook.

Kohd grunted and blinked away the sting as he uncoiled from Khaniel's rapid strikes. The shaman glared at his foe and took a threatening step in Khaniel's direction, whipping the mace toward Khaniel again. Once more the mercenary dodged the attack and redirected Kohd's own weapon back against him, then followed it with a powerful punch to the ogre's gut.

"Damn you!" Kohd growled, staggering from the human's too-quick blows. He began to mutter under his breath, and Khaniel understood all too well what the ogre attempted. In a flash, the mercenary ducked past the shaman's defenses and landed another powerful punch against the side of his head.

Kohd, stunned at the speed of the attack, faltered in his incantations. Whatever magic he had intended to call upon, the moment was lost. With a roar of rage, he tried to beat Khaniel to a pulp with his mace. The mercenary simply moved too fast. Each swing from the shaman became an awkward miss or self-inflicted wound, followed by bare-fisted strikes to the abdomen and head.

Kohd, battered and bleeding, dropped his mace and began shaking and rubbing his arms. "You are a devil," he muttered. "Innoruuk himself take you!" he shouted. He backed up a step, then turned and ran.

With a savage cry, Khaniel grabbed up his axe in both hands. He shifted the weapon behind one hip, then took one quick stride forward. He twisted his body and pivoted his shoulder, swinging the axe up and over. At the apex of the stroke, as the blade came forward and down, Khaniel released the axe, flinging it at the fleeing ogre. The axe spun through the air and struck true. Kohd arched his back in surprise and pain and tumbled forward to the ground.

Khaniel exhaled in relief. As the fight left him, weariness and ache settled into his body. The mercenary turned to his companions.

Zethamy sat huddled with her knees drawn up to her chest and her arms wrapped around them. She trembled. Bhaobuk slumped against the wall in exhaustion, his legs splayed out to either side of him. Between them, Bruigan lay sprawled out on the ground, unmoving. The remains of the dwarf's shield rested atop him. The pair's expressions made Khaniel's heart skip a beat.

"What is it?" the warrior asked, dreading the answer as he ran toward them.

"Bruigan," the ogre said.

Khaniel knelt beside his friend and pulled the remains of the shield back. Blood matted the hair on the dwarf's forehead and trickled down into his face from a huge gash. Part of the dwarf's skull, exposed and misshapen from the sundering blow, gleamed dully in the light. His glazed eyes stared upward at nothing. He still breathed, but each one came in a raspy gasp.

"Bruigan?" Khaniel said, his voice sounding small. "Talk to me," he said, suddenly feeling like a lost child. "Tell me you're all right."

"I'm sorry," Bruigan said in a near-whisper. "I tried to protect her."

Khaniel glanced over at Zethamy, who still hugged her knees. "You did, my friend," Khaniel reassured the dwarf and patted him on the shoulder. "Zethamy's fine. And you're going to be fine, too. Bhaobuk, do something. Heal him, damn it!"

But the shaman, looking defeated, shook his head. "I have nothing left to give. I exhausted all my magic fighting Kohd."

"No," Khaniel growled. "Not here. Not now, when we're almost free. Hold on, Bruigan," he pleaded. "Don't you die on me. We're going to find a way to heal you. Stay with me!" The warrior looked up. "Help me," he begged the other two. "He's dying."

A single tear ran down Zethamy's cheek, and Bhaobuk pursed his lips, unable to return Khaniel's stare. Neither of them said anything.

The mercenary rocked back on his heels and stood up, desperate to find some way of saving his friend. He jerked his gaze about, hunting for something, anything. Only ogre bodies littered the street, and Khaniel started forward toward one, hoping against hope that he might find salvation among their belongings.

The warrior stopped again just as suddenly, feeling hope drain away, replaced with sorrow. He knew. Closing his eyes and stifling a single, choking sob, Khaniel clenched his hands and turned back to face the end. He knelt down once more by his friend. Tree frogs filled the night with their songs as the warrior took the dwarf's hand in his own.

"We're going to escape, get back to Freeport. You and me," he said gently, squeezing Bruigan's fist. "We're going to sit in Hogcaller's and drink the best damn stout you ever brewed. Can you taste it?"

Bruigan reached up with his other trembling hand and grasped the edge of Khaniel's breastplate. He pulled the warrior down close to him and whispered, "No, we're not. But you lift one in my name someday, when you get back there." Khaniel grimaced and closed his eyes, overcome with anguish. The dwarf continued, his voice growing weaker. "Learn from this, lad. Be more than you think you are. Help her, take her away from here. For her sake, not for yours."

With those final words, Bruigan let out one last raspy sigh and was still.

12

KHANIEL COULDN'T FIND ANY WORDS. HIS THROAT constricted with sorrow. Then the mercenary rose to his feet and took a step backward, still staring at his dead friend. Rage and resentment overwhelmed him, and he raised his fists in the air and shouted a savage, wordless cry. When he finally had exhausted his ire, the sound echoed down the street of Oggok and faded away, replaced by the croaking song of the tree frogs. Khaniel just stood there, breathing deeply and glaring at nothing.

Why? he asked, knowing he posed a stupid question, knowing that life's sudden, erratic changes sometimes had no answers. He wanted one anyway. *Why! Why did I wait so long to escape? Why did this have to happen so close to freedom? Why!*

Nature is what it is, came the answer. *The strong survive; the weak perish. There is no why. We're all simply animals, surviving or not.*

Khaniel refused to accept that answer. *Animals don't feel guilt, don't blame themselves, don't grieve for their fallen comrades. That's just the coward talking, afraid to accept responsibility. You killed him!* That thought made Khaniel gasp in self-loathing, as surely as if it had punched him in the gut. *I bought her life with his, but his life wasn't mine to spend!* he screamed inside his head. *I'm a fool!*

Then the anger and resentment toward himself vanished, replaced by sorrow. *I'm sorry, Bruigan. I waited too long to figure it out. You paid the price.*

For long moments, Khaniel sat there, staring at nothing. Eventually, his thoughts returned to Bhaobuk and Zethamy behind him, waiting silently. "He should not be dead," the warrior said. He spoke in a flat, emotionless tone, but the words pained him. "He deserved better than to die here."

"We don't always get what we deserve," Bhaobuk said, rising to stand beside Khaniel.

"Don't quote me philosophy, ogre," Khaniel spat, then instantly regretted it. Though the shaman had probably not intended the comment as a dig at him, the warrior felt the guilt weigh him down. "He wasn't a fighter," the warrior went on in a quieter tone. "I should have protected him. He was the brains; I was the brawn, he'd always say. Not very noble, but he was a realist."

"He had enough fight in him to protect her," Bhaobuk said, gesturing toward Zethamy. "In that, he was perhaps the most noble."

Khaniel rolled his head about upon his neck and closed his eyes. *More noble than I,* he thought. *Not my life to spend.* Suddenly, the warrior felt very tired. He wished he could curl up on the ground right then, drift off to sleep, and leave his heavy heart behind. But the ogres would awaken soon. Freedom still beckoned, and he had a duty to see Zethamy to safety. He owed Bruigan that. "We should go," he muttered. "Before more guards come."

"Yes," Bhaobuk agreed. "It is unfortunate that we had to slay so many," he added, looking around.

"You know," Khaniel said, looking at the ogre with a steady gaze as rage began to mix with the sorrow. "I couldn't really care right now how many I had to slice through. If the whole gods-forsaken city woke up right this moment and tried to stop me, I'd soak the ground with their blood."

Bhaobuk grimaced. "Then let's make certain it doesn't come to that," he said, staring just as intently back. For a moment, the two locked gazes, as if trying to determine who would flinch first.

Finally, Khaniel broke the contest by turning away. "Get her," he said, pointing at Zethamy, who still crouched by the wall. She held her head cocked to one side, listening. As the shaman went to her, Khaniel went to Kohd's body and retrieved the axe. Then he returned and crouched down next to Bruigan. He grabbed the dwarf and tried to lift him up.

"What are you doing?" Bhaobuk asked. When Khaniel glanced over, the shaman looked pained. He had pulled Zethamy to her feet and had gathered up the bundles of supplies. Zethamy held one and the ogre had the other two. He prepared to lead her toward the gates.

"We're not leaving him here for them to scavenge and defile," Khaniel replied. He grunted with the effort of shifting the dwarf's weight over his shoulder. "I'm bringing him with us."

"Khaniel," the ogre began, "you cannot seriously—"

"I'm not leaving him," the mercenary said. He stared at Bhaobuk, challenging the shaman to argue further.

The ogre opened his mouth and then shut it. Whatever he had intended to say, he dismissed the whole thing with a shrug. "Do what you must," the shaman said at last. "I hope your noble intentions do not slow us down."

"Set us a pace," Khaniel replied. "I'll keep up."

The trio passed through the gates, a sad collection of travelers and their cargo. Once past the entryway, the road leading from Oggok wandered down from the hillside and moved to the northeast.

Bhaobuk paused. "The road?" he asked. "That will be the easiest, but Kizrak will send runners that way to see."

Khaniel thought for a bit. He intended to return to Freeport, and following the road was the surest overland route to make it back there. But they would draw too much attention there. The ogres would find them if they followed the road.

"For a bit," he said. "Then, after a while, we'll leave it and cut more northward."

Bhaobuk frowned. "Why not leave the road now, then?"

"Because Kizrak will expect us either to take the road or not take the road. His trackers will look most carefully for signs we strayed from the road right here, at the beginning."

"Ah," the shaman said, nodding. "But if we wait a while, they'll grow complacent, stop searching for signs of our passing, and might even miss the point where we veer away."

"Exactly," Khaniel said. Zethamy chuckled softly.

"What's amusing you?" Khaniel asked, surprised that the woman would show any emotion at all. She had remained silent and stoic since the attack.

"Freeport," she said with a hint of derision in her tone. "I should have known you'd want to go to Freeport. Can't resist taking me back there, can you? Can't pass up the promise of returning me safely home, huh?"

Khaniel frowned. "I would have thought you'd *want* to return to Freeport," he said. "Maybe be back with your order, try to find some peace."

"There is no peace for me there now," she said bitterly. "And you know it. All you want is peace for yourself, to assuage your guilty feelings about destroying everything that ever mattered in my life."

Khaniel shook his head, not knowing what to say to that. She was right, of course. But he had pinned his hopes of redemption on somehow easing her pain, too. She didn't seem to want that. "It's almost as if you enjoy your suffering," he said.

"Enjoyment has got nothing to do with it," she replied coldly. "This is what I am now. This is what I have become."

Khaniel cringed, hearing an eerie echo of his own thoughts, his own resignation from the previous weeks, in her words. He understood her bitterness. That understanding fed his sense of guilt.

"The two of you can find fault with one another later," Bhaobuk said. "Let's go."

Khaniel nodded, shifting Bruigan's weight. "Lead on," he said.

They followed the road from Oggok until the first brightening of dawn. Along the way, Khaniel considered what he expected to accomplish after freeing himself. His goal to return to Freeport had seemed the only logical choice, but of course, he had made it when Bruigan was . . . *was still alive*, he thought. *That's where he would have wanted to go.*

Zethamy tripped for perhaps the dozenth time and went down to her knees. Bhaobuk turned around and helped her up again. No word of thanks issued from her lips. The shaman had taken some rope, cinched it around her waist, and tied the other end around his own. It left about ten feet of slack between the two of them. Zethamy could follow its tug and theoretically walk unaided. But even though the ogre picked his route along the road carefully, she still seemed to have a knack for finding exposed tree roots, gullies from rain washouts, and protruding stones. Before long, her cloth armor was soiled with mud and caked with leaves. She seemed to drag her feet, plodding along without any apparent interest in what happened around her.

"Can you try to pick up your feet a little more?" Khaniel asked in as pleasant a tone as he could muster.

"I can't see," she spat back. "Or had you forgotten?"

"Look," the warrior replied, trying to hide his growing exasperation, "I'm only saying that—"

"Shh!" Bhaobuk commanded, motioning for quiet. He cocked his head to one side and stared off at nothing, listening. "Someone's coming," he said.

"Get off the road," Khaniel urged, already lumbering as best as he could down the embankment on the side of the trail, moving to disappear into the foliage. The dwarf's body still resting across his shoulders made it difficult to navigate. Bhaobuk took Zethamy by the hand and guided her down the slope, following the warrior. The three of them pushed deeper into the great trees, vanishing from sight.

When they moved deep enough into the concealment, Khaniel came to a stop and laid Bruigan's body down at the base of a tree as gently as he could. He felt the ache in his shoulders and back as he straightened again.

Bhaobuk steered Zethamy next to the tree and placed her hand against the bark. "Sit," he said quietly.

"Like a good Dakkas," she whispered back, but she squatted down and held still. Despite all her indifference to her own well-being, Khaniel could see that a will to survive and escape the ogres still lived within her. He had to make her see it, to draw it out. But right then, they had to make sure the pursuit didn't find them.

As Khaniel peered through the dense greenery of the trees of the Feerott, he spotted what had made Bhaobuk react. A handful of ogres went trotting by the point where they had left the road. Khaniel held his breath, waiting to see if the pursuers somehow discovered that fact. There was no mistaking the ogres' identities; they all displayed the insignias of Oggok on their shields. Kizrak had sent them out to find his escaped slaves.

The ogres did not move fast—clearly they looked for something—but they didn't slow as they passed their hidden prey. When they had moved down the road, Khaniel breathed easier. "I don't think they figured it out," he said quietly. "This is as good a time as any to leave the road, I guess."

"It will be much harder to travel cross-country," Bhaobuk warned. "There is more to get in her way," he said, nodding in Zethamy's direction, "and you will have a difficult time lugging him along."

Khaniel swallowed, knowing the ogre spoke the truth. Lack of sleep and the added weight of Bruigan on his shoulders hastened his exhaustion. He didn't want to admit it, but he knew he had to part ways with his old friend. "All right," he said at last. "I'll bury him out here. It probably would not be his first choice, but it's better than what would have happened to him in Oggok."

They decided to move further away from the road before making a grave. They didn't want to leave any clear signs of their passing to anyone who might decide to parallel the road in search of tracks. Bhaobuk helped Khaniel dig, while Zethamy sat on a log off by herself. The two of them used their weapons to loosen the soil, then scooped it out with their hands. Then they laid Bruigan's body in the shallow trench they had created. After covering his body with the soil, they stacked the whole thing with stones.

When they were done, Bhaobuk led Zethamy a little ways away, giving Khaniel some time by himself to say good-bye. The warrior stood there for a moment, staring down where his friend's body lay in the cold, quiet earth. "We've followed many strange roads together," he started. "And gone many other places where there were no roads. I guess it's fitting, then, that you're out here in the middle of nowhere. Maybe I've plopped you beneath a crop of some vine or berry that makes the best damn ale in the world." He chuckled at the thought. Then the smile passed, and he sighed. "I know it's not deep under a mountain, like you'd prefer, but find some peace out here, my friend." He swallowed hard, his throat thick with emotion. "I'll miss you, you old grump."

Then, with blinking eyes, the warrior turned away.

The trio traveled through the morning. It was slow going, for they had to be diligent with Zethamy, who couldn't see the limbs and vines they pushed through. She got slapped in the face a couple of times, and when the third one hit her, she sat down and refused to go any farther, accusing them both of doing it on purpose. They only got her moving again by promising to walk on either side of her and keep the branches away from her that way.

The sun had begun to warm the forest by the time the three of them next stopped to rest. Even so, the gloom beneath the heavy canopy made it feel like little more than twilight. They chose a small clearing on the bank of a gentle stream. Bhaobuk passed around some bread. It was a bit on the stale side, but Khaniel didn't much care right then. He began ripping big hunks off the piece the ogre had given him.

As he ate, Khaniel watched Zethamy. She held the bread in one hand and pulled little bits free of the crust with her other. As she chewed, she stared at nothing. She seemed listless. The warrior contemplated how to draw her out, how to get her to forget about her own miseries. He realized that he knew nothing about her. Since it seemed pointless to make small talk, he shrugged and threw caution to the wind.

"The day Bruigan and I met you, when you were out hunting for that hermit's abode in the mountains . . . ," he began.

The comment seemed to catch Zethamy off guard. She stopped chewing, as if wary, then grimaced as she turned toward the sound of the warrior's voice. "Yes," she said. "What of it?"

"Well, I pieced together how you wound up with Ghoarg," he said, "but you never asked me how Bruigan and I wound up in Oggok."

"I don't care," she said, turning away again.

"Yes, you do," Khaniel replied. "I know you do."

"And I know you're going to make me hear it whether I want to or not, since I can't get up and leave. I'm as good as your hostage, you know."

Khaniel ignored that last comment and proceeded to explain what had happened to him and Bruigan after the attack. When he got to the part where Maix Treganan appeared, she whipped her head toward his voice again.

"Maix?" she asked quietly. "Are you sure?" Khaniel thought he saw a shudder pass through her at the mention of the wizard's name.

"Yes," Khaniel answered. "It was definitely him. He is a follower of Innoruuk, in league with the Church of the Dismal Rage," he added solemnly. "He thought we might have known something about this hermit's abode. Said something about a vision you'd had, a mountain lake or something. Of course, we didn't know anything about it, but that wasn't good enough for him."

Zethamy sat very still and didn't say anything for a long moment. When she did speak, her voice sounded fearful. "He was with the cyclopes after they captured me," she said. "He . . . he demanded that I tell him where the hidden dwelling was. When I couldn't, he flew into a rage. He . . . beat me, taunted me. Used my lost eyesight as another tool of torture." She shuddered.

"You don't know where the hermit's lair is?" Khaniel asked.

"No!" she said, almost shouted it. "Don't you see? I didn't know where it was, but I could 'see' the path. At the top of every rise, at every new vista, I could tell where we needed to go next. It was as if I had dreamed about it at night, had forgotten it, and then, upon seeing it, remembered it all over again. I could just feel it. That day, in the mountains, I was leading that expedition on faith. I had a vision, a perfect image in my mind's eye, of where that lake is. I still do," she said, emphasizing those last words. "I can still see every part of it, even the remaining part of the path, the part I haven't walked yet. I can see it in here," and she pointed at her forehead, "but I can't see it out here!" and she jerked her hand out in front of herself as her words rose in pitch, showing her agitation. "He let you take my eyes from me, but he left the inner vision with me. To torture me!" And she flung the crust of her bread away with a stifled sob.

Khaniel gave her a moment to compose herself. Then he asked, "What did this hermit—this Ushiv Beor—what did he have that is so important?"

Zethamy sniffed and wiped the tears from her cheeks with the back of her hand. "Artifacts," she answered in a subdued voice. "Weapons of power dedicated to the glory of Mithaniel Marr."

"Why would this wizard want them?" Bhaobuk asked. He had sat off to one side, listening while he ate.

Zethamy shrugged. "I don't know," she admitted. "Maybe to stop us from getting them—stop the temple from getting them," she corrected herself. "Although there could be . . ." Her voice trailed off.

"What?" Khaniel asked. He doubted Maix and the other followers of Innoruuk would continue to work so hard to try and track down the locale if they merely wanted to prevent the paladins from getting their hands on the lost items. He said as much and then added, "Knowing you were the only compass to the place, I would think he would be content just to let you vanish. For that matter," the warrior added, "I would think the Dismal Rage would want him to kill you the first chance he got."

Zethamy nodded. "The hermit was a priest of Marr," she began. "Both powerful and very well respected. He spent his days at the Chapterhouse of the Fist."

"The what?"

"Today it's known as Befallen," Zethamy explained. "I'm sure you've heard of that."

Khaniel shuddered. "I've heard enough to know to stay away from that charnel house," he admitted. "I had never heard its original name, though."

"Yes. It was a powerful stronghold for the Order of the Fist who, like the Knights of Truth, served Mithaniel Marr. When the famous and terrible plague descended upon the chapterhouse and wiped it out, most of the holy warriors and priests within perished, to rise again as unnatural things. But one priest, Ushiv Beor, managed to escape. The Knights of Truth still have records of the tragedy, and included in those records are the remains of a diary that Ushiv kept, telling of the few fabulous things he managed to salvage from the carnage."

Khaniel shook his head, forgetting that Zethamy could not see his gesture. "That still doesn't explain why Maix would want them."

"Because he might have taken some other items, too," Zethamy answered. "Records salvaged from Befallen mention some tools of darkness that the chapterhouse sheltered before the tragedy. Ushiv might have feared having them fall into the wrong hands. Maybe he made off with them."

"Ah," Bhaobuk said. "And this wizard you speak of must have learned something of their existence and thought to use you and your order to get them."

Zethamy nodded. "But it doesn't matter now," she said, hunching over. "None of it matters now. I'll spend the rest of my days haunted by the vision of the mountain lake and the abode and never be able to find it."

"Stop that," Khaniel said, feeling exasperation replacing sorrow for her. "You act like your eyes were the only asset you ever had."

"Don't patronize me," Zethamy snapped. "It's not only that I am blind. It's that I was blinded. He let it happen. I trusted him, dedicated my life to him, and he failed me." Her words sounded wooden then, as if the energy she had shown before, while telling the story, had completely drained from her. "I thought I had a destiny," she said, her voice barely above a whisper. "I thought my power of vision was a gift from him, a gift to make me his champion. Instead, it's become a curse." She sniffed back tears and rubbed her fists into those unseeing eyes. "I will never fall sway to his false promises again," she mumbled.

Khaniel and Bhaobuk looked at one another. She had fallen hard and fast, the warrior realized. Her sense of betrayal ran deep. It might prove difficult to bring her back, to help her find a new purpose in her life.

"We should get moving," the shaman said. "My brother's soldiers will eventually figure out where we went."

DARKNESS HAD SETTLED OVER THE FOREST BEFORE the trio of fugitives stopped again. A chill began to fill the woods as the light failed. Bhaobuk pointed out a small hollow hard against a low, moss-covered embankment and suggested that they make camp there.

"We can build a small fire for warmth," he said, "and down in that hollow, it won't be seen."

Khaniel agreed. As the shaman began gathering wood, Khaniel searched for a way to get Zethamy involved. "We need kindling to get the fire started," he said. "Gather up some moss." He took her hand and guided it to the embankment, letting her feel for it. "Try to get the driest parts," he explained, and he positioned her hand in a place where the old growth had sloughed off and died.

"I can't," the woman said.

"Yes, you can," Khaniel argued. "Just feel it. You can tell the dry from the wet by the way it—"

"I can't!" Zethamy shouted, flinging a handful of the moss in Khaniel's direction. "I can't see! Don't you understand? I can't do *anything* any more!" and she sat down and cried.

Khaniel wanted to slap her, as Bruigan had done the night before in Kizrak's throne room. "You're not that helpless," Khaniel growled, rising and leaving her to sob. "You can do more than you think."

Bhaobuk returned with an armload of wood and dropped it in a heap nearby. "I smell rain," he announced. "We ought to build a shelter."

Khaniel shook his head in exasperation as he turned away from the woman. "I'll figure something out," he said and stalked away as Bhaobuk began to lay wood for a fire.

As Khaniel began chopping saplings with his axe, he fumed. *I want to help her,* he thought, *but she's doing her damnedest to stop me.* Then he drew up with a start. *Just like Bruigan was trying to help me,* he realized. *When you're feeling sorry for yourself, nothing anyone is going to say will change that. She's the only one who can make up her mind that there's still a reason to live. I can't force her to.*

As the mercenary continued to gather and trim the saplings and haul them back to the camp, he made up his mind not to push her any more. When she was ready to accept her situation, he would be there, and until then, he would have to try to keep her out of harm's way. Satisfied that he had focused his intentions, he got to work.

He began lining saplings up at an angle against the embankment, forming a lean-to. Then, using some vines as an impromptu rope, the warrior began lashing the saplings together like a raft, to keep them hard up against one another. Afterward, he lay the branches he had trimmed from the young trees on top of the slanted wall. He piled them on thickly enough that the leaves formed a substantial covering. The first drops of rain began to patter down just as he finished.

Inside the lean-to, Bhaobuk had gotten a fire going. The heat from it kept the worst of the growing chill at bay, and Khaniel settled in on one side of Zethamy, while the shaman sat on her other side. As the rain began to fall in earnest, they shared a repast of more bread, some hard cheese, and a few strips of dried meat.

No one talked. Exhaustion, so long staved off by necessity, overtook them quickly, and before long, two of the three of them slept soundly. Only Khaniel remained awake, forcing himself to resist sleep so that he could keep watch for anything out in the dark of night and maintain the fire.

The rain grew stronger, becoming a deluge, but Khaniel's improvised roof kept most of the moisture off them. Afterward, when the rain had stopped, he sat in the near-darkness, listening to the dripping in the forest and the tree frogs singing. He had no idea how much time had passed, but when he couldn't keep his eyes open any longer, he kicked Bhaobuk awake and dozed off.

13

First light awoke Khaniel. The glow of the dawn revealed a heavy fog that had formed during the night. He peered out past the edge of the lean-to but could only see the nearest two or three tree trunks. Everything else vanished in a haze of gray-white.

The warrior sat up and immediately regretted it. His muscles ached from the chill and dampness, as well as from the cramped position in which he'd slept. *Too many battles*, he thought as he crawled out and stood. *I feel like Bruigan*. The jolt of remembering that the dwarf had died sent a flash of grief through him. He shook it away and turned to peer back into the shelter, where Zethamy lay curled up. Bhaobuk was not there.

Khaniel, with a stab of concern, stood straight and peered about into the fog. He couldn't see farther than ten paces. The sounds of dripping water echoed all around him, but he heard nothing more. No birds greeted the morning; no breezes rustled the trees overhead. Everything remained still.

"Bhaobuk?" the warrior called, softly the first time, then repeating it a bit louder. No answer came. Growing concerned, Khaniel knelt down and retrieved his axe, then rose and began to circle the camp, stopping periodically to listen. Just when he prepared to awaken Zethamy to tell her the shaman was missing, he heard the sound of a branch pop. Something moved toward the camp, not too fast, but not taking too much care to be quiet, either. *What I wouldn't give for a bow,* he lamented. The snapping branch became a rustling bush.

"Khaniel?" Bhaobuk called from the gauzy whiteness. "Where are you two?"

The warrior sighed with relief and then answered. "Over here."

Bhaobuk appeared out of the mist a short time later. "I got lost," he professed, looking a bit sheepish.

"It happens," Khaniel replied. "What were you doing?"

"Tending to morning business," the shaman answered. "And stretching my legs after being cramped all night."

"I know how you feel," Khaniel said ruefully. "Why don't you wake Zethamy, while I scout around?"

Soon the trio ate a quick breakfast of more bread and cheese, then Khaniel began dismantling the lean-to, discarding the saplings in various places throughout the forest. Bhaobuk swept the ashes of the fire with branches to scatter and hide them. Zethamy sat by herself to the side, in as sullen a mood as before. It seemed that every little thing, from needing help finding a private spot in the woods to gathering up her goods when she accidentally kicked over her satchel, darkened her spirits further. Khaniel fought to keep from letting her self-pity dampen his own spirits, but it felt like a losing battle.

As they set off, even Bhaobuk's mood seemed oppressed by the gloom. The shaman led the way, with Zethamy right behind him, and Khaniel brought up the rear. They traveled into a range of foothills, where the land became more rolling and pitched. The ground, uneven as well as slippery from the night's rain, made footing an issue. More than once, Zethamy slipped and fell. By midmorning, she had become a bedraggled mess, coated with mud and debris, and looking miserable.

"You're going too fast," she fussed yet again, stumbling over another root. "I can't keep up."

Khaniel, frustrated at their already slow pace and weary of Zethamy's endless complaining, grabbed her by the arms and lifted her up. He spun the woman around to face him, even though he knew she could not see. "Pick up your feet," he told her, snarling more than he meant to. "You're catching your toes on things because you're scuffling your feet!"

Zethamy punched Khaniel. She did not strike him hard, but she caught him right under the chin, clacking his teeth together. He let go of her in shock and stumbled back a step. Bhaobuk, who had stopped and leaned wearily against a tree, let his mouth gape at the sight of her attack.

"Don't tell me how to walk blind!" she cried, looking furious. "You can't possibly know what it's like!"

Blinking, Khaniel rubbed his stinging jaw. Then his eyes narrowed, and he lunged at the woman. He grabbed her by her arms, keeping them pinned at her sides. She gasped and tried to recoil, but he kept his grip firm. She began flailing against him, trying to kick his shins.

"Stop it," he commanded. When she didn't cease, he shook her. "I said, stop it!" His ferocity seemed to stun the woman. She froze, her unseeing eyes going wide. "Don't presume to understand what I know," he said through clenched teeth. "I once spent an entire week with a blindfold on, training to fight without the use of my eyes. I know what it's like to walk blind." She held still, listening to his words. "I didn't bring you with me to listen to you grouse about your troubles," he added.

"Then why did you bring me?" she demanded, anger creasing her forehead.

"I don't know!" Khaniel retorted. "Because Bruigan died protecting you, and I owe him something in return! And because I owe you! I thought I could save you! But you don't want to be saved! You want to feel sorry for yourself!"

"Khaniel," Bhaobuk said, standing straight and moving toward the two of them. "Ease up."

"No!" the warrior barked, turning his glare on the shaman. "If she only wants to wallow in her own misery, I'm all for leaving her here! I've had enough!"

"Fine!" Zethamy yelled, shifting her weight and twisting her arms to break Khaniel's grip: a martial move, he realized, made on instinct. "Do it again!" the woman said, tears welling up in her cloudy eyes. "Leave me out here, blind and helpless, to die! That's what you're good at, mercenary. Maiming me and then running away!"

Khaniel swore and almost rebuked her again, but she turned and stomped off, sobbing. She stretched her hands out in front of her, feeling her way. A drop-off, half-obscured in the mist, loomed directly before her.

"Khaniel, she's headed toward—" Bhaobuk warned. The shaman took a faltering step toward the woman, but the warrior stood closer.

"Zethamy, wait," Khaniel called, lurching forward to catch at her.

"Don't follow me," she said, not turning around. "Just leave me for the ogres to find."

"Gods, why do you have to be so bull-headed?" he muttered, reaching her right before she stepped over the edge. "You're going to get yourself k—"

The ground, softened by the rains, gave way beneath their feet. Khaniel flailed and tried to reach out and grab at something to halt his descent, while Zethamy screamed in surprise. The warrior missed the closest tree, and the two of them went tumbling down the steep embankment, slipping along mud-slick surfaces. Khaniel struck an exposed tree root and bounced hard out into space. When he hit again, he heard and felt a resounding splat.

He found himself sprawled out in sloppy goop, a puddle of mud at the base of the steep incline. He tried to roll over, to peer back up at the top of the slope. The motion only succeeded in making him sink a little lower in the mud. He struggled harder, trying to right himself, and realized with dread that every effort he made only made it worse.

He was sinking in a bog.

"Bhaobuk!" he shouted. "Get me out of here!" Khaniel tilted his head back and spotted Zethamy. She clung to some exposed roots halfway down the slope. Her feet slipped against the slick surface as she tried to find some traction and pull herself up. "Bhaobuk!" Khaniel yelled again, beginning to panic. He felt himself settle a little lower in the muck. "Hurry!"

The shaman appeared finally, rope tied around his waist and the end leading back out of sight behind him. He stared down at the two of them, his lips pursed.

"Pull me up!" Khaniel cried. "I'm sinking!"

"No," Bhaobuk said.

Khaniel felt cold dread pour through him. "What?" he asked in a timorous voice. "What do you mean? Quit playing and drop me some rope!"

"No," the ogre repeated. "You two are going to have to get yourselves out."

"Are you crazy?" Khaniel yelled, panic rising. "I can't!"

"No," the ogre replied, "but she can. She can get herself out, then get you, too."

"I can't, either!" Zethamy sobbed. "I can't do it! Please help me up!"

"No," Bhaobuk said a third time. "It's time you figured out what you really want, Zethamy. It's time for you to choose."

"Choose what? What are you talking about?" the woman cried, scrabbling again against the slick ground, trying to drag herself up without success.

"Bhaobuk, you miserable worm, stop it! She can't help herself, much less me," Khaniel said. "You're going to have to pull me out with rope, and you're going to have to do it soon, because I'm going under!" he finished vehemently. "Now!"

"Zethamy," the ogre said, getting down on his hands and knees and peering at her, "you have to decide right now if you're willing to live as you are and persevere, or not. You're at a crossroads, and you must choose a path. Accept your fate and overcome it or succumb to it."

"You thrice-damned ogre, she can't! Help me!" Khaniel pleaded.

"Khaniel, you were right before. She wants to feel sorry for herself, and she wants us to feel sorry for her, too. And that's the coward's way out. She's too afraid to face the fact that everything isn't always how we want it. That sometimes, we have to overcome our own failures and imperfections. Well, this is her chance to decide. Right here, right now. Pull yourself up, Zethamy, and remember how to succeed, or let go and give in to your own self-pity."

Zethamy sobbed. "It's too hard," she said. "I don't want to die, but I don't know how to live like this!"

"You can learn," the shaman said.

The muck had reached Khaniel's ribs by then. He tried with all his will to keep from thrashing, but even so, every breath seemed to shift his body in small ways, and he sank lower and lower. Fury washed through him, focused on the ogre. He understood Bhaobuk's ploy, and it made sense, but the shaman played with their lives. It was hardly the time.

No, he realized, understanding finally. *It is precisely the time. Only when she's faced with two absolute choices, when everything else is taken away and she has the power to live or die, can she finally gain clarity. This is the only way I can save her—save her from herself.*

Making up his mind, Khaniel looked at the woman once more. "Zethamy," he called. "You can do this. You can live."

"No, I can't," she whimpered. "I don't even know where I am."

"Khaniel can guide you," Bhaobuk said, "but you must do the work."

"But I can't see!"

"That doesn't matter. You can feel, and you have strength. You're a warrior. You can pull yourself up," the shaman said.

"Come on, Zethamy," Khaniel called. "I know that arrogant, will-not-be-denied warrior I met in those mountains is still inside there somewhere. Now be her again!"

With a growl of anguish and determination, Zethamy began to pull.

Khaniel let out a shout of exaltation and relief as he saw her make the effort. "Come on, Zethamy," he muttered to himself. "You can do it."

The woman slowly, inexorably began to ascend. She hauled herself up little by little, until she had her chin above her hands.

"Good," Khaniel called out. "There's another root higher, to your left. Feel for it."

She gave a wordless yell, straining with exertion. She dug her toes into the mud and held on with her right hand as she reached up, slapping at the earth, trying to find the exposed root. When her palm hit the woody protrusion, she wrapped her fingers around it and pulled again.

"Yes!" Khaniel crowed. "Go! You're doing it!" The muck came to his armpits. "Keep going, Zethamy!"

Her cries echoed through the forest, but Zethamy climbed inch by inch up the side of the embankment. Those cries, which had once sounded with despair, became cries of determination. As Khaniel watched, urging her on, she climbed to the top and finally dragged herself over the edge. The warrior sighed with relief as he watched her collapse next to the ogre, who reached down and patted her shoulder.

"Now get me out of here!" Khaniel yelled up at the two of them.

Bhaobuk said something to Zethamy in a voice too soft for the mercenary to hear. Khaniel saw her shake her head, and then Bhaobuk nodded.

"Bhaobuk," Khaniel demanded, feeling the bog creep almost to the top of his shoulders, "stop wasting time!"

"She's got to do it," the ogre said.

Khaniel swore. "Bhaobuk, no! She pulled herself out. That's good enough!"

"No, my friend, it's not. Only when *you* truly believe that she can do what she puts her mind to, without your aid, will she actually do it. Unless you force her to believe that she is still capable, independent, she'll never find out what her limits really are, and you'll be forever trying to protect her. You're setting her up to fail because you're too afraid for her to try." Then he turned to Zethamy, but he spoke loudly enough for both of them to hear. "And you will never stop pitying yourself until you accept what happened. And I don't mean that you went blind. I mean accepting that Khaniel did it to you. Not Marr, but Khaniel. It was an unlucky strike, to be sure, but it was an accident."

"It was a curse," Zethamy began bleakly, "put on me by Mithaniel Marr."

"Why?" the ogre asked.

The question stunned Khaniel. "It's not the time for philosophy," he insisted, his voice rising in panic again. "Someone's sinking down here!"

Bhaobuk motioned for Khaniel to be quiet and asked again. "Why would your god do such a thing?"

"I don't know!" Zethamy said, her tears coming again. "Ask him!"

"No, *you* ask him," the ogre said. "If you believe he did this to you, even using Khaniel as his instrument, then you must believe he had a reason. You must have some idea why you would deserve such a thing. What is it?"

"I don't know!" the woman screamed again, pounding the ground with her fists. "You don't think I wonder that every day? You don't think I stayed awake at night, lying in Ghoarg's cage, asking myself that?"

"Certainly," the shaman replied in soothing tones. "But until you figure out an answer, you're going to continue to blame everyone else around you, whether they were responsible or not."

"Bhaobuk, I'm not sure that's helping!" Khaniel shouted. The slime had reached his neck. "She has every right to be angry with me! You're just reminding her of that."

"No, Khaniel," the shaman said. "You *think* she has every right to be angry with you and that she will be angry with you forever. You don't expect forgiveness for your mistake, because you still blame yourself. Until you stop punishing yourself for it every day, you're going to continue to pity her, even when it drives you mad, watching her feel sorry for herself."

Khaniel gasped as he sank a little lower. The ogre was right. "But I blinded her, damn you! How could anyone forgive that?" *Could I forgive her if the roles were reversed?* he thought, filled with shame.

"Don't ask me, ask her," the ogre replied.

"Zethamy," the warrior pleaded, "I don't expect you to forgive me, but please find a way to pull me out of here."

"I can't!"

"Stop saying that!" Khaniel shouted. "Yes, you can. You climbed up the mud bank. I watched you. And you can do this. You can do anything you want, if you just believe in yourself."

"But Mithaniel Marr didn't even believe in me!" She began to sob again. "If I was so special, why did my god, to whom I gave everything, permit you to strike me? My whole life was his to use as he saw fit, and instead he discarded me with one flick of an axe! What did I do to deserve that?"

"I don't know. Maybe it was a test. But I believe in you," Khaniel said. "You're all I've got. Please," he pleaded. "I'm almost under. Don't let me die like this. It's not a warrior's death. Please!"

With a last whimper, perhaps born of desperation, Zethamy yanked her satchel from her shoulder and felt around inside. She produced a coil of rope. "Help me," she asked, but she did not direct it at Bhaobuk. She spoke to Khaniel.

The bog had come up to the warrior's chin by then, and he had to tip his head back in order to keep his face exposed. He could barely move any longer. "Tie one end to a tree," he said. "And be careful that you don't get too close to the edge."

"All right," she said, feeling around until she found the nearest bole. She wrapped one end around the trunk and fumbled for a moment with the knot. "It's ready," she said.

"Throw the other end here!" Khaniel encouraged her, feeling the bog at his ears. "Hurry!"

Zethamy got up onto her knees. "Talk to me," she said. "Let me hear your voice so I know where to throw it!"

"I'm right here," Khaniel said. "You've only got a couple of chances at this, so make them count."

Zethamy threw the rope coil at the warrior. Her aim was on target, but the excess fell short of his reach. He didn't even try to squirm to it. Doing so would only doom him.

"That was close," he said, trying to sound full of patience when he actually felt panicked. "But it wasn't quite far enough out. Reel it in and try again. Quickly, now." He said, gasping. His ears submerged. He couldn't hear her reply. "I'm right here," he kept repeating. "Just throw it straight to me." He gasped for air, fighting an overwhelming need to claw his way out. His mind recoiled in horror at the thought of sinking. He didn't want to be buried alive.

Please, Zethamy.

The end of the rope sailed just past his face, dragging the line right alongside his nose. Trembling with relief, Khaniel pulled an arm out of the bog and grabbed hold of it. "You did it!" he shouted, lifting his head free. "Bulls-eye!"

Zethamy put her hands to her mouth and began to cry again, but they were tears of joy. Even from where he flailed about, the warrior could see her beaming.

Khaniel began to try to pull himself from the muck, but he could not overcome the suction and viscous nature of the slime by himself. "You've got to help," he called out. "I can't pull myself up."

"You sound like me," the woman said, the emotional release of her fears and joy making her laugh and cry all at once. "No more 'I can't,' remember?" Khaniel laughed along with her. The sheer joy of still being alive overwhelmed him. He watched as she felt for the rope and then braced herself before beginning to pull.

Together, they made headway, and when Khaniel rose far enough out of the muck that he could raise his arms overhead, he took the slack and wrapped the rope around his chest, tying it off. Then together they dragged him the rest of the way out and up the side of the embankment.

When Khaniel reached solid, flat ground at last, they both collapsed, totally spent. For a moment, the mercenary only gasped for air and reveled in the simple fact that he could do so. Breathing had never felt so wonderful in his life.

Bhaobuk sat against a nearby tree, watching them. He stood after a moment and walked over to the pair. Looking down at both of his companions, the shaman said, "I'm sorry it came to that, but I didn't think I had a choice. Learn from what you felt when you didn't think you were going to live. Never forget what it felt like to depend on each other to succeed. And let's never have to do that again, please."

Khaniel wanted to punch the ogre in the nose, but he couldn't even lift his arms. "That was a risky game you played," he said between deep breaths. "Especially when the stakes weren't yours to wager." He thought briefly of Bruigan when he said that, remembering how he had gambled with—and lost—the dwarf's life back in Oggok.

Bhaobuk nodded. "Except that you both had already lost the bet. Had I let you continue down the road of self-recrimination and pity, you would have wound up as dead to the world as if you had sunk into the bog. So I simply made you see the rules of the game a bit more clearly. Now you both understand what you could have lost." Finished with his lecture, the shaman turned back to his tree. He settled there and broke out some food, waiting for his companions to recover.

FOR THE NEXT SEVERAL DAYS, THE TRIO JOURneyed without significant event. Though they didn't know where they were within the great forest, they had a good sense of their heading and knew they made progress. At Bhaobuk's almost insistent urging, they decided to travel more northerly than easterly, avoiding the open country and harsh climes of the desert.

Though Khaniel didn't say anything to the others, he realized that they approached the southern foothills of the Serpentspine Mountains, the same range where he and Zethamy had first met. If they continued on and crossed the range to the northern side, they might very well come close to the same valley. He grimaced at the irony of passing near that point. Fear that they might encounter the cyclopes again plagued him, too.

Each day that passed seemed to take them farther and farther from the threat of Kizrak's pursuit, and it occurred to Khaniel that it no longer felt as if they fled at all, but rather as if they simply traveled through the wilds. He found himself enjoying the journey immensely, almost as much as he had once enjoyed traveling with Bruigan. He missed the dwarf daily, especially when he would spot a stand of brush or a certain kind of vine that the two of them had hunted for during their days together. The mercenary realized how much he had learned about brewing from his friend, and it surprised him. He decided that someday, when he could no longer swing an axe, he would settle down and continue Bruigan's legacy. That thought made him grin.

As they got farther from Oggok, and their sense of urgency dissipated, they spent fewer hours actually hiking and a bit more time toward the end of each day resting. Khaniel began to train Zethamy in some rudimentary methods of fighting without the use of her eyes. Recalling how he had dealt with wearing a blindfold for an entire week made him a little wistful, thinking about the Bunker; but being able to put the knowledge to practical use boosted his spirits far more.

Zethamy still had her moments of self-doubt and self-pity, but Khaniel could sense a profound change in her. For the first time since he had freed her from that cage in Kizrak's throne room, she seemed to have an eagerness about her, a desire to try things. And she picked up many of his tricks at fighting blind so quickly that he even felt a little jealousy at her prowess. She was, of course, far from a deadly warrior, but she could grasp the nuances of using her other senses to find and move with her opponent.

One evening, after the sun had dropped well out of sight and they finished a meal that included fresh fish that Bhaobuk had pulled from a stream, Zethamy found her way next to Khaniel. "The day you fell into the bog, when you convinced me to pull you out, you said that you thought Mithaniel

Marr had permitted your strike to blind me as a way of testing me. What did you mean by that?"

The warrior thought for a moment. "Before I answer, are you willing to hear me out?" When she nodded, Khaniel continued. "You keep looking on the events of that day as some sort of defining act of your god. Whether you see it as callous disregard or punishment for some as-yet-unknown transgression, your whole world centers around the notion that your god controls events in your life. Everything you do, every ability you possess, is a blessing from him.

"I don't view it that way. To me, Mithaniel Marr has no responsibility for what happened. I'm a trained, finely honed fighter. I should have been in total control, should have known where all allies and foes were at every moment, and I should have made a more precise strike. It was my own shortcoming that blinded you. I was less perfect than I needed to be. I went into a rage, lost control."

"That's pretty arrogant," she said with a sniff. "Even the best warriors aren't perfect."

"You promised you'd listen to the whole thing," the warrior admonished.

"I am."

"You say that's arrogant. Perhaps. I'm coming to see that, actually." He took a deep breath. "Before

Ghoarg brought you to Oggok, I had sunk pretty low, myself. Bruigan wanted to escape, had concocted plans, brewed up sleeping beer, the whole works, but I wasn't interested."

"You thought that's where you belonged," Zethamy said. "You thought that was the only life you were fit for."

"A caged animal whose only use was as a feral killer. Sound familiar?"

"Yes," she answered, hanging her head.

"We see things from opposite perspectives, Zethamy. You believe that everything you do, every decision you make, is divinely inspired and that you have the tacit approval of Marr. And I am convinced, or at least I *was* convinced, until our unfortunate encounter, that I am my own man, that if I train hard enough, master the techniques well enough, that I can be perfect. We both think of ourselves as superior in every way, even if it's for different reasons. It makes us both haughty, unwilling to listen to anyone else's viewpoints."

"And that's why Mithaniel Marr was testing me? Because I am arrogant?"

Khaniel shrugged. "I made a desperate comment at a moment when I found my life balanced on the tip of a sword. But yes. Has it ever occurred to you that you had your faith all backward? From where I sit, it seemed that you spent all your time absorbed in what Marr was giving you, rather than what you gave him. You became so wrapped up in all the glories you wanted to have heaped upon you that you forgot that your gifts were supposed to be used in his service." Khaniel coughed then, feeling embarrassed that he had spoken so plainly. "Bruigan told me once that there was nothing wrong with pride, as long as I didn't let it go to my head. He claimed that being a perfectly honed warrior was all well and good, but it wasn't the sole measure of me as a person. And when he died, he told me that I should save you for your sake, rather than my own. I think I've finally begun to figure out what he meant, because it's the same thing I'm telling you. Measure yourself by your most selfless acts, not by those you perform for your own benefit."

Zethamy sat silent for a long while after that. Khaniel couldn't tell if she was angry, brooding, or something else. But when she turned to him again and spoke, she reached out and squeezed his hand. Her words startled him.

"I need to find the hermit's refuge. Will you help me?"

14

IT HAD GROWN COLDER. KHANIEL PAUSED TO peer up through a break in the trees. The sky glowed with a gray color that hinted at rain. If rain was all the three of them had to deal with, he would consider them lucky, but he knew better than to count on that. They had traveled into the lower slopes of the Serpentspines by then, leaving the Feerott behind as they ascended the foothills and entered the lower elevations of the mountains themselves.

With Bhaobuk in the lead, they crested a ridge, and Khaniel got a good look at the line of mountains ahead of them in the distance. He began to regret their decision to cross the mountains so late in the year. They didn't know the best route, and as snow already blanketed the high slopes and peaks, they might already find the passes closed by the weather. He hoped he was wrong.

The morning after Zethamy had made her plea to the warrior, he insisted that the three of them discuss it together. They had fled Oggok without anything other than the few supplies Bruigan and Bhaobuk had scrounged together for the impromptu journey. Though they had managed to fish a bit and set some snares for fresh meat, they tempted nature, he knew. He did not want to cross the mountains ill-prepared, so he had to make it clear to the others what they would need to do to get over the mountains, what they should expect during the journey, and the dangers they were likely to face.

"It's bound to be snow-covered," Khaniel explained. "That means tough going and little cover. This late in the year, the weather can turn nasty very fast. A blizzard could hit us while we're caught out in the open.

"And in the open," the mercenary continued, "we will be more visible to predators. Some pretty fierce things live in those mountains, things like drakes, the smaller cousins of the great dragons. Drakes hunt creatures twice our size for snacks. And there are big hunting cats and maybe bears."

"I think bears sleep in the wintertime," Bhaobuk said.

"That means we have to be careful about their caves, too. We're going to need to stay vigilant.

There's a reason folks don't often try to cross the mountains."

Even understanding the hardships, Zethamy wanted to try, and Bhaobuk seemed willing to trust Khaniel to help them survive the journey.

When the three of them agreed, the mercenary began preparing. They spent three days camped in one spot while Khaniel and Bhaobuk hunted. Khaniel would have preferred a bow, but he managed to fashion a handful of throwing spears to make do. He considered them crude, with stone tips tied with gut, but assisted by the shaman's spells, they served well enough, and Khaniel and Bhaobuk managed to down several deer.

Each evening, they returned with the carcasses and skinned them. Khaniel taught Zethamy how to tan the hides by using the brains to soften and stretch the skin. He showed her how she could measure her progress by feel as easily as sight. During the day, while the mercenary and the shaman hunted, she gathered rotten wood. She tied a rope to a tree in the middle of the camp and tied the other end to her ankle, and then she began methodically feeling along the forest floor, finding downed limbs and branches.

Finally, Khaniel smoked the hides, and all three of them stitched pieces together for warmer clothing. The meat they also smoked, knowing they would not find much to eat on the slopes. After that third day, the trio each had a pair of warm fur boots and a simple but effective hooded cloak to wear.

Khaniel would have liked to have made them some hats, too, but he began to grow uneasy the longer they stayed in one spot. He couldn't explain it, but he felt as if something watched them. More than once, while he hunted, he suddenly got the impression that others hid in the bushes not too far away. But when he stopped and peered about, he never spotted anyone there.

The others seemed to share his unease. Once, when Zethamy had ventured off to find a private spot in the woods, she got lost and grew nervous, shouting Khaniel's name until he found her standing near a large tree, whipping her head back and forth as if listening.

"What is it?" he asked, reaching for her to calm her down.

"I felt . . . eyes, watching me," she answered, trembling. "I was certain I wasn't alone."

Khaniel frowned and peered about as they both stood still and quiet. But there was no one there. "Did you hear anything?" he asked.

"I'm not sure," the woman replied. "Maybe my mind was playing tricks on me."

"Maybe," the warrior said, but he knew his doubt was audible. "Let's get back to camp."

Another time, Bhaobuk sat straight upright during an evening meal and conjured a crackling ball of flame in his palms. He hurled the conflagration right into some bushes shining at the edge of the campfire's glow.

Khaniel lunged up and grabbed for his axe, while Zethamy gave a yell and toppled over to the side, quivering. "What in the gods' names are you doing?" the warrior demanded, shifting his gaze back and forth between the shaman and the burning shrubs.

Bhaobuk, his staff clutched in his hand, did not shift his stare away from the gloom. "I thought I saw something there. A face, perhaps." Finally, with a shake of his head, the ogre relaxed. "I guess it was nothing. I'm sorry."

The incidents unnerved them all. Zethamy insisted that Khaniel step up his training for her, and she spent every moment of her free time practicing with the blade. She also began to take a turn at watch, not by herself but in concert with the other two, overlapping the end of Khaniel's and the beginning of Bhaobuk's. "Just for an extra pair of ears," she explained. The warrior admired her determination, but the reasons behind her intensity worried him sufficiently that he decided to forgo the hats and just get them all moving.

Besides, he convinced himself, *we want to get through the passes before the snow gets heavy. The hoods will be good enough.*

Yet as they moved higher up the flanks of the Serpentspines, he began to doubt anew that they had made the right decision. They still had time to reconsider, to turn and head east. If they paralleled the range, they would reach the desert and cross there before doubling back and coming to the hermit's valley. That route would take longer, but he knew they would find it far less treacherous.

"I don't think this is a good idea," the warrior said, voicing his concerns. "The weather in the higher elevations looks worse yet," he added, pointing.

Bhaobuk glanced that way and shrugged. "We've come this far," the shaman said. "I don't think we have a choice now."

"We do," Khaniel insisted. "We can turn and head east. I know it isn't the quickest way, but it—"

"No," Zethamy said where she stood between them. "We can't wait that long."

"Why?" Khaniel asked. "Why the hurry?"

The woman shook her head. "I don't know. I can't explain it, but I feel like we're racing to beat something. I wish I could make it plainer, but that's all I can tell you."

"We may be pushing through snow up to your hips before we're over the pass," the warrior warned. "We may freeze and die up there."

Zethamy shook her head again. "I don't think that will happen. I think Mithaniel is somehow coaxing me that way." She took a deep breath. "I'm trying to learn to trust him again," she added. "Please, don't veer off the route. This is the right thing to do."

Khaniel sighed, feeling helpless. He found himself torn between gladness at seeing Zethamy finding her faith again and fears that her faith was unfounded. *I can't tell her that,* he thought. He looked at Bhaobuk.

The shaman shrugged. "I think we should keep going," he said. "But you're the wilderness expert."

"Fine," Khaniel said at last, giving in. "We'll keep going. But we may have to turn back, regardless of Zethamy's feelings."

They pushed on, working their way through a thinning forest interspersed with heath-filled meadows that eventually became stands of scrubby trees scattered along the slopes. By mid-afternoon, they had broken out of the trees altogether, reaching the timberline. They climbed a little higher, where a steady wind buffeted them. Khaniel called a halt and turned back to study the route they had taken to get there. The view behind them took his breath, and he soaked it in for a moment, but he felt a pang of guilt at mentioning it out loud when he knew Zethamy couldn't see it.

"Describe it to me," the woman said, moving to stand beside the warrior. She looped her arm through his own and turned her face to the south, as if staring at the vista herself.

"Are you sure?" he asked in an uncertain voice.

"Yes," she said. "Be my eyes. Tell me everything you see."

With a reluctant glance at Bhaobuk, Khaniel began to describe the terrain spread out below them. He mentioned the rolling, tree-covered hills and the flatlands beyond them. He conveyed how the clouds hung low overhead, seemingly so close that he could reach out and touch them.

"Show me," Zethamy asked, sticking her hand out at arm's length. "Move my arm like you're pointing with it."

"Zethamy," the mercenary began, not wanting to discourage her newfound enthusiasm but fearing to dash her fragile hopes. "I don't think this is such a positive thing."

"How are we going to find the hermit's refuge if you can't give me an accurate picture of where we are?" She turned to look at him, those haunting, clouded orbs studying him, and Khaniel felt as if she stared intently into his inner being. "I can only see what's in my mind. You have to be the bridge that connects me to the world. You have to help me 'see.' That's the only way I can guide us there. So get in the habit of telling me what it looks like now. We have to find a connection, your words and my inner pictures."

Khaniel swallowed and began again. He threw everything at her: colors, shapes, levels of clarity. He tried to describe motion and depth. Through it all, he stood behind her, guided her hand, pointed with her finger. When he faltered at last, not sure what to say, she lowered her arm and smiled at him.

"Good," she said. "That was a fine start. We'll keep working on it."

The warrior had to temper his elation with the understanding that they still had a long way to go, and prohibitive weather to overcome, before his burgeoning skill at description would become useful. "Come on," he said, taking her hand. "We've got to keep moving. Those clouds aren't going to hold back much longer, and we need to find a spot to hunker down if they open up."

The trio pushed on through the afternoon, until the first large drops began to spatter them. Khaniel peered desperately all about, seeking anything—some low-lying bushes, a rock face even partially leeward from the wind, or, if fortune truly wanted to smile upon them, a shallow depression or cave where they could huddle until the storm passed. But he found nothing.

"Keep going!" he said as the spatters became a steady thrum. "It's only rain right now, but it could become sleet or hail!" He drew his hood up over his head and pulled his cloak more tightly about himself with one hand. With his other, he continued to lead Zethamy. They stumbled forward, following the shaman, picking their way around scrub brush and loose rock. Ahead of them, a steep rise loomed, the side of a saddle between two higher ridges. To continue in that direction, they would have to scale it; no way around existed. Already, Khaniel could see rivulets of water cascading down the face of the slope.

Zethamy stumbled, tripping over the detritus scattered on the ground. Khaniel kept lifting her and pulling her along, trying to keep her upright while still searching for some sort of shelter. Finally, he spotted an outcropping of rock jutting from high up one side of the slope, where it curved around the base of the right-hand peak that formed the saddle.

"There!" he said, shouting to be heard over the pounding rain. Bhaobuk peered up where the mercenary pointed, then nodded once and angled his ascent to reach it. "Hurry!" Khaniel said. As if to support his sense of urgency, tiny pebbles of ice began pelting them and turning the ground white all around them.

As they climbed, the slope became more treacherous, slick with rain and sleet. The onslaught of precipitation came harder, and soon Khaniel had to use his hands as much as his feet to make progress. Beside him, Zethamy worked hard to keep up, but he could see that she grew tired, her strength flagging because she exhausted as much energy grabbing poor handholds as good ones. He doubted she could finish the climb.

"Bhaobuk!" Khaniel called to the ogre, who moved several paces above them. Through the deluge, the mercenary could barely make out the shaman. He couldn't even see the outcropping anymore. Bhaobuk turned at his call. The warrior motioned for him to wait, and dragged Zethamy the remaining few feet between them. "Help me!" he said, putting his mouth near the shaman's ear to be heard.

The ogre took one of Zethamy's hands, and Khaniel grabbed the other. Together, they practically hoisted her off the ground, as they would a small child who didn't want to go with her parents. Moving like that, they tackled the slope once more. The rain and sleet stung Khaniel's exposed skin. The cold felt raw, and the wind whipped his cloak about, sending shivers through him.

Finally, Khaniel caught sight of the jutting point of rock. In their blindness, they had gotten a little off course, angling too far to the right. He pointed and steered them toward shelter. The last 15 feet or so became really steep, so much so that they had to help Zethamy find every foothold by hand. Khaniel felt his fingers become raw and bleeding as he hoisted one of her feet up and planted her toes in a crack in the stone.

Already, though, the mercenary could sense that the pounding from the downpour had slackened a bit. They stood beneath the outcropping. He squinted and peered up, trying see if they could gain better shelter by climbing higher. He could see a narrow shelf perhaps another 20 feet above them, at the top of a vertical face. Zethamy could never climb that unaided. He wasn't sure *he* could do it, as wet as it looked.

"Stay with her!" he called to Bhaobuk and then pointed overhead. "I'm going first. Then I'll lower a rope down for her!"

Again, the ogre nodded in understanding and pressed himself flat against the face of the bluff, protecting Zethamy so she wouldn't fall off. Khaniel turned his attention to the ascent. Rain pelted his face and stung his eyes, but he ignored it and grabbed a handhold, determined to reach that ledge. One handhold after another, he carefully pulled himself up. The dampness of the rock made his grip suspect. Once, he nearly lost his hold, and he made the mistake of looking down. Bhaobuk and Zethamy weren't directly below him, and the fall looked much worse, all the way back down the side of the saddle.

Don't look down, he belatedly told himself, clinging with only one hand. Taking a deep breath, he steadied himself and continued.

Khaniel finally reached the ledge and discovered he had made a good choice. Though they would be unable to stand upright, the cleft in the rock ran back deeply enough that they would be completely out of the elements. Scrambling on his hands and knees, he found a position where he could brace himself and tied a rope around his waist before dropping it down over the side.

A moment later, he felt the rope twitching and then felt two sharp tugs on it. He dug his feet in against the uneven surface of the stone and began to pull. Bit by bit, he hauled the rope up until Zethamy's hands appeared on the edge of the ledge. He kept dragging the rope, giving her the support she needed so she could find solid grips. With one last tug, he managed to get her weight on the ledge, then reached out and took her hands in his. She crawled next to him and collapsed.

"Don't stand up," Khaniel cautioned her as he untied the rope from her waist. "The ceiling's too low here." He tossed the line back over the side. The rope wiggled and twitched a moment, and then the signal tugs told him the shaman was ready. Khaniel leaned hard into his pulls. He dragged the much heavier ogre more slowly, and though Bhaobuk could help his own cause more than Zethamy had, his lumbering bulk must have impeded his ability.

Suddenly, the rope slipped, nearly jerking Khaniel off his seat. He began to slide, losing ground. "Damn!" he cried, scraping against his will toward the edge. "Zethamy, help me!"

The woman rolled upright and reached for Khaniel. He felt her arms grab his cloak, and then she got hold of one of his arms. Scrambling behind him, she sat down and wrapped her arms fully around his waist, giving him extra anchor weight. Together, they held on while Bhaobuk started to climb again.

When the ogre finally appeared, Khaniel's arms shook from the strain. The shaman tumbled over the lip of the ledge and rolled in, away from the edge. He lay on his back and gasped for air, while Khaniel and Zethamy slumped down together.

"I thought we'd lost you," Khaniel said finally. "And maybe me, too."

"That would have been a fine mess," Zethamy panted. "The two of you gone over the side, and me without a chance in all the hells of getting down again."

"Still want to go over the mountains?" he asked. Out beyond the safety of the outcropping, the deluge still raged unabated, and the sleet had turned to hail. The thunderous roar of ice pounding rock reverberated in the crevice.

Zethamy made a face of distaste, but she nodded her head. "I know it sounds crazy, but we're going in the right direction." She pointed up and to the right. "We're almost to the top of a slope, and there's a saddle there, isn't there?" she asked.

Khaniel gave Bhaobuk an incredulous look. "Yes," he said, amazed. "You know this?"

"I can see it," she said. Her voice sounded odd, and Khaniel realized she barely held her emotions in check. "He's giving me another chance," she whispered. "He's showing me the way."

Khaniel reached out and squeezed her hand. "All right, then. Over the mountains."

"I wouldn't mind if we waited until the sky stopped falling down on us, though," Bhaobuk said. "That wouldn't bother me at all."

Khaniel gave the ogre a brief smile. "I think we're here for the night," he said. "By the time this lets up, it will be too dark to travel."

The wind continued to whip about, growing colder as the sun settled to the west. The trio of travelers sat and watched the landscape beyond the outcropping grow white from hail and sleet until the chill got to be too much. They ate a cold meal of bread and dried meat, and then they gathered as many loose stones as they could from around them on the ledge. They put them into a pile, and Bhaobuk worked his magic, heating the pile, letting the rock absorb the warmth. Once he finished, all three curled up around the stones and began to drift off to sleep.

Khaniel lay awake for a little while, staring up at the night sky. He had hoped the rain would dissipate, but it continued to drizzle, even after the worst of the storm passed. *Oh, well,* he thought, *at least the cloud cover will keep it from getting too cold.* A cold night might freeze the dampness and glaze everything with a rime of ice. But even if it did, he decided, Bhaobuk could use his magic to thaw them a path.

Eventually, the wind slacked off. Khaniel scooted closer to his two companions, sharing their warmth, and wrapped the hood of his cloak about his head, then drifted off to sleep.

KHANIEL AWOKE IN DARKNESS. HE SAT UP, shivering. It took him a moment to remember his location. His teeth chattered as he reached over and tested the rocks with his hand. They no longer felt warm. He listened for a moment and caught the slow, even sound of Zethamy's and Bhaobuk's breathing. *Why is it so cold?*

The chill made him feel sluggish, slow to think. He blinked and peered out beyond the edge of the ledge. The whole world had been swallowed in a curtain of white. Dazed by the odd vision, he rubbed his eyes and looked again, and when he realized what he stared at, his heart leaped into his throat.

The moon glowed only the slightest bit, fighting its way through the cloud cover. It illuminated a heavy snowfall tumbling from the sky. Khaniel watched as huge, wet flakes fell silently past. He crawled to the edge and looked down to see how much snow had accumulated. He couldn't tell the depth, but he couldn't make out any protruding rock by the dim glow.

Damn, he thought. *Not good.*

The warrior turned around and scurried over to the other two. He nudged Bhaobuk, who came awake slowly. The ogre sat up, rubbing his face with his hands. "What?" he grunted.

"Can you reheat the rocks?" Khaniel asked. "We need warmth right now, or we're going to freeze to death."

The shaman mumbled something Khaniel didn't quite catch, but went to work with his spells once more. Soon enough, Khaniel could feel warmth radiating from the pile. "Good," he said. "Go back to sleep. I'll stay awake, and when they cool off again, I'll wake you and let you take a turn at watch."

The ogre was already snoring.

MORNING HAD ARRIVED WHEN KHANIEL AWOKE again. He felt stiff, and when he stirred, pinpricks skittered across his skin. He stretched and sat up, tugging his buckskin cloak more tightly about himself. Zethamy still slept, but Bhaobuk was sitting up, working over the pile of stones. Khaniel realized the ogre had heated the stones again and had laid out strips of dried meat on them. They sizzled and popped and gave off a mouth-watering aroma.

When Bhaobuk saw Khaniel awake, he flipped a slice of the jerky in the warrior's direction. Khaniel caught it and immediately took a bite. "I hate eating it cold," the ogre explained.

Khaniel nodded. "It's good."

The mercenary turned and looked out over the landscape. Though the sky radiated a clear blue, a great deal of snow had fallen during the night, it seemed, for the whole world appeared blindingly white. Only the most distant lands far below did not wear a hoary blanket. They had a difficult hike ahead of them, and the warrior said as much.

"It's a couple of feet deep, at least," Bhaobuk commented. "Might make it hard for her to walk."

Khaniel looked over at Zethamy, who began to stir. "She'll make it," he said. "She's driven now."

"Did someone forget to close the windows last night?" she mumbled, sitting up. "By Marr, it's cold!"

"Grab a stone and hold it in your hands," Bhaobuk suggested. "Those on that side aren't too hot any more."

Zethamy felt around until she located a rock that she could handle, then brought it close to her body. "You have a few good uses, shaman," she said, smiling.

They finished breakfast quickly, for Khaniel wanted to get started. "We'll be lucky if we can make it through the pass and down the other side before it gets dark. Hiking through that much snow is going to be slow and tedious."

With Bhaobuk's magical aid, Khaniel found a way down from the ledge. He sank up to his hips in snow, but he judged that it had piled up against the bluff because of the wind. The ogre lowered Zethamy with the rope, then came down last.

As the mercenary had predicted, they traveled slowly, but they made it to the top of the saddle by mid-morning. They discovered a deep blue mountain lake on the other side, which they skirted to reach another slope on the lake's far side. Khaniel and Bhaobuk took turns in the lead, pushing through the snow and clearing a path for the others. By midday, they had gotten very near what Khaniel presumed was the summit of the pass. On either side of them, jutting peaks impaled the deep blue sky. The wind had picked up, slicing through the pass, and it whipped a cloud of snow off the caps overhead.

The snow had piled up fairly deep when they slipped over the final ridge. Khaniel led then, and the white stuff came almost to his navel. Exertion kept him warm, but he feared stopping to rest, for his body heat would dissipate quickly if he stood in so much snow. Even so, when he crested the pass and got his first look at the northern side of the Serpentspines, he gasped at the beauty of it.

"What is it?" Zethamy asked, puffing up next to him.

"I wish you could see this," the warrior replied. "It's extraordinary."

"Are we at the top of the pass?" she asked.

"Yes."

"Then I already do," she told him, tapping her forehead with her finger. "And you're right; it's wonderful."

Khaniel smiled. Bhaobuk drew up beside the two humans and looked out, too. "All my years in Oggok, I had no idea such marvels existed elsewhere in the world."

Khaniel clapped him on the shoulder. "Now you do," he said. "Which makes leaving everything you knew behind a little more palatable, I'll wager."

"Indeed."

"Do you see a low ridge, somewhat to the right?" Zethamy asked, gesturing vaguely with her hand. "Where two peaks are close together and look like teeth?"

Khaniel looked in that direction, and sure enough, he saw the ridge the woman described. The warrior confirmed it to Zethamy.

"That's where we need to go," she replied. "Just to the right of those two peaks."

Khaniel snorted. "Can't argue with that," he chuckled.

The three of them set off again. They waded single-file through the snow as they descended the pass. They pushed through to the head of a narrow valley flanked by steep ridges. At the far end, the two peaks rose like beacons, drawing them closer. The land became flatter, and the snow shallower there, only up to Khaniel's knees.

The warrior felt pleased. *We might get out of the high elevations before sundown after all.*

A shadow flashed across the snow. Khaniel turned and looked upward, toward the sun, and spied a winged shape circling overhead. It glided lazily around, banking so that it swooped in their direction, coming at them from behind. Khaniel could see something reptilian and white, its teeth-filled maw wide open.

"Drake!" Bhaobuk shouted. "Run!"

15

BHAOBUK TURNED AWAY FROM THE APPROACHing drake and bulled his way through the knee-high snow, blazing a trail for the other two to follow. Even for the ogre, the going was much too slow. And they had nowhere to run, could reach no shelter or defensible spot within the narrow valley to make a stand against the flying menace. That didn't stop them from trying.

Khaniel loosened his axe from its ties on his back. "Keep going!" he shouted to the other two. He spun around and watched, twirling his axe nervously into the air. The drake accelerated as it approached. It came in low, skimming right over the snow. The warrior crouched, trying to make a small target.

The long, slender creature looked very much like a dragon, though smaller. Its angular head extended forward on a long and flexible neck, which gradually thickened into a body sporting a pair of strong, leathery wings. The beast's tail fluttered along behind it, whipping about as the drake made small corrections to its course.

Just as the winged creature neared him, it veered slightly to the side. Khaniel lunged up out of the snow and tried to slice at the drake, but it banked barely enough to stay out of reach.

Clever bastard, Khaniel thought as he tumbled back down. He watched as it soared past and then saw the reason for its evasive move: it headed for his companions. "Down!" he shouted to them, but the warning didn't come quite fast enough. Bhaobuk turned to look back over his shoulder just as the drake reached him. The dragonlike creature didn't get in a bite, but it made contact, and the high-speed nudge sent the ogre sprawling in the snow.

The drake whipped past, buffeting Khaniel's companions with its wings as it climbed into the sky and began a long, wide bank to come around again. The circling reptile took the turn far enough out that it would again approach from the head of the valley. Khaniel would be its first target once more.

If it doesn't shy away again, he thought. The warrior turned and began to churn through the snow, trying to catch up to the others and make some headway down the valley. Ahead of him, Bhaobuk had regained his feet and pulled Zethamy along behind him. Slowly, Khaniel closed the gap. Periodically, he would glance behind him to see how close the drake had come. When the beast reached the head of the valley and dropped low, Khaniel knew it was time.

The mercenary turned to face the approaching drake, planted his feet, and waited. That toothy maw loomed closer, the jagged teeth inside flashing in the sunlight. When the creature began to veer away again, Khaniel acted. Rather than trying to lunge up and reach the target, he flung his axe. The blade spun up into the air on a collision course with the drake. The edge of the axe scraped along the beast's torso, gouging a line that blossomed with bright red blood.

The drake screamed and jerked itself high into the air, trying too late to evade the deadly axe, which tumbled away, knocked to the side by its contact with the monster. The weapon landed on the ground some 20 paces away from Khaniel. Red rain sprinkled the ground as the drake thrashed about while it hurtled through the air, bellowing in pain. Then finally it seemed to regain some control and rolled over, banking sharply.

It came right at Khaniel, and its eyes blazed in fury.

Oh, hells, the warrior thought. He spun and began plowing through the snow as fast as his legs could push through it, running toward his axe. It suddenly seemed impossibly far away. The drake closed in, streaking toward the mercenary like a bolt from a crossbow. The gash along its chest showed in stark contrast to the beast's pale white scales, as blood streamed out of the cut and trickled along its flanks.

Khaniel still had five or six feet to go before reaching the axe when the drake reached him. He threw himself sideways, evading the snapping jaws of the beast, but he didn't get far enough out of the way to avoid one raking claw. He felt a single talon rip through his cloak and snag the flesh of his shoulder. As the talon dug in, Khaniel felt himself hoisted from the ground. But the drake's grip lasted only a heartbeat, and as the talon tore free, the warrior fell to the earth again, plunging into the snow and skipping across the ground like a skimming stone on water.

The drake flipped about in midair and came at the warrior again.

Khaniel lay gasping in the snow, his shoulder burning with pain. He reached up to determine the severity of the wound and felt mangled flesh. Groaning, he sat up and looked for his axe. His impromptu flight in the claw of the beast had dragged him through the pristine snow, scattering the stuff and obscuring the landing point of the weapon. It could have lain anywhere along the path.

Khaniel scrambled to his feet and saw the snow where he had sprawled tinged with red. He knew he bled badly. Trying to ignore the pain, the warrior began backtracking, scuffling his feet, hoping to bump into his weapon, but he never turned his back on the beast coming at him.

When the drake got near, it drew up and settled in the snow. It lifted its head high into the cold, crisp air, towering twice as tall as Khaniel. It screamed a triumphant cry heavenward, then snaked its long neck down again, giving the warrior a cold glare that made him shiver in trepidation. He continued to back up, still hoping to find his axe.

The drake took one stride forward, closing the gap between it and its prey. That serpentine neck shot forward, driving the head right at Khaniel. The warrior recoiled as the jaw snapped shut only inches from his face. He scrambled backward again as the drake took another step. The head swooped down once more—just as Khaniel discovered his axe by tripping over it.

The warrior caught his heel on the weapon and fell hard on his rump. The monster's teeth sheared through the air where Khaniel's head had been. He flopped the rest of the way down, onto his back, reaching beneath himself for the handle of the axe. When he found the grip, he executed a rolling backflip. The effort made his shoulder throb, but he came up on his feet anyway, as the drake strode forward, trying to bite him a third time.

Khaniel whipped the axe up with his good arm, snapping the blade against the beast's snout. The strike sliced flesh from the tip of its nose. The monster yanked its head back, screaming a high-pitched wail. Khaniel saw an opportunity to close in for the kill, but he had no energy. He felt light-headed. *The blood loss*, he realized. He stumbled forward, trying to fight through the wooziness, but he moved too slowly.

The drake reached out with one talon and swatted at the warrior. Khaniel had enough presence of mind to bring the axe around and deflect the strike with the flat of his blade, but the beast's attack sent him sprawling face first into the snow. He collapsed in a heap, grunting as the wind was knocked out of him. His skin crawled along the center of his back as he braced himself for the fatal strike.

The blow did not come.

The drake screamed above Khaniel. The warrior gasped for air and managed to shove himself over onto his back with his good arm. He dragged the axe in front of himself, hoping he could fend off the beast until he could suck in enough air. He fought down panic as his lungs slowly recovered from the blow.

By the time he could breathe again, Khaniel saw that Bhaobuk stood nearby, gesturing at the beast. Zethamy crouched a few paces behind the ogre, holding the shaman's staff. They had come back to him instead of continuing to flee to the end of the valley. Khaniel felt relief course through him, thankful for his friends' help.

The drake reared up on its back legs, thrashing about. Flame engulfed its head, a magical effect courtesy of the shaman. Khaniel struggled to his knees and then clambered to his feet. His wounded arm hung limp at his side. The pain began to fade, replaced with a cold numbness.

Got to kill this thing now, he thought grimly. *Can't last much longer.*

As the fire faded from the beast's head, the drake struggled away from its attackers, floundering through the snow. It managed to get airborne, flapping its wings furiously in an effort to climb fast. It seemed wobbly, but it leveled off as it picked up altitude and soared toward the horizon.

For a moment, Khaniel let out a sigh of relief, thinking the creature had clearly had enough and intended to find easier pickings. But then he saw the drake begin circling, coming back. The beast was up to its old tricks again, skimming low across the surface and building up speed, racing toward them. He gasped, realizing the angle was off. The creature wasn't heading toward the ogre and him.

It had singled out Zethamy.

"It's going after her!" Khaniel tried to shout, but it came out more of a croak. Bhaobuk seemed to understand, though, for he hesitated and looked back over his shoulder. The woman stood by herself in the snow, oblivious.

A stabbing pain erupted in Khaniel's shoulder. He twisted in agony, clutching at the wound. He bellowed, a primal yell of rage at feeling so helpless. The anger began to overtake him, fury at not being able to get to Zethamy in time. With a growl, he grabbed his axe and took a step in her direction.

"Khaniel, wait!" Bhaobuk shouted as the warrior stormed past him. "Let me heal you!"

But the mercenary could no longer hear his friend. He craved the battle. He found that inner strength and drew upon it, berserk with battle lust. He sprinted toward Zethamy, determined to intercept the drake before it reached her. Each step became longer, more powerful. The burning drive to fight overcame him, and he lost his reason.

The world became a swirl of colors, white and red and steel. He saw what happened only peripherally. Somewhere in the haze of his consciousness, he saw himself lumbering toward the woman, heard Bhaobuk shouting at her to get down. He felt the axe as an extension of himself, felt it in his hands and wanted to drive the thing deep into the beast. Then he jumped.

For long moments, everything turned to black and wailing and shrill screaming. He couldn't differentiate his voice from his companions' or his foe's. But slowly, he began to come out of his battle lust, to grow cognizant of his surroundings.

He clung to the axe embedded in the drake's flank, its head buried almost to the haft. He bounced against the beast's torso and realized it still moved.

No. It flew, and Khaniel was airborne with it.

Gods, the warrior thought, terrified of what he had done. The drake didn't soar so much as careen through the air, twitching and jerking. It screamed as it buffeted both of them along, craning its neck, trying to reach back and bite at its unwanted rider, but the pain made it crazed, and it could do no more than snap near Khaniel. The warrior knew it could not stay aloft much longer.

The wind howled in the mercenary's ears as he bumped against the beast. Khaniel wanted to climb atop it, to find a place on its back and ride, but his strength, his berserk burst of power, faded again.

With a gasp of terror, Khaniel felt his grip slipping from the axe. As the drake tumbled, thrashing, toward the ground, the mercenary finally lost his hold on the axe handle and slipped free. He and the monster hit the snowy ground at about the same time, both of them bouncing and rolling across the white surface. Clouds of snow kicked up at the impact, and Khaniel lost sight of everything in a curtain of white. Then he came to a stop, dazed and woozy once again. A few paces away, the drake shuddered and screamed one last time and then settled its head on the snow and lay still.

"Damn," Khaniel said as he watched the drake die. His vision blurred, and the world teetered around him. "Bhaobuk," he called, not knowing how far away his companion might be. "Where's Zethamy? Is she safe?"

With those words, Khaniel's world went dark.

KHANIEL CAME TO IN DARKNESS. HE FELT AS IF he were floating, that all the weight of his body had been taken away, leaving only his inner presence. Total relaxation wafted through him, and he began to close his eyes again. Then he remembered battling the drake. With a gasp, he tried to sit up.

"Easy," Bhaobuk said. The shaman, only a silhouette against the glow of outdoor night, placed his hands against Khaniel's chest and forced him back down. For a moment, the warrior tried to fight it, but he felt a twinge in his shoulder, and he realized he had too little strength to resist the ogre. The warrior felt that odd, sickly taint wash through him. Soothing warmth spread through his shoulder. The effect calmed him.

"You're still hurt," Bhaobuk warned. "You need to rest."

Khaniel swallowed and nodded. "Zethamy," he tried to say. His throat, he discovered, was parched. The woman's name came out in a rasp.

"I'm here," Zethamy answered from Khaniel's other side. He rolled his head in that direction and saw a mound of fur cloak shift and rise. The woman sat up and reached out to him. She found his hand with her own. "We're all fine," she said. "But you scared us."

"Water," the mercenary pleaded. Bhaobuk placed a skin in Khaniel's hands and helped him sit forward enough to drink. When Khaniel had his fill, he lay back down, fatigued.

"Sleep now," the shaman commanded. "You lost a lot of blood. In the morning, you'll feel better."

Khaniel nodded and closed his eyes, letting his drowsiness take over. The last thing he remembered was Zethamy shifting slightly, moving closer beside him.

MORNING BROUGHT WITH IT THE SOUND OF birds and the glow of bright sunshine. Khaniel lay still for a few moments, keeping his eyes closed, listening. When he did finally open them, he discovered that he lay within a natural bower of evergreens. The branches overhead made a fine roof, and he rested atop a nest of soft needles. He drew in a deep breath, absorbing the cold air and the scent of pine. He felt strong, vibrant.

Bhaobuk and Zethamy slumbered on either side of the warrior. Careful not to disturb them, Khaniel crawled out from the shelter. Snow lay on the ground beyond the trees. He scrambled out into it, climbed to his feet, and looked around.

They had come a long way from the alpine valley where the drake had attacked. The high peaks rose in the distance to the north, their snowy caps brilliant white against the sapphire hue of the morning sky. The land seemed gentler, not so steep and open. Evergreens of different varieties filled the bowl where they had stopped, and an icy stream gurgled nearby.

How did we get here? the warrior wondered. *Did the two of them drag me all this way?*

Shaking his head in amazement, Khaniel further surveyed the trio's campsite. Someone had brushed away most of the snow in one spot, leaving an open pit where a fire had burned, though nothing but gently smoking ashes remained by that point. A few bits of wood still sat in a pile near the last of the fire, so Khaniel scooped up a couple and stirred the ashes. He uncovered a few embers and sprinkled some pine needles on them. The fire smoked and sputtered a bit, but then the needles ignited, and soon after, Khaniel had the fire crackling again. He began to wander about the immediate area, gathering more wood to burn. A dusting of snow covered everything, but he managed to find enough additional branches that they could enjoy the warmth of the flames until at least mid-morning, if needed.

As Khaniel fed the fire and enlarged it, Zethamy crawled out from beneath the copse of trees. "Khaniel?" she called, swiveling her head about uncertainly, listening.

"Right here," he called to her. "I'm getting the fire going again."

The woman smiled and moved toward him. She squatted down beside the blaze and stuck her hands out to warm them. "Feeling better?" she asked.

"Much," the warrior replied. "How did we end up all the way down here?" he asked.

"We carried you half the night," Zethamy explained. "Bhaobuk didn't want to risk remaining in the open, and he wanted a fire to keep you warm."

Her expression grew serious. "We almost lost you yesterday, Khaniel."

"I don't remember," he said. "What happened?"

"Bhaobuk said you should have already been unconscious, but somehow, you charged the drake as it bore down on me, jumped on it, and hacked at it while riding on its back. You finally slipped off right before it crashed to the ground. Bhaobuk didn't understand how you could even still be alive afterward. He nearly exhausted himself trying to heal you. Even when he had done everything possible, he wasn't sure you'd make it through the night."

Khaniel didn't know what to say. "That's what happened the day you and I . . ." He didn't finish. Though he was finally coming to terms with what he'd done and Zethamy seemed to be moving past it, talking about it still pained the warrior.

"Yes," Zethamy said. "I remember how bestial you looked. Your eyes seemed to be those of an animal. Something inside you takes over, drives you past what your body could normally handle. It's quite a gift."

"That's not the term I would use for it," the mercenary said wryly. "I don't particularly like losing control that way."

"It saved my life, this time," the woman said. "I'll take whatever blessings I can get these days."

For a while after that, they didn't say anything. Khaniel stirred the glowing coals with a stick and occasionally threw another bit of wood onto the fire. Eventually, Khaniel spoke again. "So you and Bhaobuk brought me all this way from the pass? Are we still headed the way your images tell you?"

"I hope so," Zethamy replied. "Bhaobuk doesn't quite have the same descriptive ability you do, but from what he could tell me, it still seems right."

"How close are we?"

The woman shook her head. "I don't know. I get no sense of time from what I see, only the knowledge that it's there."

"Well," Khaniel responded, rising, "I guess we'll see how much farther we can go today, if Bhaobuk is up to it. I don't know how much it took out of him, working his healing magic on me last night."

Khaniel crawled back into the bower and retrieved the satchels of supplies. While there, he nudged the ogre, waking him. "Come on, shaman, we've got miles to cover today." The ogre grumbled and rolled over. Khaniel nudged him again. "None of that," he scolded with a smile. "Get up."

"Go away, or I'll roast you on a spit," Bhaobuk growled.

"Suit yourself," Khaniel replied. "Zethamy and I will be moving on as soon as we finish breakfast. Catch up if you can." He crawled back out to the sound of an exasperated sigh from the ogre.

After a quick meal and an invigorating splash of water to the face, the three of them prepared to head out. Bhaobuk warned Khaniel that he would probably tire easily, but the warrior assured the shaman that he felt fine. Nonetheless, he grew weary more quickly than usual, and they stopped regularly. The warrior's voracious appetite seemed a sure sign that he was slowly regaining his stamina.

For two more days, they wandered down through the mountains, following Zethamy's mysterious mental map. After the first morning, they had moved out of the snow. By the middle of the second day, they had entered deep forest again, and evergreens gave way to broadleaf trees. Toward the end of that second full day, the terrain started to look somewhat familiar to Khaniel. When he commented on it, Zethamy grew quite excited.

"I think we're getting close," she said.

That night, they reached the valley where the warrior and the paladin had their fateful encounter. Despite the darkness, Khaniel felt certain. Though he didn't mention it to either of the other two companions, he also grew more tense. He feared running into the cyclopes. They found a hollow to make camp in, but Khaniel advised against lighting a fire. When his friends quizzed him, he finally admitted his worries.

"I think it would be better not to draw attention to ourselves here," he said. Reluctantly, the other two agreed, and they spent the remainder of the night subdued. When they finally began to bed down, Khaniel took the first watch, as always. He had no trouble staying awake, for he jumped at every night sound, rising and peering about regularly but finding nothing. He desired to remain awake the whole time, but he knew that an entire night without sleep would make him sloppy tired the next day. Reluctantly, he woke Bhaobuk so the ogre could take a turn.

Once after he had gone to sleep, Khaniel awoke with a start. He sat up and stared around. He could not see Bhaobuk. Alarmed, the warrior climbed to his feet and grabbed his axe. He began walking the perimeter of the camp, traveling in widening circles, calling to the ogre. Finally, after several minutes, he heard the sound of something moving through the forest. He took a defensive crouch behind a tree and waited, axe in hand.

Bhaobuk emerged from a thicket, walking toward the camp. With a loud sigh of relief, Khaniel rose from his spot. "You scared me half into the next life," he scolded. "Where were you?"

The shaman seemed abashed. "Sorry. I thought I heard something, went to check it out. Nothing but a deer."

Khaniel frowned and nodded. "You're as nervous as I am out here," he said.

"I know," the shaman admitted. "It's eerie. Go back to sleep. I'm fine," Bhaobuk assured him.

The warrior crawled back into his bedding and lay there, but sleep took a long time coming.

The next morning, the three travelers arose bright and early. Zethamy hardly ate. She was too eager to get started, Khaniel sensed. The warrior finally told her to carry some bread with her while they walked. He began to describe the surroundings to her as Bhaobuk broke camp. The woman listened intently as Khaniel went into exhaustive detail, asking him questions from time to time. When he could think of nothing else to say, he noticed she frowned.

"What is it?" he asked.

"It doesn't sound right," she complained. "I know you're telling me what's there, but it's not what I expected. I don't understand it."

"Maybe it's the wrong time of day," the mercenary offered. "Or the weather's off."

"No, that's not it," she answered, biting her lip in thought. "Explain to me again how the hills run along each side of the valley." Khaniel started describing the terrain once more, but it didn't seem to help.

Bhaobuk came to stand next to them. "Having trouble?" he asked. When Khaniel and Zethamy described the disparity, he laughed. "It sounds to me like you're looking at the wrong end of the valley," he said.

Zethamy gasped. "That's it!" We need to be more in the middle, like the day I first came here!"

They hurried through the valley, following the same trail that Khaniel had traveled with Bruigan only months before. The whole thing gave the warrior a surreal sense, compounded by his continuing and growing unease about lurking dangers.

When they reached the spot where Khaniel and Zethamy had met, Bhaobuk slowed down. "Maybe here?" he asked.

Khaniel shivered. "Zethamy," he said, "this is the exact spot where it happened."

Her face grave, the woman said, "Describe it now. Everything, exactly as you see it."

Khaniel did as she had instructed. Almost immediately, she began to nod.

"There's a low ridge to the right, and a really tall tree that juts up higher than the others," she said with certainty.

"I see it," Khaniel answered.

"That's where we need to go next," she claimed.

The three of them marched through the woods, Khaniel on the lookout for any signs of danger, for most of the morning. At each landmark, Zethamy would latch on to something else that the warrior would describe—a rock, a stand of trees, or even a waterfall—growing more excited with each successive discovery.

Finally, after a quick midday meal eaten while hiking, they clambered up a steep ridge and stood at the top, peering down into a hidden valley. Khaniel could see a quiet lake in the middle of it, with an open stretch of shore on the left side.

"That's it," Zethamy whispered. "That's where his refuge will be." She shuddered. "We're here."

16

It didn't take long for the trio to find the hermit's simple home, though its appearance proved disappointing. It sat nestled in a stand of smooth-barked aspens well back from the shore of the hidden lake. Overgrown bushes and the ravages of time and weather hid the remains of the abode. The structure had rotted to little more than a pile of timbers, gray lengths of wood covered in moss and grassy sod. True to his nature, Ushiv Beor had lived a simple and rustic life after fleeing the destruction of the Chapterhouse of the Fist.

As they approached the decaying dwelling, Khaniel made a point of describing it and its surroundings to Zethamy. She listened attentively to everything the warrior said, but she frowned and shook her head more than once. "I know we're in the right place," she said, "but I don't have any feeling about what it should look like. Nothing you're describing seems familiar."

"Do you see something else?" Khaniel asked. "Another spot on the shore of the lake? Facing a different direction?"

"No. It's strange... I don't have a preconceived notion of what anything looks like now, but I have the oddest feeling I'll know something is significant when we reach it."

Khaniel spun in place, staring at everything within sight, but he could see nothing else to describe to her. He raised his hands in the air helplessly. "I don't know what else to tell you," he said. "That's all that's here."

"There has to be something else," Zethamy insisted. "Remember, he brought treasures with him, old artifacts very important to his order. He wouldn't have left them in the cupboard of his cottage; he would have hidden them somewhere."

Khaniel nodded. "All right. You and Bhaobuk stay here and poke around the cottage some more. I'll search the area."

As the ogre and the woman began examining the remains of the dwelling, the mercenary strolled through the trees, scrutinizing everything. He searched for odd details, strange shifts or patterns in the ground that would indicate a foundation or hidden opening. He scanned the trees overhead on the possibility that the hermit might have camouflaged something in the branches. He found nothing. The warrior widened his search, circumnavigating the ruined house in an ever-widening spiral. He walked back down to the shore and began to pace along the water's edge, peering into its crystal-clear depths.

No evidence of any other building or cache of artifacts appeared.

Khaniel returned to where his two companions sat on a log, talking quietly. "There's nothing in the vicinity," he admitted, sitting down next to them. "Whatever this Ushiv did with the things he brought from the chapterhouse, he hid them well."

"Maybe he simply buried them," Bhaobuk suggested, standing and pacing. "Maybe he dug a hole in the ground and dumped everything in it, then covered it up and built his home right on top of the spot."

Zethamy pursed her lips. "That doesn't . . . 'feel' right," she said. "He would have wanted to keep them safe and away from enemies who might come looking, but he would have wanted to get to them in a time of need, also. No, he didn't intend to bury them forevermore. He put them somewhere, somewhere in this valley. We simply aren't looking in the right place, yet."

"What about a cave?" Khaniel asked. He stared at the ridge that ran behind the cottage, on the side opposite the lake. It looked more like a rock shelf than a mere hill, and Khaniel suspected it could hold a subterranean chamber or two. He hadn't made any effort to search it, because he had been thinking about a building, another structure the hermit might have built. The slope of the ridge was too steep to accommodate any sort of construction.

"Maybe," Zethamy said, tilting her head sideways. "Where would this cave be?" Khaniel described the ridge to her. "That could be it," she said, not sounding totally sure but seeming intrigued nonetheless. "Let's take a closer look."

Khaniel led the other two through the trees and to the base of the steep-sided ridge. Once he had a better idea of what to look for, it didn't take him long to spot a subtle but unmistakable alteration in the exposed rock of the slope. "There is a set of steps carved into the face of the ridge," he said excitedly. He described the cuts to Zethamy, who nodded as if amazed. "That's it," she breathed. "Lead me to them."

While Bhaobuk guided the woman to the base of the camouflaged steps, Khaniel began to ascend them, to see how far up they would go. He found the climb surprisingly easy. The hermit had done an amazing job of creating footholds without making them obvious to a casual observer. After a rise of 30 feet, Khaniel came upon a narrow ledge. The way the stone had formed, the strata of the rock tilted at a slight angle, and the ledge followed that incline for another ten paces. Where it finally petered out, the warrior discovered a narrow and jagged fissure in the rock. It did not face straight out, thus making it difficult to see from the ground.

"I found it," he called back. He returned to where the ogre and Zethamy slowly made their way up the steps and began to explain in more detail what he had seen.

Zethamy grew more and more excited with each word. "Yes, yes, that's it! That's what we've been looking for!"

Together, they worked their way up the last few steps. Zethamy clung to the wall as she navigated the ledge, with Khaniel in front of her and Bhaobuk behind. When they reached the cave entrance, she paused and ran her hands over the lip of the passage, feeling the stone edges with closed eyes. "Ushiv came here many times," she said, almost whispering. "It made him happy when he was here."

"We might have a problem," Bhaobuk said. When Khaniel looked over at the ogre, he saw him eyeing the opening doubtfully. "I'll never fit through that," the shaman said. "It's too narrow."

Khaniel compared it to the ogre's girth and had to admit that Bhaobuk was right. It would be too tight a squeeze. "I'm sorry," he said. "I know you really want to know what's inside."

Bhaobuk shrugged. "I got to accompany you this far," he said. "Perhaps it's better this way. I will remain out here and keep a lookout. You two go in. But be careful, and promise me you will describe what it looks like when you return."

"Now you sound like me," Zethamy said with a chuckle.

Khaniel grinned and clasped the ogre's shoulder in friendship. "Absolutely," he said.

"Oh," the shaman added, grabbing up a rock from the ledge at his feet. He passed his hand over it a couple of times and muttered some gibberish in a low voice. Then he handed the stone to Khaniel. "So you can see," he said.

Khaniel smiled his thanks. Then he turned to Zethamy. "Are you ready?" When the woman nodded, he turned and took her hand in one of his. Using his other hand to hold the stone aloft like a torch, he squeezed through the narrow opening.

The interior of the fissure widened almost immediately, and Khaniel pulled Zethamy beside him. Though the sunlight from outside still made it bright enough to see, the rock Bhaobuk had enchanted glowed with a soft pearlescent light. Khaniel thrust it forward so he could see deeper into the blackness. The passage tilted slightly to one side and angled down as it plunged farther into the ridge. Khaniel described it to his counterpart as he led her along. Zethamy ran her free hand along the smooth wall of the route, and Khaniel noticed that she couldn't stop smiling.

"You're enjoying this, aren't you?" he asked as he cautiously followed the fissure.

"It's indescribable," she replied. "Before, when I led the paladins from Freeport here, I felt similar feelings, but they were different. They were intermingled with pride, a sense of entitlement. I felt like reaching this place was my birthright."

"And now?" Khaniel asked. The glow of sunlight grew dimmer as the opening receded behind them.

"I feel very blessed," Zethamy answered. "It's humbling, being allowed to intrude on this sacred place. The sense of history, of finding out what happened to Ushiv firsthand, is almost overwhelming."

Khaniel chuckled. "It's odd," he said.

"What is?"

"I find the sense of irony particularly strong."

"You mean you being here with me?" Zethamy offered.

"Yes," Khaniel said. "You coming to this place blinded—most people would look on that as a rotten twist. But if you hadn't suffered the loss of your sight, you wouldn't feel quite the same about finally being here as you do. And I'm the link. Not that I take any pride in what happened," he added hastily, "but it almost feels like everything that's happened has been for a reason."

"So perhaps you're willing to believe that Mithaniel Marr guides your footsteps after all."

"Maybe," the warrior said doubtfully. "Maybe not. But if he does, he's got quite the twisted sense of humor."

The fissure had begun to narrow again, and Khaniel had to take the lead so they both could continue moving. Just when he began to fear that the gap would become too narrow for them to go on, he came to an opening on the left side. He paused, looking back up the route one last time. The faintest hint of sunlight made it that far into the interior. He turned and shone the glowing stone ahead, into the opening. What he saw made him gasp softly.

"What is it?" Zethamy asked. Her hand dug into his more tightly.

"There are steps here," the warrior explained. "This looks like it was cut out of the stone, like it wasn't a natural opening."

"Where do they go?" the woman asked breathlessly.

"Let's find out," he replied and pulled her forward, helping her find the first step. Together, they began to ascend, taking it slowly. Khaniel found it easier to see if he kept the stone a little behind himself, so he had Zethamy hold it above his shoulder. With each step, he strained to see ahead. Her grip on his hand grew tighter by the moment.

Khaniel suddenly spotted an end to the climb. A pair of wooden doors lay across the path, lying flat like the exit from a storm cellar. He told Zethamy as much.

"Doors?" she asked. "He built doors in here?"

"Apparently so," Khaniel answered.

They reached the portal, and Khaniel drew to a halt. He balled one hand into a fist and gently pushed against the wood, which felt dry and rough. It shifted slightly but didn't open. He pressed harder. The doors swung open a finger's breadth and then stopped. Something blocked them from the other side.

"They seem to be locked," he explained.

"What? How?" Zethamy demanded.

"Something on the other side is barring them, keeping them from swinging open."

"Can you force them?" she asked.

"I can try," he said. "Go back down a couple of steps, give me some room."

When Zethamy stood clear, Khaniel turned, moving into a crouch beneath the portal. Bracing his back against the wood while keeping his knees flexed, he raised up, putting pressure on the doors. He heard them groan, along with the faint sound of popping. He pushed harder, straining to force them upward. Finally, with a loud crack, something gave, and the twin doors flopped open with a crash.

Khaniel whistled softly, for a glow of natural sunlight shone from the space beyond.

"What? What do you see?" Zethamy demanded.

Khaniel didn't answer her immediately. He reached down and took her by the hand and led her up the last of the stairs. At the top, the two of them stood in a large, domed chamber. Most of the stone surface was natural, but in other areas, the warrior could see that someone had worked it, smoothing it and widening the space and making it generally round. The unnaturally flat floor sloped slightly toward the center, where a hole in it sat directly beneath a similar opening in the ceiling. Sunlight came through that second hole.

Khaniel found himself most amazed by the accoutrements of the place. The builder had outfitted it like a home, with wooden furniture set up in groups to form different areas. Nearest to the two interlopers, a table and two benches stood near a rock fireplace built against one sloping wall. The short chimney stopped after the curve of the wall became too great for it to stand steady, the stone above it blackened by soot in a path up to and out the hole in the ceiling. To their right, a writing desk with a high-backed chair stood against another part of the wall, and a couch sat next to them. Further back, against the far wall, Khaniel could make out the shape of a bed. The top of it seemed vaguely mounded, giving the mercenary a sudden sense of disquiet.

Perhaps feeling him tense, Zethamy hissed, "What do you see?"

"It's his home," the warrior explained at last, describing the features of the chamber to her. "He lived here," he said. "And I think he died here, too."

The woman's breath caught in her throat. "What? You see him?"

"I think so," Khaniel answered. "There's a form on the bed. He might have died in his sleep." He could feel a shudder pass through Zethamy. "He probably built the cottage outside initially, while he worked this place into shape. He did some impressive stonework to make it big enough. And all the furniture! None of this would fit through the passage. He must have brought the timbers in one at a time and built everything right here."

Zethamy took a deep breath and said, "Lead me over to him."

Khaniel did as the woman asked, guiding her through the different sections of the chamber, closing in on the bed. As he steered them both in that direction, he peered around the room, getting a better look. The large space had a surprisingly cozy feel to it. Numerous lanterns hung from iron hooks driven into the wall, and a couple of others sat on the writing desk and the table. He saw several wooden dishes and a pair of iron kettles on the mantel of the fireplace, and a rack with several pegs on it set into the wall nearby. The tattered remains of two or three cloth items hung from some of the pegs. The warrior also spotted a number of cabinets, armoires, and shelves, some against the wall and some in the middle of the room, defining divisions between different areas, almost like interior walls. The pit in the center held water, though Khaniel didn't move close enough to it to determine its depth. All those things Khaniel described to his companion.

At last, they drew near enough to the bed to see that it was, indeed, occupied. The bedclothes had mostly rotted away, leaving only scraps of fabric, dark and stained, draped across the framework of the wooden berth. A skeletal corpse in rotted animal-hide clothing rested in a natural sleeping position, on its side with one arm drawn up and tucked beneath its head.

"I suppose it's him," the warrior said, feeling a sense of respect and also very much like an intruder. "He's lying peacefully, as if he went to bed one night and never woke up."

"How sad," Zethamy said, moving closer and kneeling down. Her sightless eyes seemed far away to Khaniel as she ran her hand over the frame of the bed. "To live out here, all alone, and to pass like that, without anyone ever finding him."

"Until now," Khaniel said.

"Yes," Zethamy agreed. "After so many years, we've come at last to offer him a prayer for resting and peace." She bowed her head then, her lips moving without making a sound. Khaniel stood quietly by, for though he found no real value in the ceremony, he respected that his companion did.

When Zethamy finished, she rose to her feet and asked, "Do you think we should bury him?"

Khaniel shook his head, forgetting for a moment that she could not see the gesture. "No," he said. "This was his place of rest in life, and it should be in death, too. Besides, we would have to move him all the way back out through the tunnel and down the slope, and I don't think we could keep him in one piece. The bed is too big to tote," he added, grimacing at his macabre description. "And no one else is ever likely to find this place."

"I suppose you're right," Zethamy said. "So the only thing left to do is figure out where he hid the artifacts."

"There are plenty of spots in here," Khaniel said. "I see a few cabinets and whatnot, and the pit in the center of the floor might be deep enough to stash weapons and armor."

The woman shrugged. "They are as good a place as any to start," she said. "I wish I could help you."

As Zethamy fidgeted in anticipation, Khaniel began going through the different storage places. He found all sorts of tools, rotted cloth items, ink vials, scroll cases with dust inside them, and the powdered remains of herbs, spices, and other flavorings in the cabinets and on the shelves. But no hidden cache of artifacts turned up.

"Even in here, he would have very carefully hidden the treasures away," Zethamy said, tugging at her lower lip with her fingers, "in case someone did find his refuge after he had died. He wouldn't want someone accidentally stumbling upon them. He would want them to go to followers of Marr."

"So, where does that leave us, then?" Khaniel asked, looking around doubtfully.

"Maybe under something," the woman replied. "Beneath a heavy piece of furniture, perhaps?"

Khaniel thought for a moment, taking the whole chamber in one more time. His eyes settled on the bed. "What about right underneath him?" he asked in sudden inspiration. He squatted down to get a look at the space beneath the frame.

"Yes," Zethamy said eagerly. "He would have felt safest resting close to them."

Khaniel stood up and took hold of the frame. Very gently, he began to slide it away, dragging it across the floor. The squeaking sound it made grated on the mercenary's ears, and he felt very irreverent for the act, as if he defiled a grave. "Sorry, Ushiv," he felt compelled to say.

Khaniel could see that a large section of the stone had a seam surrounding it, and a little iron ring had been hammered into the interior piece of stone along one side. The warrior described it out loud before trying unsuccessfully to lift it alone. "I'll need your help," Khaniel said, threading rope through the ring and handing one end of it to Zethamy. "We'll have to pull together."

"How could Ushiv have managed to lift it by himself?" she asked as she positioned herself to assist the mercenary.

"Probably with some pulleys hung from a frame," Khaniel answered. "Which he later disassembled and used for other things." He counted to three, and together, they hauled on the rope. With a deep groan, the stone lid rose and slid to the side, revealing a dark recess beneath it. When they had dragged the lid far enough out of the way that Khaniel could work, he got down on his knees and shone the still-glowing rock into the space.

The hole measured perhaps three feet wide by five feet long. A single wooden chest sat inside it, filling the space. Khaniel considered how to lift it out, but there didn't seem to be any external handles on it anywhere, so he concluded that the hermit had lowered it by the lid first and then filled it before sealing it away.

"Well, this is it," he said to Zethamy, who knelt down beside him and felt around with her hands. "Are you ready for me to crack it open?"

"Yes," the woman answered, her unseeing eyes wide with impatience. "Please!"

Khaniel reached down and tilted the lid of the chest back.

The soft pearly glow of the magical light reflected off gleaming metal. Khaniel looked closer and saw a silver cudgel resting atop a purple linen cloth. Both the weapon and the fabric appeared carefully preserved. Very gently, the warrior reached down and took hold of the cudgel. He took Zethamy's hand, which shook, and laid the handle of the weapon in her palm. "Here," he said, placing her other hand on the larger end. "Do you know what this is?"

Zethamy gave a soft, choking gasp. "Yes," she said, tears of joy streaming down her face. "It's the scepter of Lord Fekrand the Luminous. I'm holding the scepter of Lord Fekrand the Luminous!" she muttered to herself, seemingly stunned by the reality of it. "It must be beautiful."

Khaniel started to reach for the purple cloth, recognizing it by then as a folded cape, but a noise from behind the two of them caught his attention. He glanced over his shoulder and let out a strangled cry.

The skeletal remains of Ushiv Beor rose from the bed.

17

THE ANIMATED CORPSE OF THE PRIEST OF Mithaniel Marr issued a low, rumbling moan as it came to a sitting position. The skull of the long-dead hermit pivoted to peer at the two intruders, and Khaniel saw a cold-burning blue flame in each eye socket.

"Oh, Brell's beard!" he swore, the dwarven curse coming to him unbidden.

"What in Marr's name was that?" Zethamy asked, turning toward the unnatural sound behind her. Her voice quavered in dread.

Khaniel didn't bother to waste time in a reply. Instead, he grabbed the woman by the elbow and pulled her to her feet before dragging her several paces away across the floor. Only then did he explain. "Ushiv seems to be unhappy that we disturbed his cache," the warrior said, slipping his axe free of its bindings. "I don't think he wants us to have his secret trove."

Zethamy's breathing became sharp and rapid. "He's . . . moving?" she asked, her face going pale. "Undead?"

"Stay well behind me," Khaniel ordered, giving his axe an experimental swing. "I don't want to catch you in a backswing."

"Khaniel, wait," the woman said, but the warrior had already advanced on the rising corpse.

Not wanting to wait until the remains of the priest could get fully to its feet, Khaniel stepped into a full two-armed swing of his weapon, intent on cleaving the undead thing in half where it still sat. With a grunt, he slammed the axe into the bones of Ushiv's ribcage—and caught the full force of a thunderous burst of energy that erupted on impact. The mercenary found himself in a heap on the floor several paces away. His ears roared, and bluish light swam in his vision. He blinked and shook his head, trying to clear it of cobwebs. In a daze, he tried to rise to his feet as the frightful creature across from him did likewise. Somewhere in the distance, he heard a faint voice, calling his name. But he couldn't quite place it or hear it clearly.

The corpse stood upright with its bony feet planted on the floor. It seemed unsure, peering around the chamber, looking for something. When it spotted Zethamy, it uttered another long, low moan and took a step toward her. Khaniel wanted to charge across the space between himself and the grotesque abomination, but he could not find his balance. His took uneven steps, his body tottering as he staggered to protect the blind woman.

"Khaniel!" Zethamy shouted, and the warrior finally realized it was her voice he heard. The roaring in his ears had muffled the sound. "Are you all right?"

"It's coming at you," he said, moving closer. "Don't move."

"Stop!" she shouted.

But the mercenary was too caught up in trying to interpose himself and keep her safe. He raised his axe as he closed the last few steps. The skeleton paused and looked at him, lifting an arm defensively. When Khaniel yanked his weapon down and forward, intending to shear the bone clean in half, the undead thing never even flinched. To his amazement, the strike bounced off without any effect at all. Khaniel gawked as the corpse turned toward him, its icy-flamed eyes staring right through him.

With a menacing growl, Ushiv's remains jabbed both bony hands out, pointing them at Khaniel. Twin streaks of bluish light flashed from desiccated fingertips and pierced the warrior's chest. Agonizing cold erupted at the points of contact, and Khaniel arched his back, dropping his axe as he stumbled backward and down. He hit the floor hard, his head bouncing against the stone. He writhed in half-conscious anguish as the icy pain radiated throughout his body.

The skeleton turned and began to close with Zethamy once more.

"No!" Khaniel growled, his voice hoarse. "Zethamy, it's coming for you! Get out of here!"

The woman, who stood uncertainly in the middle of the floor, gasped and took an involuntary step back. She turned her head back and forth, trying to listen for the telltale sounds of the approaching corpse.

Khaniel rolled to his knees, dizzy. The back of his skull throbbed, and he felt nauseated. He wanted to stand, but his body wouldn't cooperate, and he curled up as the residual effects of the frigid arcane blast gripped him. He closed his eyes, trying to get his world to stop spinning.

The undead creature emitted another deep howl. Khaniel heard it shuffle closer to Zethamy.

"Run," the mercenary croaked again, despairing over his inability to aid her. "Get Bhaobuk."

"No," she replied.

Khaniel pounded his fist against the floor in frustration, bloodying his knuckles. The new pain enraged him, and he felt that hidden reserve of strength beginning to well within. With a savage snarl, he found the power to climb to his knees. He crawled across the floor, wobbly still, and grabbed his axe. "Come here, you damned thing!" he shouted, trying to swing his axe as he crept toward the skeleton once more.

"Khaniel, for the love of Marr, stand down!" Zethamy cried. "You can't destroy it like this!" She reached out, feeling her way toward him as she spoke.

Somehow, despite his rage, the warrior heard his companion's words. He wanted more than anything to beat his fists against the skeleton, to smash the flat of his blade against it and watch its bones shatter. Fighting through that animalistic fury was the hardest thing he could remember doing, but something in Zethamy's voice got through to him, convinced him to trust her. With a sigh of frustration and waning strength, he stopped trying to reach the skeleton and sagged down to the floor once more.

"Whatever you're going to do," he muttered, his voice barely audible, "pray that it works. I can't help you." And with that, he hung his head, woozy again.

"Precisely," Zethamy answered. Khaniel managed to look up in time to see her kneel down on the floor, right in the path of the approaching thing. She still held the scepter that Khaniel had pulled out of the chest, and she placed it in front of herself, as if in offering. Then she closed her eyes and began to speak softly.

Khaniel rubbed his eyes and watched. The living corpse advanced, walking with awkward, jerky steps, until it stood directly in front of the woman. It reached out with both clawlike hands. Bony fingers extended as if to grab at Zethamy's neck, but instead, they closed around the scepter.

When Zethamy felt the touch, she shivered, but she did not let go of the scepter. Instead, she lifted one hand free of it and let Ushiv's hand rest upon it unhindered. Then she closed her own hand around the skeleton's.

To Khaniel's amazement, the scepter began to glow. It radiated a gentle light, similar to that of the magical stone Bhaobuk had created, but richer, warmer. Its glow spread between the two figures, radiating in Zethamy's face and permeating the skeleton's fragmentary torso. The woman continued to mouth soft words that Khaniel could not quite hear. Whatever she said, it seemed to have an effect on the undead creature.

The glow from the scepter grew brighter, infusing both of them with its radiance. The mercenary realized that the glow emanated not only from the item itself, but from both of the figures touching it. And then, to the warrior's amazement, the glow surrounding the skeleton took solid shape, transforming from a vague brightness to a semitransparent body. The harshness of the skull softened beneath the facial features of a bearded man with sad eyes. Those sad eyes gazed at Zethamy, radiantly beautiful in that moment.

As Khaniel watched, the ghostly image of Ushiv Beor reached out with one pale, luminescent hand and touched the woman's cheek, stroking it. A single finger brushed her eyelid, wiping away a tear. Then, bowing his head once more, the apparition and its more substantial skeleton faded from sight. A smattering of dust wafted to the floor, all that remained of the corpse that had risen from the bed.

Zethamy sat very still for a moment longer, as if enraptured. Khaniel found her expression to be totally serene, at peace. Then whatever spell had held her broke, and she drew in a long, shuddering breath and sagged down. The glow from the scepter faded, and she sighed.

"So much sadness," she mumbled, another tear running down her cheek. "He was here by himself for so long, was so lonely." She opened her eyes then and blinked. The cloudy orbs turned in Khaniel's direction, peering about uncertainly once more. "He was only doing his duty, Khaniel. He thought we were tomb robbers, come to steal the objects of that duty. He didn't understand."

"But you explained it to him," the warrior said in wonder. "You found a way to communicate with him."

"Somewhat," she answered. "The scepter let me fill myself with the glory of Marr, and he could feel it, too. When he realized what I was doing, he relaxed, and there was a sharing of . . . emotions. I could sense that he felt relieved, he could finally go to his rest, turning his duty over to me."

"So he's gone?" the warrior asked, though he already knew the answer in his heart.

"Yes," she said, rising to her feet. "He's with Marr now." She took a few tentative steps in the mercenary's direction. "Are you hurt?" she asked.

"Not badly," Khaniel answered, "but I smacked my head pretty hard, and I feel dizzy."

"Stay where you are," the woman instructed, and she began to make her way over to where the warrior sat. When she reached him, she extended her hands and found his face. She ran her fingers over the top of his head and to the back. Her touch felt gentle but sure. She spread her fingers wide and placed her palms over Khaniel's skull. Almost immediately, he felt a cool, soothing relief seep into him. The shock of it nearly made him jerk away.

"You—" he began, unsure he could trust his own perceptions, "you're healing me!"

"Yes," she said simply, and a faint smile played across her face. "Does it feel better?"

"How can you—?" He left the question hanging, amazed. She didn't answer him, but he saw then that she cried softly. They were happy tears, though. She helped him to his feet, that soft smile not leaving her face.

"You reconciled with him," Khaniel offered. "Regained your holy touch."

Zethamy didn't answer for a long moment. When she did speak, her voice sounded quiet but firm. "No," she said, "not reconciled. Surrendered. I stopped fighting him, struggling to try to negotiate and dictate the terms, and I found joy in the humility of being at his service, in whatever he needs of me." She took a long, slow breath. "I had forgotten how sweet his presence could be."

Khaniel hugged the paladin. "I'm happy for you," he said.

"It took me so long to finally understand," she said. "It took looking inside Ushiv's soul to see what I blocked out. Now, it seems so clear to me. Ushiv's devotion was complete, unconditional. He came out here, brought those relics with him, because he knew that's what Marr needed from him. There was no glory in it, no pat on the back. It was hard and lonely, but he did it because he wanted to give himself completely.

"My devotion to Mithaniel Marr was a false devotion before. I said once that all his gifts to me felt like a birthright. I didn't truly appreciate them; I felt entitled to them. And I saw my service in his name to be a means to glorify myself. I considered what he provided me as a measure of my courage and honor."

Khaniel raised his eyebrows in surprise. "That's not an easy thing to admit to," he said, impressed.

Zethamy went on. "I realize now that courage and honor are hollow when everything is stacked in your favor. It's easy to be a champion when you don't have to struggle to succeed. Mithaniel brought me low so I could understand that and learn to appreciate what I took for granted before," she said, her voice soft, earnest. "I saw these artifacts as treasure, power and glory for my benefit. But that's not what Mithaniel wants from me. He wants me to be their caretaker, to ensure their safety and their legacy as gifts to our order."

Khaniel nodded. "So what do we do with them now?" he asked.

Zethamy's face clouded. "I also understand now why Maix wanted to find this place," she said. "Ushiv didn't only bring holy relics here for safekeeping. He also secreted away a tainted thing, an item of corruption and dread power. The Chapterhouse of the Fist had long kept such things locked away from those who would use them for selfish ends. In many ways, it was more important for those artifacts to escape the carnage of Befallen."

"That's in there, too, then," Khaniel said, pointing toward the chest, remembering again too late that Zethamy could not see the gesture. "And the Church of the Dismal Rage knows it."

"Yes," Zethamy replied. "We have to get whatever it is back to Freeport before Maix finds it—and us."

"Well, then," Khaniel said, "I guess the sooner we take everything out of here and get on our way, the better."

The two companions returned to the chest. A quick survey proved that the wooden container would not fit back down the hallway. The warrior surmised that Ushiv had either constructed it inside the chamber or had lowered it through the hole in the ceiling. Since they could not get it back out that way in a short amount of time, they agreed to go through the chest's contents and see how best to carry the relics individually.

Khaniel began to unpack the items, pulling them out of the container one by one and handing them to Zethamy. The paladin ran her hands over each piece, exclaiming in delight when she recognized one. They discovered a magnificent suit of plate mail armor fashioned from steel dyed the color of sunlight. It bore the symbol of Marr upon the breastplate.

"You should wear it," Khaniel suggested. "It was probably his, but it will fit you well enough until we can get it back to Freeport and have some adjustments made."

Zethamy laughed. "That won't be necessary," she said, slipping the breastplate on. Right before Khaniel's eyes, the piece of armor shifted and molded itself to fit its wearer, finding harmony with one of Marr's servants.

He shook his head in amazement. "That solves that," he said, pulling out several tomes. "What are these books?"

"Oh," Zethamy said breathlessly, reaching out so that Khaniel could place one in her hands. "I didn't dare hope—" She ran her hands lovingly over the leather binding, feeling the embossed cover. She opened it and felt the pages, which were surprisingly supple despite the tome's age.

"What are they?" Khaniel asked, noting that the paladin had tears glistening in her eyes once more.

"Ancient texts," she whispered. "Guides for imbuing weapons and armor with powerful enchantments, long thought lost to the order. Some of the elders at the temple often expressed hope that Ushiv had taken them with him, but no one knew for sure. Oh, I wish I could read them!" she finished, hugging the book to her chest.

In addition to the armor, scepter, and books, Khaniel found a magnificent sword, expertly forged. He placed it in Zethamy's hands and watched as she took a few practice swings. He could see the bittersweet expression on her face, knowing she felt joy for having recovered the weapon, but sadness that she could no longer wield it with the skill she once possessed.

"In time," he said, his voice gentle. "You will learn again in time."

"I know," she said, smiling. "I just need patience, that's all."

Zethamy donned the rest of the armor, and Khaniel fastened the purple cape over her shoulders. With the sword in her hand, she presented an imposing figure to the warrior.

He took one last look in the chest, but it was empty. He frowned. "There's nothing else," he said. "Where's this dangerous relic you learned about?"

Zethamy shrugged. "It should be there," she said doubtfully. "Feel around and see if there isn't a false bottom or something."

Khaniel hopped down into the chest and did a thorough search. He didn't come up with anything, but then, on a whim, he examined the lid. Sure enough, when he rapped on it with his fist, it gave a hollow thud. He found a small depression and managed to pry a false panel out of the lid, revealing a small box inside. He pulled the container free and climbed back out.

"This might be it," he said, working to open the box, made of a highly polished black wood. The lid tipped open and revealed a pendant nestled against velvet. Khaniel whistled at the beauty of the jewelry.

A master craftsman had fashioned it of silver, the filigree elven-fine and perfectly sculpted. Numerous sapphires had been set into it, including a large central one the size of a walnut. It was stunning and undoubtedly priceless.

Khaniel reached for it, to lift it out, but Zethamy stayed his hand. "Close the box," she said in a commanding voice. "You don't want to touch it."

"Why?" Khaniel asked, feeling a little put out with the paladin. "I only want to look at it."

"Khaniel, just do as I ask. Right now."

Khaniel started to retort, but something in the tone of her voice worried him. With a shrug, he closed the box and immediately felt a weight of anger lifted from him. "Sweet mother," he said in a near-whisper. "That was unnerving."

"The Pendant of Hatred," Zethamy said. "I can feel its taint even now." She shuddered. "Don't open the box again. Please hide it away."

"No wonder Maix wanted to find this place so badly," the warrior said, slipping the ebony box into his satchel. "Such a thing could start a street riot in a matter of moments."

"Yes," Zethamy replied. "Our burden is greater than I imagined." She took Khaniel's hands in her own. "I can't see you, but look at me and listen carefully," she said. "You are still my eyes, Khaniel. I can't do this without you. No matter how dark things seem to become, I need you to help me. All right?"

The mercenary exhaled slowly. "I'm not going anywhere," he said. "I've got your back, all the way to Freeport."

Zethamy nodded. "Good. Then let's go."

The pair made their way to the entrance to the chamber. Zethamy halted and turned back. "Describe it to me one last time," she asked. "I want to remember this place."

The warrior obliged her.

When he finished, Zethamy gave a simple salute toward the middle of the chamber. "Goodbye, Ushiv," she said. "Rest and peace to you." Then she turned and felt her way down the steps.

Khaniel followed the paladin out, pulling the wooden doors shut behind him. They walked in silence back up the fissure toward the sunlight. Khaniel's thoughts swirled. Zethamy had changed. She seemed confident, regal. She had found her purpose once more, he realized, and she reveled in it. He felt genuinely happy for her, and it reinforced what he was coming to believe about himself.

He would never go so far as to assume that a god, Mithaniel Marr or otherwise, manipulated events surrounding his life. To do that might make it seem as if Bruigan had needed to die in order for everything else to fall into place, and he simply would not accept that. But he began to understand that working for a greater cause, helping Zethamy succeed in her own quest, brought him greater satisfaction than anything he had done before. Maybe the dwarf had been right; maybe he had needed to love someone else more than he loved himself, for him to become a better man.

Is that what I'm feeling? he thought in wonder, watching the woman walking beside him in all her splendor. *Love?*

As they neared the opening, Zethamy slowed. "I can feel the sunlight on my face," she said, grinning back at the warrior. "Come, lead me out. Bhaobuk will be eager to hear the good news."

Khaniel stepped past the paladin and squeezed through the opening into brilliant daylight. He turned back and took Zethamy's hand, and he felt a little excitement when he held it that he had not noticed before. He shivered, wondering what he was getting himself into.

The warrior guided her through the entrance and onto the ledge. Once out, he turned back around, blinking as his eyes adjusted, looking for the ogre. But Bhaobuk did not wait for them on the ledge as the warrior had expected.

"He must have gotten tired of standing up here and gone back down," the mercenary decided. "Come on."

Together, they followed the ledge back to the point where the stone steps descended to the ground below. Khaniel went first. He turned around and climbed down as if on a ladder. He had Zethamy do the same, guiding her feet with his hands. When they reached the bottom, Khaniel peered around.

He still saw no sign of the shaman.

"Bhaobuk?" he called, trying to look through the trees toward the lakeshore and the disintegrated cottage. The ogre didn't answer.

"Where is he?" Zethamy asked, sounding worried.

"I don't know. Let's head toward the cottage. Maybe he's there."

They began to walk toward the dilapidated structure together, hurrying as much as they could. The warrior knew Zethamy shared his uneasy feeling. When they broke through a thick stand of trees and underbrush, they spotted their companion. Bhaobuk watched them approach.

But he was not alone.

Kizrak stood beside the shaman, along with perhaps half a dozen ogre warriors. Khaniel jerked to a stop, eliciting a gasp from Zethamy.

"What is it?" she asked fearfully. "Is he all right?"

Khaniel didn't answer, for at that moment, more ogres stepped out of hiding places within the underbrush, weapons in hand. At least two dozen or more of Kizrak's warriors surrounded the pair.

Khaniel felt his stomach knot up. "Kizrak and a hunting party are here," he said.

Zethamy stifled a gasp. "Where?"

"Pretty much all around us," he said, knowing his voice reflected his shock and dismay.

Khaniel couldn't believe it. Somehow, the ogre king had followed them, had found them. Poor Bhaobuk didn't stand a chance by himself while

Khaniel and Zethamy explored the hidden refuge. But, Khaniel suddenly realized, his ogre companion didn't seem too distressed.

In fact, the shaman grinned.

Khaniel felt vertigo overwhelm him. He became wobbly on his feet, trying to comprehend how he could have misjudged the ogre so completely. "Bhaobuk set us up," he finally managed to say. "He led Kizrak here."

"Oh, no," Zethamy breathed, the color draining from her face. "No," she repeated, as if pleading.

"Actually," the shaman said, taking a couple of steps forward, "Bhaobuk's been dead for several weeks now." With a wave of his hand, the ogre's physical form shimmered in the air, became indistinct, and then solidified once more as an entirely new person.

Maix Treganan.

18

"THE LOOK ON YOUR FACE IS PRICELESS, WARrior," Maix said, strolling toward Khaniel and Zethamy in the most carefree way. "Your dazed expression is everything I've been imagining, everything I had hoped for."

Khaniel felt Zethamy's hand clench abruptly, her nails digging into his skin. "That's Maix!" she hissed. "I recognize his voice!"

"Yes," Maix said, leaning against a tree and folding his arms casually across his chest. "It really is me. Surprised you, didn't I?" he added, chuckling. "Oh, I'm so glad this charade is finally *over!*" he bellowed, sounding relieved. "I'm sick to death of all your blasted camaraderie and sincerity."

Khaniel's mind froze. Nothing made sense. He couldn't catch his breath. "What—?" he began, unable to form a coherent thought. How was it possible that Maix was Bhaobuk? That Bhaobuk was dead? "What are you talking about?" he finally asked.

"Oh, this is the part where you want to understand what happened, isn't it?" Maix said. "Fine, but pay attention, because I don't want to go through this more than once. You, warrior, ruined everything. For some fool reason, you decided it would be nice if Zethamy went blind, so you sliced her eyes out. Oh, wait, you both know that part already." He peered up into the trees as if thinking, tapping one finger against his chin. "Let's see . . . ah, yes. I worked very hard to arrange it so that you two wound up together again, and I planted myself in the middle of it so that you would bring me along, and we could all find the hermit's hideaway together. Clever, isn't it? Now, give me the pendant."

Khaniel steadied his breathing, trying to grasp what he heard. Arranged? By Maix? Nothing made any sense!

"Where is Bhaobuk?" Zethamy demanded, clenching and unclenching her fist against Khaniel's hand to the point of drawing blood. "What did you do with him?"

Maix rolled his eyes. "Will you please try to keep up? I killed him before either of you ever set foot in Oggok. I got there before you, Khaniel, and took his place. And I did Kizrak here a favor in the process, didn't I?" he added, looking over at the king. "Such an embarrassment, that sniveling little whelp, and it was the perfect disguise, because no one but the king and I even knew we'd done it. Now, the pendant?"

"Why?" Khaniel asked, knowing it was an inane question, but feeling so helpless, so lost. "You knew I didn't have any clue where this valley was. Why go to all that trouble?"

Maix shook his head and sighed. "Oh, please. I knew this would be difficult to understand, but I never thought you would be so slow! It doesn't really matter, does it? We're all here now, and that was the point. I got you to convince Zethamy to believe in herself again, and she so thoughtfully led us here. I think the best part was when I got to sit there, pretending to be exhausted of magic while Bruigan died. 'I have nothing left to give,'" the wizard intoned, using Bhaobuk's voice.

Khaniel gasped at the revelation. Bruigan had died. Maix had let him.

"Now, I want that damned pendant!" Maix shouted. "Bring it here, Khaniel," the wizard instructed, holding out his hand. "Now."

Khaniel shook his head in a rage. "No," he said, yanking his axe free. "Never. I'll slice you from head to toe for that, wizard," he promised.

All around them, the ogres grew wary, raising their weapons a bit higher.

"Fool," Maix chided him. "I'll simply order them to kill you both and take it anyway. But if you go down fighting, I suppose you might fulfill some misguided sense of honor, and I'll thoroughly enjoy snuffing out your pathetic life. I guess that has to go for you, too, Zethamy. After all, you did spill beer on the king."

"Burn you, Maix," Zethamy snarled. "You're a stinking little worm, and if you get too close, I'm going to snap your neck."

"Ooh, there's the Zethamy I remember from before. Finally got a little of your old fire back, did you? Well, you'll be sorry to know that I don't need to get close to do what I do best. That's what I've got Kizrak here for. No, I'll stay back here and send your friend Khaniel to miserable, horrible oblivion while you stumble around, wondering where the next club swing will come from. Watch. Oh, sorry," he said, chuckling, "I forgot. Well, listen, then."

The wizard gestured at Khaniel, who braced for some sort of dazzling magical effect, but nothing seemed to happen. Then, a small ache, like a growing disease, resonated in his chest. It expanded, radiated out from the middle of his torso. Khaniel grunted and doubled over in pain. Every wound dealt him suddenly seemed to reemerge, sapping him of life and strength. With a shrill cry of absolute agony, Khaniel fell to the ground, squirming and writhing. He thought he would die from the pain; he almost wanted to. He tried to speak, to plead with Maix to cease, but the pain reduced his words to raw screaming.

"Stop it!" Zethamy yelled, dropping down beside Khaniel and trying to hold him still. "Whatever you're doing, leave him alone!"

Maix laughed. "But I'm not doing anything," he said innocently. "At least, not now. But before, when he kept getting himself hurt, and you thought I was healing him, well, I don't really know how to do that. I'm a wizard, not a shaman, remember? But with this nifty amulet"—he withdrew a silver pendant on a chain from his shirt—"I can mask pain and hide damage, even from the body itself. It comes in quite handy for torturing people: I can tell their minds there is no pain—and then let it return." He finished, his tone icy with menace. "Khaniel's dying from all those cuts and broken bones he suffered during his journey. It may take a long time."

Khaniel thought his body was ripping apart. He heard himself screaming still, though it had turned into a kind of horrible croaking by then. Zethamy huddled over the warrior, frantically trying to calm him. Then, suddenly, she grew still, and Khaniel thought he might mercifully black out.

Right when Khaniel felt as if he had no more air to scream with, a cool gentleness entered his body. Somewhere, as part of his conscious awareness, Khaniel realized the sensation came where Zethamy's hands pressed against his flesh. She sent healing into him, blessed relief. He sucked in a great gulp of air, but instead of screaming, he let it out as a choking sob, so thankful that the unendurable pain had abated at last.

In the next couple of heartbeats, Khaniel found the strength to concentrate on that sliver of relief, to cling to it. He clawed at it, drew it into himself as fast as he could. He felt Zethamy shudder over him, sensed her slump down with the strain of effort, trying to feed him every bit of energy she could give.

"So much pain," she mumbled, shaking. "So deep."

"Zethamy," Khaniel heard Maix say, "if you give me the pendant now, I'll let him die quickly, no more suffering. What say you?"

Zethamy snorted but made no other response. Then, suddenly, the mercenary could think clearly again, could calm his twitching, cramping muscles. He drew one very long, shuddering breath as the last of the misery left his body, and he stopped clinging to the soothing powers.

Zethamy gasped, then took a long, ragged breath of her own, and whispered, "That's everything I can give you. There is no more." And she collapsed atop him.

"Come now, Zethamy, I can't imagine you want to see him like this," Maix called. "Give me the pendant, and I'll end his suffering."

Khaniel shook his head, pride taking over, refusing to let the two of them succumb to Maix's scheme without a fight. He struggled to rise, pushing Zethamy up with him until they both rested on their knees, face to face.

Somewhere beyond, Maix snarled in anger. "Kizrak," Khaniel heard the wizard say, "would you and your warriors kindly fetch my *damned pendant for me!*"

"Kill them!" the ogre king ordered.

Khaniel took Zethamy's head in his hands. "Do you trust me?" he asked.

"Yes," the paladin replied, her body trembling with exhaustion, "I do."

"Then also trust yourself," he said, "And keep your faith. Reach down inside and find that hidden well of energy, that strength that comes from knowing Mithaniel Marr is with you, that righteous anger that you feel, knowing what Maix has done. Draw on it, embrace it, and let it wash over you. Tell yourself right now that it's not going to end this way, with you down on your knees, too weak to fight back."

The paladin panted, trying to find the reserve he spoke of. She nodded and, grunting with determination, climbed slowly to her feet beside him.

If she feels half as bad as I do . . . Khaniel tried to keep his knees from wobbling out from underneath him. *It buys us a couple more moments, anyway,* he thought, seeing the ogres closing in, warily tightening their noose around the two. *There's always a chance.*

He leaned in close once more, whispering final instructions to his counterpart. "We fight together, Knight of Truth and Steel Warrior side by side, truth and steel as one. Stay low and close to me, and I mean *close:* back to back. When you feel me shift, shift with me, Zethamy. Trust that Mithaniel is giving you everything you need to succeed. All you have to do is have the courage. Can you do that?"

"Yes!" she said, smiling. "Whatever happens, thank you."

"For what?" he asked, puzzled.

"For helping me find my way back," she answered, and she leaned forward and kissed him once, quickly.

The warrior beamed in the warm glow of affection he felt for Zethamy. Then he let go of her and turned to the nearest ogre as he hefted his axe, ready to die by her side. "So you want that pendant, Maix?" he called out as he flashed his weapon.

"Come and take it," Zethamy finished for them both as she took out her sword and turned to stand back-to-back, as the mercenary had instructed.

Maix chuckled. "You've both got courage, I'll give you that. What a waste. Kizrak," he said, "please hurry. I'd like to get back to Freeport before the sun sets."

"Attack, you cowardly dogs!" the ogre commanded. "Hurry up!"

If Marr cares about us at all, the warrior thought as ogres closed with him, *he won't let us die here. If he truly wants to see these relics returned to Freeport, and she is his true servant, then somehow, he will give us a fighting chance. And if he won't . . . if not, then I'll still be my own man,* he reasoned. *Though fat lot of good it's going to do me.*

The first ogre rushed at Khaniel from the side, raising a spiked club in the air. Khaniel swung his axe up and deflected the blow, then brought the weapon back around and forced another ogre to retreat. He felt Zethamy shift slightly, knew she had lunged out at something, and heard an ogre shout in pain. Somehow, she could tell where her enemies stood, in a way that went beyond the minimal training he had provided her. It was something more, perhaps something divine.

The mercenary couldn't help but smile to himself. *I thought so. All right, Zethamy, let's do this.*

The next few moments became a fog to the warrior. Ogres came at him from all sides, trying to flank him, trying to get inside his defenses, but Khaniel never let up for a moment. His axe hummed through the air as he shifted it back and forth, up and down. It became a wall the ogres could not breach. More than once, one of his foes would get too close, would think he had a chance to dart inside Khaniel's reach to strike a blow, and each time, the ogre would have to leap away, howling and clutching at a ruined hand or arm.

Behind the mercenary, Zethamy was fluid motion. Khaniel somehow knew what she did almost the moment she did it. He rotated with her when she needed to pivot, and she with him. When he had to shift to the side suddenly to avoid a jabbing half-spear, she bent like a reed with him. They had become attuned to one another through that connection she had made. A conduit beyond mere senses, it proved deeper, more mystical, than any familiarity they could have achieved in weapons-yard practice. They were as one, linked in spirit, in mind. It felt glorious.

More ogres rushed at them, timing their attacks, trying to draw the two humans away from one another. With each strike, each thrust, Khaniel delivered counterattacks. He continued holding them all at bay, but he could sense the last vestiges of his strength evaporating. Khaniel could tell that Zethamy faltered, too.

And still more ogres came.

Too much to overcome, he thought, losing hope. *The skeleton, the wracking pain. Damn Maix! I hate how he played us for fools the whole way! He—*

Khaniel, too caught up in his desperate musings, allowed a feint to draw him out, and another ogre slashed him on the forearm. The cut didn't go too deep, but the crease burned. It angered him. He didn't want to give in, but he could feel it coming. Already, Zethamy stumbled, backing into him more than moving with him. Their connection wavered, growing weak. He could sense her deepening despair.

No, he thought, trying to send feelings of hope to her. *No!*

And then it happened. He felt the buildup come quickly, the anger that threatened to overwhelm him. He knew what it meant, knew what it had cost him and Zethamy before, but he didn't hesitate. He surrendered to the rage, let it engulf him.

Like a crazed animal, Khaniel struck outward, again and again. Ogres that had gleefully pressed the attack scrambled back before the vicious whirling axe blade that spun anew in the warrior's hands. Something struck him on the thigh, dug a gouge in his flesh, but he felt no pain. There was only fighting and death all around.

Khaniel found a part of himself detached from it all, a portion of his mind that watched, calm and calculating. That had never happened before. He witnessed his own berserk rage. He didn't so much control it as flow with it, letting it overwhelm the ogres. He reveled in it.

When the bodies began to stack deep all around him, Khaniel kept slashing. When ogres tried to scramble over the corpses to flee from him, he kept slashing. And when the last vestiges of Kizrak's warband either fell dead or fled, he kept slashing.

Then, in a moment of clarity, Khaniel realized his rage had begun to subside. He recognized that his body had reached its limit, that he had pushed it far beyond anything it should have been able to withstand. Exhaustion replaced ferocity; quavering muscles replaced driving fury. And in that instant, that moment of reawakening, he sensed a prescience. Khaniel knew, without knowing how he knew, that his axe swung around, toward Zethamy's head. He saw the blade, parallel with the ground, glide right at her.

And he did not worry.

The paladin, completely spent, struggled even to stand. But where before they had fought as individuals, contesting for supremacy over one another on a fateful day many weeks previous, on this day they had become one. And she knew, without him having to tell her, to duck.

In that one act, that one reaction, so natural, so in tune with Khaniel's action, Zethamy moved out of harm's way, revealing Maix. The wizard stood right behind her, reaching out for her, his hands and forearms crackling with purplish spidery energy. With Zethamy clear, only Maix stood in the way of Khaniel's axe.

The mercenary never let up.

The axe passed cleanly through the wizard's neck.

His head, eyes wide with startled surprise, tumbled away, leaving the body to teeter for a heartbeat before falling to the ground.

Khaniel could no longer stand.

He slid down to one knee, right next to Zethamy, who sprawled out, gasping for air. She couldn't even hold her head up. Khaniel wanted to join her, to collapse on the cool ground and rest for an eternity. But they were not safe yet.

With great effort, the mercenary remained upright. He twisted his head around and spied Kizrak. The ogre king stood with perhaps half a dozen others, warriors of his hunting party. Many of them suffered grievous wounds. They gawked at the two humans, many with great dismay filling their eyes. It seemed that they were all that remained of the two dozen or more that had accompanied Kizrak.

"Come meet your doom," Khaniel bluffed. He knew that, if the ogre king should decide to take up the challenge, he would be a dead man. He didn't have the strength left to lift his axe. But he knew Kizrak's heart. The ogre king wanted nothing more to do with him.

Kizrak shook his head, and he and his remaining warriors turned and shuffled off, leaving Khaniel and Zethamy to themselves.

19

Epilogue

Khaniel stared into the cool, clear waters of the pools in the courtyard of the Temple of Marr in Freeport. He thought it interesting that he did not feel more impatient. He relaxed, at ease, content to wait. No one paid much attention to him, a well-muscled man in simple traveler's garb. He might have been a supplicant come to ask for favors or a manservant waiting for a highborn lord or lady to exit the temple. The potential for those sorts of misconceptions did not concern him in the least.

No, Khaniel contented himself with studying his own reflection in the water, taking note of the person he saw. There was a lot there he didn't understand. For the first time in his life, his own needs didn't seem quite so important. For the first time, he cared more about someone else than himself, found himself willing to sacrifice everything on another's behalf. It struck him how odd that felt, but it didn't trouble him. He could figure out what it meant in time.

A short time later, Zethamy appeared from within the temple. Watching her, Khaniel felt a surge of joy, of delight. Dressed simply, like Khaniel, she strolled along the path accompanied by two men, one at each arm. They clearly felt the need to aid her in walking through the gardens. Zethamy's cloudy eyes flickered in occasional annoyance, but she did a good job of not letting on. When the three of them stopped before Khaniel, Tholius Quey, standing on Zethamy's left, spoke. "Here is your Khaniel, Zethamy." The woman reached out, and Khaniel took her hand in his own. She squeezed his fingers, a loving touch.

"It's done," she said, smiling. "The relics are being thoroughly researched and the priests have sealed the pendant in a vault, away from scrutiny."

"Good," Khaniel said, feeling a sense of relief. "I hadn't realized how much the burden had weighed on me until today."

"Nor had I," Zethamy agreed. "But it's done. We can go."

The man on Zethamy's other side, Valeron Dushire, leader of the Knights of Truth, shook his head. "I wish you would reconsider, Zethamy," he said. "I fear for you in your condition. Your place now is here, finding new ways to serve Marr."

"No," the woman replied, her voice firm. "Other places need me, too. Let go, Lord Dushire. My blindness is not a limitation, only a challenge. Marr permitted it because he knew I was capable of overcoming it. It just took me a while to understand that."

"As you say," Valeron said, bowing. "But I will worry for you nonetheless." Then he turned to Khaniel. "Have you decided whether or not to petition for reinstatement? After everything you've accomplished by Zethamy's side, I don't see why Cain would turn you down."

Khaniel smiled in appreciation. "No," he admitted. "There was a time when I would have jumped at the chance to rejoin the Steel Warriors. It was the sum total of my life. But I don't know if that's enough anymore. There's more to a man than his physical prowess, his martial talents. I'm content to just be for a while, figure out what will make me happiest. A lot of it will depend on Zethamy, what she feels the need to do. There's always time to come back later, if I decide to petition."

"Very well," Valeron said. "I wish you well, then, both of you." Then he took Zethamy's free hand in his own and kissed it once, lightly. "Take care of yourselves."

Tholius hugged Zethamy briefly, then followed the elder knight back into the temple.

"So," Zethamy said, "we suddenly have nothing to do."

"That's not true," Khaniel replied, chuckling. "I can think of plenty of ways to while away the afternoon, back at the inn. Whatever your heart desires."

Zethamy groaned. "Stop it," she playfully chided him as they turned and strolled out of the temple grounds and into the streets of Freeport. "At least until we're out of earshot," she added, tossing her head back over her shoulder in the temple's direction.

Khaniel chuckled again. "All right," he conceded. "I'll behave." His smile faded as the two of them crossed paths with a handful of Freeport Militia. The soldiers sauntered along the street, looking smug. Khaniel itched to draw his axe free, but he had wisely left it at their room in the inn that day, not wanting to draw undue attention to himself.

"Easy," Zethamy said from beside him. "You can't fight all the battles at once. D'Lere and his militia will be dealt with in due time."

Khaniel gawked at her. "How did you know?" he asked, feeling surprised.

"Because I know what eats at you night and day," she answered.

"I wish we could find out more about the Church of the Dismal Rage," he said, keeping his voice low. "I know D'Lere has to be aware of them. Maybe he's even in league with them. But they sure do keep a low profile."

"We'll discover something eventually," Zethamy said in soothing tones. "Be patient."

"Maix had friends," Khaniel said firmly. "That priest and his guards were only a small part of a bigger group. I don't know where they're hiding, down in those sewers, but I want to meet them. I owe them one, for Bruigan's sake."

Zethamy didn't say anything for a long while. When she finally did speak, her question sounded familiar to Khaniel. "How did he fool us both so well? How could he pose as a trusted companion for so long without revealing his duplicity?"

"I think about that all the time," the warrior replied. "If you really scrutinize it, it doesn't seem so far-fetched. Like when he kept taking those early-morning walks. He was obviously meeting with Kizrak. But it was innocuous enough behavior, so neither of us thought much of it then. But other incidents—such as the day at the bog that turned everything around for us—I think about what he did, and it stuns me. Forcing us to come to terms with our inner struggles as a means of restoring your faith was quite a risk. It must have galled him to do that. On the other hand, he didn't have anything to lose by trying."

"Well, thank Marr he didn't get his hands on the pendant," Zethamy said as they strolled into Hogcaller's. "In the end, Marr's glory outshone Innoruuk's hatred. That's the important thing."

Khaniel found them a table and ordered two mugs of some of Bruigan's finest ale before turning back to Zethamy. "If you say so," he said.

"What does that mean?" she asked, turning to meet his gaze.

"It means, whether it was Marr's glory or blind luck"—he grunted when she punched him in the arm—"you got what you wanted. I'm happy that you're happy. Nothing else really matters to me." And he leaned over and kissed her.